W9-ALM-131

WITHDRAWN

DEBORAH MARKUS

Sky Pony Press
New York

Copyright © 2018 by Deborah Markus

All rights reserved. No part of this book may be reproduced in any manner without the express written consent of the publisher, except in the case of brief excerpts in critical reviews or articles. All inquiries should be addressed to Sky Pony Press, 307 West 36th Street, 11th Floor, New York, NY 10018.

This is a work of fiction. Names, characters, places, and incidents are either the products of the author's imagination or used fictitiously.

Sky Pony Press books may be purchased in bulk at special discounts for sales promotion, corporate gifts, fund-raising, or educational purposes. Special editions can also be created to specifications. For details, contact the Special Sales Department, Sky Pony Press, 307 West 36th Street, 11th Floor, New York, NY 10018 or info@skyhorsepublishing.com.

Sky Pony® is a registered trademark of Skyhorse Publishing, Inc.®, a Delaware corporation.

Visit our website at www.skyponypress.com.

10 9 8 7 6 5 4 3 2 1

Library of Congress Cataloging-in-Publication Data is available on file.

Cover design by Kate Gartner
Cover image credit Sarah DiBlasi-Crain

Print ISBN: 978-1-5107-3405-0
Ebook ISBN: 978-1-5107-3406-7

Printed in the United States of America

Interior design by Joshua Barnaby

To Dominick Cancilla and Markus Cancilla,
who were with me every word of the way.

"The past is not a package one can lay away."
—Emily Dickinson

The Letting Go

NOTEBOOK 1

(in some particular order)

One need not be A Chamber—
to be Haunted—
One need not—be A House—

The corpse that showed up yesterday was a stranger. I can't figure out if I'm supposed to be relieved by that or not.

I haven't seen it. Him. They won't let us, of course.

Even the picture they showed us was from before it happened. His driver's license. He had his wallet with him when he was left here, which I suppose was lucky for all of us.

There might be pictures later, online, of how he looks now, but I don't want to look at them.

If I were supposed to see, wouldn't he have been left somewhere just for me? Or am I old enough now that I'm expected to take a certain initiative with this sort of thing?

I didn't know him. None of us knew him.

Ms. Lurie didn't know him, but she found him anyway.

There's something awful about that—not just for her, but for him. Dying shouldn't be like that. Being practically tripped over by a stranger is a terrible way to start your death. It makes everything you did in life hardly count at all. It makes you "the body" forever after.

3

Of course it couldn't have been very pleasant for Ms. Lurie, either. She was just taking one of her usual early-morning walks. She always comes back from them looking even dreamier and kinder than usual, talking at breakfast about how beautiful a morning is when no one else has seen it yet.

I wonder if she'll ever talk like that again.

Maybe she will. Maybe she'll think about the hundreds of walks she's taken without seeing any corpses at all. Statistically speaking, this particular morning doesn't even signify.

I'm not sure that's how people think about things.

I've never been any good at understanding how normal people think.

I do know Ms. Lurie always tries to focus on the positive.

There's a lot of that to focus on in this case, though she may not realize it. She may have already learned, for instance, that it's a good thing everyone here knows she's always up and around at five in the morning. Maybe she was a suspect for a few minutes—finding the body always makes you look bad—but it was probably just a formality.

She's also lucky that the body she found was shot in the back of the head. That's fairly tidy, as murders go. Though I suppose that depends on what you have to compare it to.

It was a stranger. Not one of her students or teachers, not a friend, not family. Not someone she loved.

And of course she only found the *one* body.

I couldn't tell her how lucky she is even if she'd be willing to listen, though. That isn't the kind of luck anyone feels thankful for. It's all about what isn't true rather than what is.

4

Plus I'd have to tell her how I know so much about this particular subject.

I wish I knew if this is my fault.

Is it starting again, or could it just be coincidence?

Is murder ever a coincidence?

I didn't know him. I know I didn't know him.

As usual, no one's rushing in to tell me what the rules are. ~~If this is supposed to be a sign that they've changed~~

The problem with writing in ink is that when you don't know how to end a sentence, the beginning just sits there staring at you.

I love ink and paper—that's part of my project at Hawthorne—but they're not always very convenient.

I hope Stephen James (former artist, current corpse) doesn't mean I have to stop playing with them here.

I like Hawthorne. It's pretty and quiet and safe.

Or it *was* quiet, until yesterday.

I wish he hadn't come.

———

It's Easy to invent a Life—
God does it—Every Day—

They let me keep my first name when they changed everything else. I don't know if they were being nice to me or just practical.

Probably practical. They wouldn't want to go to all the work of changing things only to have me give it all away and make them do it all over again. And it's hard to learn to react naturally to a new name. It looks bad if there's a big pause when someone says your name, or if you look surprised or puzzled by it.

Not that many people speak to me, but there will always be a few. Especially now, while I'm still in school. Even this school.

Emily is a common enough name that they must have decided it wouldn't be an automatic giveaway.

They let me pick my new last name, because I suggested something completely different from my old one and also completely ordinary.

I didn't want a middle name, but most people have one so they said I should, too. The whole point of my new name is to disarm suspicion, after all. It was their idea, so I left it to them to choose. It's not as if I'm ever going to use it.

Maybe it was fun for them to get to play around with names for a change, instead of their usual legal mumbo jumbo.

I'm not even just Emily to anyone here. I don't have any friends, of course, and the day I met my assigned mentor I told her to call me Miss Stone. She looked as if I'd just given her a fresh frog sandwich, but tried to smile at me anyway. "That's a little formal, isn't it?" she asked.

"I can write it down for you, if you need to practice saying it," I answered.

She leaves me alone now. If I want to talk to her, I know where to find her.

I was named Emily after my mother's favorite poet.

I guess saying Dickinson was her favorite poet is misleading, since my mother didn't actually like any other poets. She thought most poetry was boring, trite, or pretentious—sometimes all three, if the poet really worked at it. But my mother was assigned some Dickinson in high school, and she was hooked. Just fell in love. Extra hard, the way you maybe feel when you never expected to even *like* anyone and then you find yourself wanting to propose five minutes after the first hello.

She told my father he could choose the names for any boy babies they might have, and she let him pick my middle name, but she always insisted that if their first baby was a girl, she had to be an Emily.

That was me. Their first child, who turned out to be their only child.

Maybe they were planning on more.

Maybe I wasn't supposed to be this alone.

Maybe I was supposed to have a sister, like Dickinson did.

Maybe my mother would have tried to convince my father to name her Lavinia, after Dickinson's sister. Maybe she would have pretended to insist on that name, just for the fun of hearing my father say she could name his child Lavinia *over my dead body*. Maybe she would have replied *who said it was YOUR child?* And he would have pretended to stomp out in a huff and she would have called him back laughing and said *all right, we can name her whatever you want—how about William? I've always liked William.* Just for the fun of seeing him stomp and huff again.

I was too young to hear about their plans in the child department, and then their plans died with them.

I suppose my Dickinson project is a way to connect with my mother. And partly a way to thank her for giving me the one name I'd be allowed to keep.

If you're reading this, whoever you may be, I'm safely dead and can stop lying to the world. That's what this diary is: a place where I can tell the truth and not have to worry about what might happen next.

That doesn't mean I'm not allowed to lie to myself for the fun of it. My life needs a rewrite more than most.

All that nonsense about who I was named for is a story I felt like telling myself today. I've loved Dickinson ever since I stumbled across a poem of hers when I was little. I liked her because we had the same first name, and then because she'd written what was supposed to be a letter from a fly to a bee.

For all I know, my mother hated Dickinson.

But that's not the story I want to be in.

No one is ever going to tell me about my mother, so I can make up any kind of origin story I want.

My name is Emily, and I'll never know why. I only know it's mine.

When everyone else was taken away, I got to keep Emily.

———

Of Tolling Bell I ask
the cause?
"A Soul has gone to
Heaven"
I'm answered in a
lonesome tone—
Is Heaven then a Prison?

We all woke up to the sound of the alarm.

I've heard it before, but only during drills. For a few seconds I thought this must be just another test, but then I woke completely and saw what time it was. Early morning; barely light.

Either this was the real thing or we were supposed to think it was.

There's a Sherlock Holmes story where he makes a woman think her house is on fire just so he can see what she tries to take with her when she has to flee the building. In my case, I had a collection of Dickinson's poems next to my bed, and while I'm not sure I would have fought my way through flames for it, it was comforting to take it with me.

I didn't smell smoke, or see any whispering its way into my room. I touched the door before I opened it and it didn't seem hotter than usual.

I noticed all this in a leisurely, distant sort of way. Either I was genuinely calm or I was numb with terror.

I remember being glad, as I opened the door and saw other students filling the hallway, that the clothes I sleep in are actual clothes—sweatpants and a long-sleeved T-shirt, in this case. And I'd automatically stepped into my fleecy moccasin slippers.

The girl in the room next to mine, on the other hand, was wearing only a long white nightgown, complete with eyelet lace and bits of pink ribbon at the cuffs and neck. She was barefoot. I hate being barefoot, even when it's hot out. She didn't seem to mind, though, or even to notice that in the dim hall she looked like the ghost of a wedding dress.

"Is it a fire, do you think?" she asked me, sounding conversational.

I shook my head.

Hawthorne Academy is proud to have room for only a couple of dozen students—"independent scholars"—but just then it seemed as if there were hundreds of us, all pouring out into the same narrow hallway and wondering what to make of it all.

"I don't smell smoke," another girl said authoritatively.

"Then let's go to the lounge," the girl in the white nightgown said. She was answering the other girl but looking at me. "We're supposed to gather there if there's an emergency."

I looked away. *Gather there?* What century was she from?

She was right, though. And just then, Vera, one of Hawthorne's teachers—"mentors"—joined our group.

"Let's go, girls," she said. "Everything's fine. We just have to get to the lounge, okay?"

"If everything's fine," one of the girls protested in a panicky voice, "why do we—"

"Follow Lucy, please," Vera said, nodding toward the girl who had mentioned the lack of smoke. Lucy nodded importantly in reply and turned to lead us away. Vera added, "I'll be right there. I just want to check the rooms and make sure everyone's up and out."

We all started moving in the indicated direction—not exactly running, but almost. Only the girl in the gown seemed unruffled, gliding along with the rest of us as if she were caught in a current.

"It's probably just a mistake," she said to me in a confidential tone. "Probably the alarm went off by accident and they'll be bending over backwards to apologize for waking us so early and depriving us of our salubrious sleep." She smiled mischievously. "I see quality baked goods in my future."

I didn't answer. We reached the lounge, and even before anyone told us anything, two things were clear: there wasn't a fire, and this wasn't a drill.

———

A Prison gets to be a
friend—

There are no grades at Hawthorne Academy for Independent Young Women. No classes, no teachers, and certainly no homework. Or maybe it would be more accurate to say there's nothing *but* homework. Which isn't so bad when you're the one assigning it to yourself.

We do what we want here, at our own pace and setting our own goals. We work in our rooms or the lounge or the library or under a tree. (Ms. Lurie draws the line at letting us actually climb the trees, to the deep disappointment of one budding artist.) We have access to a decent number of books and all manner of art supplies—and Ms. Lurie is always happy to order more—but mostly we have peace and quiet and solitude. Kind of like a convent, but without any pesky praying and people calling you "Sister Emily."

Most Hawthorne students end up going Ivy League—it's all in the brochure—but that doesn't happen automatically and it's not supposed to be the point. The point is to give a certain kind of artistic type the space she needs to develop her talents and realize her visions and find fulfillment in this quiet, beautiful, rural setting.

Also in the brochure, and also surprisingly true.

Coming to Hawthorne after all those dismal boarding schools was like walking into a rose garden from an unlit cellar.

We mostly get painters and writers, but every now and then there's a composer or a potter to mix things up a bit. Once we had a violinist, but she started pining away and they had to send her home.

Ms. Lurie started this school almost twenty years ago. At first it was just her big rambling house in a little artist's colony of a mountain town in coastal California. Ms. Lurie raised her four daughters here following the same recipe she uses on us now: never telling the girls what to do, just listening to their ideas and giving them guidance and letting them decide how they wanted to live their lives.

It turned out that they wanted to live their lives as two famous actors, a famous singer, and a famous artist. So Ms. Lurie decided to make a career of nurturing sensitive souls in a secluded setting, and up until this week it's worked out fine for everyone involved.

It's making me a little crazy trying to figure out if her luck ended on my account or if dead bodies sometimes just turn up where no one expects them.

———

1 Pound Sugar—
½—Butter—
½—Flour—
* 6—Eggs—*
1 Grated Cocoa Nut—

Mrs Carmichael's—

Dickinson used to write poems on almost anything—a chocolate wrapper, edges of envelopes, even the back of a recipe she'd jotted down. Or maybe the poem was supposed to be the front. Nobody knows which was more important to her: a poem about the things that can never come back or a friend's recipe for coconut cake.

She loved baking, so maybe she loved the recipe and the poem equally.

There was a stack of flyers in the lounge that morning, and some pens. So I was able to write down some of what happened while it was happening.

It would have been tidier to copy those scribbles into this notebook, but I thought it was more in the spirit of Dickinson to tape them in here.

I guess it was also very Dickinson of me to scribble my thoughts on whatever scraps of paper were at hand. At the time, though, I felt like an idiot for having left this notebook back in my room.

At least it was in a drawer. The police wouldn't have been looking for a murderer or maybe another dead body in my night table. They wouldn't know to care about anything I've written down.

No one knows I'm at Hawthorne except Aunt Paulette and a few other people who don't care where I am as long as it's nowhere near them.

———

They Shut Me Up in Prose
As when a little Girl
They put me in the Closet—
Because they liked me "still"—

Nobody's told us anything yet. They look like they wish they didn't have to tell us whatever it is that's going on. They just want us to sit still and know nothing.

Ms. Lurie came to talk to us for a few minutes. She was trying to be both comforting and vague, which is a frightening combination. It means the truth is too scary to tell.

She said *Something's very wrong* and she said *Don't worry, you're all safe, everyone's all right,* and you could tell she wanted to be able to say them at the same time.

"Why did the alarm go off?" a girl asked, sounding as if she were trying not to burst into tears.

"Alarms don't go off all by themselves, genius," another girl told her. "Somebody *set* it off."

"That's enough, Sarah," Ms. Lurie snapped, and that frightened us more than anything so far this morning.

Ms. Lurie never snaps. She sighs sometimes. She gives Improving Lectures that would sound straight out of the nineteenth century if they weren't so laced with urgings to be Present. She smiles a lot, which would be annoying except she actually means it. Before this morning, I'd never heard her say anything harsher than *Is there another way you could have phrased that, Emily?* And believe me, I've given her plenty of reasons to say plenty worse.

And now she's snapping at us.

And that, more than the unfamiliar slant of light and the memory of alarm bells, made Hawthorne a strange and terrifying place.

———

This is My letter to the World
That never wrote to Me—

Phone reception is spotty at Hawthorne. Everyone who comes here figures out pretty quickly where the good spots are, and none of them are in the lounge.

I don't have anyone to call, of course, but some of the girls are crying. One of them practically threw a fit about being allowed out of the lounge *just for a* minute, *why can't we go for just* one *minute?*

The only thing the teachers will tell us is that everyone at Hawthorne is fine, but something terrible has happened and we all have to sit tight for a little while longer and let the police do their jobs.

"*What* jobs?" the girl practically shrieked. "What's going *on?*"

No answer.

It must be starting again.

But who could it be?

I've been playing by the rules. For years I've played by them—certainly the whole time I've been at Hawthorne. I barely even know anyone's name here—and, anyway, they said it isn't anyone at the school.

~~I thought it would be safe here~~

~~I felt safe here~~

~~I want to be~~

The girl in the white nightgown is sitting and watching me scribble. I glared at her once, but she just smiled until I looked away again.

I think she's new here. She has to be. Everyone else has gotten the message to leave me alone.

The last thing I need right now is to have to fend off yet another friendly, well-intentioned idiot who doesn't know what fire looks like.

Not that this girl looks friendly, exactly. More like amused, I guess.

It's hard to write with someone watching my every pen stroke. Not that she's anywhere near close enough to see what I'm writing, but the way she's staring makes me wonder if it's possible to read pens the way some people can read lips.

If so, I hope she can read this message that's just for her: <u>Piss off.</u>

'Tis not that Dying hurts us so—
'Tis Living—hurts us More—
But Dying—is a different—way—
A Kind behind the Door—

The Southern Custom—of the Bird—
That Ere the Frosts are due—
Accepts a better Latitude—
We—Are the Birds—that stay.

Still here on lounge lockdown.

The police are everywhere, looking for maybe even they don't know what.

They'll want to speak to us at some point.

I'm not looking forward to having to try to seem shocked at the idea of murder.

Not that anyone has told us that's what happened, but what else could it be?

———

MINE enemy is growing old,—

All right, I admit it: I thought it might be over by now. It's been so long since the last time.

I thought maybe I was safe now.

Not that I've been taking any chances. Of course I wouldn't. I've grown used to living like this. It's almost all I remember. (Almost.) It's practically a point of pride now—being unspeakably rude to someone and seeing that look on her face: *Did she really just say that?* And me thinking, *Yes. Yes, I did. And you'd better hope you never learn how big a favor I just did you.*

It's funny how startled people are by rudeness. If you asked a random person out of the blue, they'd probably say, *Oh, yes, people are horrible and good manners are dead and that goes double for teenagers. Triple for rich ones.*

But then say to them, "If you have to be a moron, I'd appreciate it if you could at least be a *quiet* moron," and watch how shocked they look.

I guess it's just that people are used to there being some kind of reason for things. They don't have to *like* the reason; they just want to know it's there.

My nonstop unpleasantness must seem completely random. Like Iago: Why was he such a jerk to Othello from scene one? You can read the whole play and then read it again and not be any the wiser.

Maybe Iago just enjoyed being cruel.

I don't, but I've gotten used to it. Anyway, it beats the alternative.

But now it's started again. Maybe.

(Could they just *tell* us, already?)

I've been so careful for so long.

Was it all for nothing?

Othello killed his wife for a reason. It was a completely wrong reason, and it would have been a bad one even if he'd had his facts straight, but the motivation was there. He wasn't just lashing out at whoever happened to be next to him.

People can learn to live with almost anything if they think there's a reason for it. Something *like* a reason, anyway. A rationalization. Even just a pattern.

I thought this killer was an Othello, and now it seems he's an Iago. What am I supposed to do?

———

God gave a Loaf to every Bird—
But just a Crumb—to Me—
I dare not eat it—tho'
I starve—

Hawthorne is all about letting us find our own paths and go our own ways, but those ways had better bring us to the breakfast table at 8:30, lunch at 12:30, and dinner at six o'clock sharp. Prompt and regular appearance in the dining room is practically the only rule here. Hawthorne isn't just about the joys of self-discipline and the freedom to follow one's own motivation, Ms. Lurie says. It's about building community and fellowship and everything else they talk about in the brochure.

Breakfast at Hawthorne is usually whole-grain porridge, whole-grain toast, fruit, grass-fed milk, and honey made by proud local bees. No bacon, no refined sugar. Coffee only on Sundays; tea the rest of the week.

Today, while we were still huddled in the lounge, Ms. Young and Vera brought in take-out cups of hot chocolate, lots of paper napkins, and pink boxes of what turned out to be the most beautiful pastries I'd ever seen.

(Breakfast the morning after my mother was murdered was Lucky Charms cereal. I don't think they did it on purpose.)

The girl in the nightgown laughed. "Looks like my crystal ball is working," she said.

"Things are a little . . . disordered in the kitchen right now," Ms. Young said.

"Still crawling with cops, she means," the girl murmured.

"So we had this sent from Sunrise Bakery," Ms. Young continued, ignoring or not hearing her. "Please try to eat something, girls. You should be able to go back to your rooms and get dressed soon."

"I don't *want* to eat!" a girl cried. It was the same girl who was yelping before about the police and their jobs. She's pretty pale on any ordinary day. This morning her skin looked whiter than nightgown-girl's nightgown. "I want to know what's going on! I want to talk to my mom!"

She shook her friend's arm off her shoulders and stood before Ms. Young. "Tell us what's going on!"

Ms. Young is one of the mentors. She's also Bianca Young, the poet. She lives the writer-as-wide-eyed-waif stereotype, and looks as if a baby's breath could carry her away. She looked at Vera, who's a sculptor and is built like one of her own sturdy statues. Vera met her eyes bleakly and then turned to the rest of us.

"We'll tell you more as soon as we can," she said.

———

It would have starved a Gnat—
To live so small as I—
And yet I was a living Child
With—Food's nescessity

Opon me—like a Claw—
I could no more remove
Than I could modify a Leech—
Or make a Dragon—move—

I was scribbling away when the girl in the white nightgown sat down next to me.

"I took too much and you didn't take any," she said. "Here." She put a covered paper cup of hot chocolate on the arm of my easy chair, and then a chocolate croissant on top of a paper napkin.

I glared at her. "I don't want anything." I should have left it at that, but like an idiot I added, "Anyway, I don't like chocolate. Or croissants."

(The part about croissants is true, anyway. If I want to eat plastery flakes, I'll gnaw on a wall.)

Her expression brightened. "Oh, good. More for me."

She took the croissant back and left a small, soft apple pastry in its place. "Better?"

"No."

The terrible thing was, in spite of everything, it looked wonderful. I caught a whiff of cinnamon and cloves. This was exactly the kind of thing I might pick up for a treat on one of our field trips into town. And it had been a long time since dinner last night.

"Oh, come on," she said. "We have to enjoy this while it lasts. We won't see the likes of *this* breakfast again. Not at Hawthorne, anyway."

I couldn't help noticing that several of the other girls seemed to share her philosophy. The low-level terror that had dominated the room had subsided into bafflement and a bit of carpe diem. So much refined sugar at Hawthorne was as foreign as the police presence, and the consensus seemed to be that if we had to put up with the one, we might as well enjoy the other.

And could things really be that bad if they were feeding us like this?

Even the girl who'd been making such a fuss was sitting in a consoling circle of friends, with Bianca Young next to her offering little sweets like a tiny mother bird.

"I could have gotten something for myself if I'd wanted it," I said, hoping my stomach wouldn't choose this inopportune time to growl.

"I figured you were just being polite and leaving plenty for the rest of us," she said.

A girl sitting across from us snickered. "Being polite isn't exactly Emily's hobby," she said.

Which was so accurate that I didn't bother replying or even glancing up. The girl in the nightgown, however, looked at her wide-eyed for a long moment. "That's fascinating," she said.

"What?" the other girl asked suspiciously.

"The way you really seem to believe anyone's interested in your opinion," she replied. "Why is that, do you think? Have you been clinically diagnosed as delusional, or are you just an idiot?"

I sat frozen, trying not to let my jaw drop and break something. This must be what trying to start a conversation with me is like, except I'm sure I don't sound that nineteenth century.

The girl across from us glared. She's white, but her skin is kind of brown, with nutmeggy freckles. "You're new here, right?" she asked in a patronizing tone.

"This is my first year, yes."

"Well, since you obviously haven't had time to figure it out on your own yet, I'll do you a favor and tell you that Emily isn't exactly worth defending."

The girl in the nightgown was gazing at her with almost scientific interest. "Sorry—what did you say your name was?"

"I didn't," the other girl said, "but it's Madison."

"That is *such* a coincidence!"

"Why?"

"There's a bitch at my *school* named Madison!"

Madison's face flushed deep red faster than I would have thought physically possible. Without answering, she shoved her chair back, picked up her pastries, and stomped off to sit with a small group of girls across the room.

"And speaking of coincidences," my strange companion went on to no one in particular, "just last week I was telling my mother how glad I was my name doesn't relate to a city where she forgot to use birth control."

The Madison group was whispering and casting glances in our direction. "You shouldn't have done that," I said in a low voice.

"Why not? It was fun. I can see why you make such a habit of it."

So she *had* heard about me.

"I don't do it for fun," I said.

"No? Why, then?"

The room felt colder all of a sudden. I wanted to cup my hands around the hot chocolate she'd brought me for warmth, but that would have looked weak.

"Just leave it alone," I said instead. My book was next to me, and I opened it at random. You can do that with poetry and it works fine, even if you really are reading. "Leave *me* alone, while you're at it."

She didn't look shocked, or hurt, or angry, or all three, the way other people do when I talk to them. She just looked curious. "Why?"

I gritted my teeth. "I don't know. Maybe because the bitch named Emily at your school said to."

Most people are happy to stay away from me just because I'm aggressively unpleasant. I don't usually have to go in for attempts to sound menacing. I guess my lack of practice showed, because she laughed.

"Actually," she said, "there are *two* bitches named Emily at my school. And don't look now, but one of them's sitting right next to you."

———

for several years, my lexicon was my only companion.

My independent study project focuses on Emily Dickinson.

The best thing about Hawthorne, other than the fact that up until recently everyone here was willing to leave me the hell alone, is that I don't have to say much more than that about what I do all day. I'm drawn to Dickinson's work, and I want to read it and explore it and learn about her life as well as her writing and see where that takes me next.

That's the kind of language that gives the staff at Hawthorne a thrill. It also happens to be true.

Most of the actual writing I've done isn't anything I can show my mentor or Ms. Lurie, since it's mostly things I'm not allowed to share. But Hawthorne *is* giving me a peaceful place to work, and they say that's what they want to offer their students.

Emily Dickinson wanted, for reasons only she knew, to keep her poetry mostly to herself.

That's the strangest thing about her, and maybe the most famous part of her life. People who don't know anything else about Dickinson know she was quiet and mostly stayed at home, and that she wrote ridiculously brilliant poems and shut them away until her death gave them to the world.

She did publish a few poems while she was alive, though. Not many people know that, but it's true.

I guess it isn't quite right to say *she* published them. They *got* published, but no one seems quite sure how. And she didn't sign her name to them.

Maybe Dickinson just needed the world to know she had a voice, even if in the end she was too shy to sing for a living.

Maybe that's why I show my mentor some of my writing now and then. Not much and not often, but some.

I want to know if I'm any good.

Not that it matters, since the only story I really want to tell is the one I need to keep to myself until death sorts everything out.

I keep scrawling things down in weird bursts that sometimes barely make sense, even to me. I stick them into this notebook any old way.

I like the look of so many random scraps of paper, all different sizes and colors. It's comforting, like a quilt.

Maybe I'll edit them someday, or stitch pages together the way Dickinson liked to sew some of her poetry into little booklets. Maybe I'll write different versions of the same event the way Dickinson kept different versions of the same poem and didn't tell anyone which one she liked best.

Maybe no one will ever care about what lies under all my enforced nastiness, but there have been books written about the events that caused it, so it's not conceited for me to think someone will be interested in what I have to say someday.

I wish there were better reasons for people to want to read about me. I wish I were a brilliant poet, or a brilliant anything; but all things considered it's probably best that I'm not.

I'm tired of considering all those things.

———

Surgeons must be very careful
When they take the knife!
Underneath their fine incisions
Stirs the Culprit—<u>Life!</u>

Everyone stopped talking when Ms. Lurie came into the lounge. Before she could say anything, two senior girls rushed up to her. "What's going on?" one asked loudly. "What happened? When do we get to—"

"You can go back to your rooms whenever you're ready, girls," Ms. Lurie said, putting her hand on the girl's shoulder in a silencing gesture. "Finish your breakfast and then go in pairs or small groups to your rooms and get dressed."

We all looked at one another nervously. I don't know what anyone else was thinking, but I was hoping Ms. Lurie wasn't going to be too insistent on the pairs-or-groups part of those instructions. I also hoped she'd let me bring breakfast with me rather than making me finish it here, since I now desperately wanted the apple pastry—but there was no way I was going to eat it in front of that other Emily.

"When you're finished, come back out here," Ms. Lurie continued. She hesitated, then: "A detective would like to speak to each of you, one at a time. Just for a few minutes. I'll be there, of course."

The stunned silence was broken only by the sound of hair swishing as heads whipped around to see if everyone else had heard this. My stomach clenched.

"Tell us what's going on," someone said. The voice was so sure of itself that for a minute I thought it was a teacher. But then I saw that it was Lucy, the bossy girl from the corridor. "We need to know. We've waited long enough."

Ms. Lurie looked at her, and then at the girl whose shoulder she was still holding, and gave a little sigh.

"Yes," she said. "Yes, you're right."

She squeezed the girl's shoulder gently and let it go, then smiled at her and tucked a curl of hair behind the girl's ear in a caress that looked like a farewell.

Considering the news I was fairly sure Ms. Lurie was going to be giving us, I would have expected her to look frightened or confused or at least grim. Instead she looked around with an expression of pity.

"Sometimes," she said, "even wanting to protect someone can be selfish. If you take it too far."

She looked at us again, lingeringly, as if this were the last time she'd ever see us.

Which it was, in a way. She'd never see this same group of girls again. Everyone else in the room was about to have her life sliced cleanly in two. After this morning, after Ms. Lurie finally broke the damned news to us, disaster wouldn't be something that only happened to other people anymore. Everything that happened from now on would be measured as coming before the catastrophe or after.

Must be nice to have a dozen-plus years of that kind of arrogant ignorance.

I had four.

———

Eclipse—at *Midnight*—
It was *dark*—*before*—

One of the books—the one that managed to get a really big publisher—insists I must not remember that first time. Maybe I remember my father, and certainly Violet and Zoë; but of *course* I must have forgotten my mother. Any "memories" I might think I have of her could only have been glued together from other people's words.

Yes, I was young. Yes, I probably have some of the details wrong.

But please let the record state that there are things no one can forget. Not if you're old enough to wander out and find those things yourself.

I have not forgotten finding my mother that night. And I have not forgotten her.

I never will.

I think Ms. Lurie would believe me, but she's the last person I'd ever tell.

Second to last, now.

I give that detective pride of place.

———

The name they dropped opon
my face
With water, in the Country
Church
Is finished using, now,
And They can put it with
My Dolls,
My Childhood, and the string
of spools,
I've finished threading—too—

"It's a very common name," the other Emily said.

I glared at her. She'd followed me when we were herded out of the lounge. Now she was in my room. Sitting on my bed.

Everyone else had worn the impact of the news visibly. Some of the girls were staggering, clutching best friends like stuffed animals. Others were stiff and straight. One particularly young-looking girl had stared at the floor so hard I would have thought the directions to her room were printed there.

This new, unwanted Emily had moved as quietly and naturally as she had when trailing me to the lounge. She wasn't unmoved by the news, exactly. Her bright eyes were as solemn as a bird's. But she wasn't panicked and she didn't take the announcement as the sort of assault everyone else had.

I wanted to ask if this was her first murder, but I was afraid of being overheard and also afraid she'd take it as an invitation to conversation.

I didn't want her here. It wasn't even about the rules, for once. I *wanted* to be alone.

So of course she didn't let me be.

In this small, enclosed space the scent of her perfume was pronounced. Something dark and sweet. Violets? And when had she had time to put it on this crazy morning? Or was it a reflex for her on getting out of bed?

I almost rolled my eyes. A terrible alarm goes off, and *that's* your priority? "I looked it up when there were three other Emilys in my English class at the last school I got kicked out of," she went on. "It's actually the most popular girl's name in the country. Lucky us. My parents have never been very original. Other than coming up with me, of course, but I'm not sure how much credit I give them for that."

"You don't give your parents credit for making you," I said. "I'm guessing they kicked you out of that school for failing biology?"

"Oh, I know the basics," she said, unruffled. "So do my parents, apparently. I just don't think I was quite what they had in mind when they decided to go in for the whole baby-making venture, you know? Otherwise they wouldn't keep shipping me out and looking so disappointed when I turn up again. Which I tend to do."

I said nothing. Hostility wasn't working—if anything, she was taking it as encouragement. Instead, I turned to my closet and started browsing through my clothes. As if it mattered what I wore today.

Although it might, really. Today wouldn't be the day to throw on a BE HAPPY! T-shirt. Not that I own one, but another girl here does.

The police would be talking to us. A detective. I'd be making an impression on someone.

I had to pretend to be startled—terrified, if I could manage it— by the proximity of a murder victim.

What would a frightened but innocent bystander wear?

"Schools are funny," Emily went on. "So often, all you have to do to get expelled from one is walk out. They don't seem to see the irony at all. 'You want to leave? We'll punish you by *making* you leave.'"

"Is that how you're planning to get kicked out of here?" I asked hopefully.

"Oh, *here's* all right," she said, flopping down and lolling across my bed. Ick. "Here's wonderful. Recent events notwithstanding, there's nowhere I'd rather be."

"Great." I picked a dark, lightweight, long-sleeved blouse, and then a pair of jeans.

"This is the first place I've gone where the teachers know more than I do," other-Emily said, staring up at my ceiling. "About some things, anyway. I can ask a question and get a useful answer. It's amazing. And the best part is, unless I'm asking them something, they stay out of my way and let me do what I want."

"What is it you want to do?" I asked without thinking.

She actually shut up for a second and looked at me with a pleased expression. I closed my closet with more force than necessary and turned to my chest of drawers. "And could you please go do it and let me get dressed?"

"Ms. Lurie said to stay together," she said virtuously.

"She didn't say we had to get married," I said, pulling out socks and a bra. "Whatever she's worried about, I'll be just as safe with you outside that door as in it."

She grinned knowingly at my clothes and rolled over on one side, facing away from me. "There," she said. "Can't see a thing. Carry on. Unless of course you're planning to drag me out of here."

Ordinarily, I wouldn't have minded doing exactly that. Today wasn't a day to attract attention, though, even by acting like my usual self. I glared at the back of her head, hoping I had undiscovered powers and her hair would start smoldering. Sadly, she seemed perfectly comfortable, so I turned my back on her and started getting dressed as quickly as possible.

"Painting, mostly," she said as the chill morning air touched my skin.

"Excuse me?" I snapped my bra and pulled my blouse on. Backwards. Damn it.

"You asked what I want to do here," she reminded me as I struggled like a toddler with my top. "Art. I love painting, but I like to draw, too. And sometimes I tear things up and put them together again, only different and better this time."

I would have liked to hear more about that. It sounded like what *I* wanted to do at Hawthorne.

"*You're* not an artist, though," she said rather than asked. "*You* like to write."

"I don't know if I *like* to write, exactly," I said. "It's just what I do."

"But why do it if you don't like it?"

I sat down on the bed as far from her as possible to pull off my sweats and pull on socks and jeans. "I don't *not* like it," I said. "And I have to do *some*thing if I want to stay here. Writing's the only thing that doesn't take any talent."

She startled me by bursting into silvery, unabashed laughter.

"Could you possibly keep it down, please?" I asked, standing up and going to the closet again. I'd forgotten a belt. "People will hear you."

"I don't care."

"I do. And you should."

"Why on earth should I? Why do you, for that matter? You certainly don't *act* like someone who cares what people think of her."

"This isn't about what people think," I said. "Not the way you're talking about, anyway."

"What, then?"

I pulled a light sweater over my blouse. "Someone *died* today. Someone was murdered. I *do* care about that, thank you."

"Of course," she said, surprised. She rolled over to look at me without asking if I was ready for her eyes. "So do I. But if you say something funny, I'm going to laugh. There's nothing wrong with that. We could all use some cheering up on a day like this."

"Yes, you've really had the worst of it, haven't you?" I asked. "How was that second croissant, by the way?"

"I never said I was the victim in this play," she said calmly. "But I have my share of worries, thanks. Corpses at the door aren't my idea of a lovely start to the morning."

I flinched.

"And," she went on, pulling herself up to sit cross-legged, "this could be a disaster for Hawthorne."

"What do you mean?"

"Oh, come on," she said. "Think about it. How are the parents who are shelling out Hawthorne's tuition fees going to feel about their little darlings being exposed to actual violence? A police investigation? A dead body one of *us* might have found? If there's enough publicity, and if enough parents freak out, they might even have to close the school."

"No," I said. It came out louder than I meant it to.

"I don't want it, either," she said. Her voice was quieter now, almost gentle. "I'm just saying it's possible. Ms. Lurie's certainly old enough to be thinking about retirement. Maybe she'll take this as an excuse—close Hawthorne before anyone can force her to."

"But—" I stopped, choked by bewilderment that threatened to become terror. It was one thing to know I'd have to *leave* Hawthorne someday. Next year, to be precise. I didn't like to think about that, but I had it as a concept. But *close* Hawthorne? It felt impossible, as if someone had threatened to "close" the mountains Hawthorne nestled in, or the ocean we could see from town on field trips.

Close the ground under my feet and the sun in my sky while you're at it.

"She wouldn't do that," I said.

"She wouldn't *want* to do that," the other Emily corrected. "That doesn't mean she might not have to."

I said nothing. Ms. Lurie had always laughed if anyone mentioned retirement. Hawthorne *was* her retirement, she always said.

But things were different now. Maybe Ms. Lurie would have to be different, too.

That shouldn't have mattered to me.

Thanks to California emancipation laws, I was a legal adult already. I couldn't quit school, but I could finish out the year using one of those online education programs. And I could live all alone while I did so. Which would make it that much easier for me to follow the rules.

So much easier than it was now, living in a house full of people who would be friends—or at least friendly—if I gave them half a chance.

"So don't tell me I'm not taking things seriously enough, Little Miss Cakes and Ale," the other Emily concluded.

I stared at her.

"*Twelfth Night*," she said. "I played Viola two years ago. That was the closest I ever came to finishing the school year at the same place I started. 'Dost thou think, because thou art virtuous, there shall be no more cakes and ale?'"

For the second time that bizarre morning, I wondered what century she lived in. "Look, I never said I was *virtuous*—"

"Good. I find virtuous people very boring."

"What is *wrong* with you? Not everything's about what *you* think, you know."

"Of course it is. Everything important, anyway."

I made a rude noise. "What a wonderful, selfless philosophy."

"Oh, come on. You of all people can't claim you're always thinking of everyone else's welfare first and foremost."

And then I said the stupidest thing I'd said all morning. Probably in all my life.

"As a matter of fact, that's *exactly* what I do," I said. "That's all I *ever* do. And I'm sick to death of it."

I think I would have killed her if she'd laughed. She didn't. She just looked at me quietly, as if waiting to hear more. I stared back, paralyzed by how much I'd already said.

Then she smiled and stood up. "My turn to get dressed, I guess," she said.

I turned to the door without answering. Today had brought the worst news almost everyone at this school had ever heard, and here my hands were feeling strange and shaky because of something *I'd* said. Almost said.

The old familiar panic was flaring up. I couldn't blame it. I'd practically called it by name.

She didn't seem to notice anything amiss. "I partnered you," she added, "so you have to return the favor."

"Not going to happen."

"We're not supposed to be alone right now," she reminded me.

"You're a big girl. I'm sure you'll be fine."

"Shall I tell Ms. Lurie you said so? After she explicitly told us—"

"Oh, shut *up*," I said. "Just shut up about Ms. Lurie. Shut up about everything, while you're at it. You can find someone else to go with you if you're afraid of your own room."

"I wasn't worried about me."

Oh, please. "If it's *me* you're so concerned about, you can do me a big favor and leave me the hell alone."

She just smiled at me again.

"Not going to happen," she said.

———

I had some things that I called mine—
And God, that he called his—
Till recently a rival Claim
Disturbed these Amities—

"Call me M," she said in her room. "As in the letter M, not Auntie. It'll make the whole Emily/Emily thing a little easier to take. Anyway, it's what I make everyone call me, even my parents."

I was staring at her door, waiting for the second I could open it and leave. Her room smelled like that flowery perfume and a dozen other scents besides. Nothing fake or intrusive. I caught lavender and lemon balm and others I couldn't quite identify. It was like standing in the best-disguised garden in the world.

(I notice scents a lot. I guess it's a natural consequence of not liking to meet people's eyes. Once I've memorized the floor, my other senses get bored and start taking notes.)

I heard her open her closet. "I kind of hate my given name," she added. "No offense."

"None taken," I said. "And no offense right back, but I'm not actually planning on calling you anything at all."

There were a few soft thumps behind me as she tossed items of clothing onto her bed. "Well, that might be awkward," she said. "But if you're looking right at me, I guess I'll know who you're talking to."

I rolled my eyes. "You'll know who I'm *not* talking to. That would be you."

"Oh, of course," she said. "As opposed to all those other people you're not talking to. Do you like my work?"

"Excuse me?" I asked, startled.

"On the door. I noticed you were looking at it."

I wasn't. I'd only been glaring at the plank separating me from freedom. But now that she pointed it out, I realized there were strange pictures taped up all over it.

"Ms. Lurie drew the line at letting me paint *on* the door," M said. Her voice was muffled for a few words, and I began to realize that the only thing worse than having someone else in the room while *I* got dressed was (as M put it) returning the favor. "But she doesn't mind where I tape things up. As long as I keep them in here, of course. No fair scaring the neighbors."

"Scaring?"

She laughed. "You really *aren't* looking at my pictures, are you?"

I was. I just didn't find them frightening.

I liked them. Which, for me, is its own kind of frightening.

One that caught my eye was of an elegantly dressed girl with gold, curling hair and an impish smile. She looked a lot like M, in fact. She was wearing a pair of glasses, but they were pushed down low on her nose and she was holding them on with one hand and peering over them. Or would have been, except that where her eyes belonged there were only dark shadows. A pair of beautiful blue eyes gazed up from the lenses of the glasses.

"That's Lucy," M said. She was standing beside me—suddenly, or maybe I just hadn't been paying attention.

"Lucy?"

"Not the girl down the hall. *Saint* Lucy."

"She doesn't look like a saint," I said.

M laughed. "Of course not. She looks like me. But the picture's based on the *story* of Saint Lucy. Bits of it, anyway." She looked at me. "You don't know it, I gather."

I shook my head.

"Saint stories are wonderfully weird," M said. "I love them. Lucy's is one of the weirdest. There are lots of different versions, but the best one is where this guy was pestering her to marry him. He kept saying how beautiful her eyes were. So she mailed them to him with a note saying they were all his now, and would he please leave the rest of her alone?"

"That's going pretty far just to break things off with a guy," I said.

"You'd think," M agreed. "But it turned out okay. That part, anyway. God healed her up and made it look like nothing had ever happened. That's why in most paintings you see her looking perfectly fine, except she's carrying a plate or something with a couple of eyeballs on it."

"Ugh."

"My favorite picture is one where she's holding what look like opera glasses, but really it's a pair of eyes on a flower stem."

I looked some more at M's picture, which now seemed almost tame in comparison. "And this is what you do here? Your project is learning about creepy saints and their creepy stories?"

"Yes," M said. "It's fascinating. I know it sounds awful—"

"It *is* awful."

"Well, people don't get to be saints by living long, peaceful, boring lives, you know."

I thought about the man Ms. Lurie had found this morning. The man who wasn't going to be living any kind of life now, boring or otherwise.

"It isn't just about saints," M said, in a sort of determinedly matter-of-fact voice. I got the sense that her thoughts had gone the same direction mine had, and she was hauling them back. "My project here, I mean. I'm not religious. I study all kinds of myths and legends. The point for me is what they mean—why people still love them and think about them and pray to them, even when they're bizarre."

"Or disgusting," I said.

"Not everything in Lucy's story is gross," M said. "She's a symbol of resistance."

"How is mailing your eyeballs to somebody resistance?"

"Well, it *is* how she resisted marrying the guy. But that's not the only story about her. Some versions of her life don't even mention

39

it. It just shows up in paintings a lot because that's the kind of thing that makes a picture more interesting."

"How nice," I said. M was wearing jeans and a pale peach blouse that matched her skin so perfectly it took a minute to see she was wearing anything at all. And she was still barefoot. Maybe she preferred that. "Are you dressed? Can we go?"

"Almost. I need another layer," she said, wandering back to her closet. No hurry in her steps. Looking at her, you'd think it was just another morning at the lovely Hawthorne Academy.

I turned away again, this time fixing my eyes on the floor. "Lucy's a symbol of resistance," M said again. I heard her sliding hangers around. "She didn't want to get married, so she didn't, even when her fiancé threatened her. She wouldn't make sacrifices to the Roman emperor because she was a Christian, so they tried to punish her by making her work in a brothel. That happens to a *lot* of female saints, by the way. Usually they manage to stay miraculously pure. But Lucy wouldn't go, and they couldn't make her. Look."

She was standing next to me again—does she move more quickly than most people, or am I just not used to anyone being close to me? She pointed to another picture on her door—not one of her own creations, but a postcard from a museum. "See? They're trying to drag her away with a herd of oxen, and she's not budging."

I couldn't help smiling a little. The men around her were furious, muscles straining as they struggled to get the cows all going in the same direction. Cattle as far as the eye could see, all lashed together and then lashed to Lucy. And there she knelt, looking so impossibly patient and immovable that she might have been a granite statue.

"So it's not such a horrible story after all, is it," M said rather than asked. "That's why I like her. She doesn't let anyone push her around or change her mind. She stands up for what she believes in."

M may not be religious, but she sounded pretty fervent when she said that. "Why does that matter so much to you?" I asked. "What do *you* believe in?"

"I don't know," she said. She was still barefoot, but she had a bright red sweater over her blouse now. It looked like the one in the picture she'd painted of herself as Saint Lucy. "I'm still figuring that out. But while I do, I'm not just going to go along with whatever they tell me to."

They were her parents, I assumed. Or maybe just the world in general.

We looked at each other. I knew I had to say something. It was time to be snarky and cruel, so we could get on with this horrible morning and M could get over any idea she might have that we could be besties.

I didn't want to.

I wanted to stay in this strange room with this strange girl and listen to more creepy inspirational stories about people who might or might not have lived and died a long time ago.

Ms. Lurie might have been right to worry that M's pictures would scare her other students, but just now this room was the closest thing to a haven I'd ever seen.

What was I *doing?* Or *not* doing, which was just as bad?

I had no right to words like *haven.* I was stuck with phrases like *oh, look—murder* and *yes, again.*

M was looking at me curiously, and I realized the silence had stretched to an awkward length.

"Are you going to put on shoes or anything?" I asked.

She glanced down. "Oh, yes. Thanks. Sometimes I forget I'm barefoot."

She went to her chest of drawers and started rummaging through an inordinate number of socks. She must really hate doing laundry.

"So, what happened to Lucy?" I asked. "Did they give up on the whole brothel thing when a herd of cattle couldn't budge her?"

M smiled over her shoulder. "Yes. They decided to burn her at the stake right where she was standing instead."

"That's a little extreme."

"Well, this *was* ancient Rome."

I decided to take her word for it. That's not a time period that's ever interested me.

"It didn't work, though," she continued, sitting down on her bed to pull on a peculiar pair of socks. They looked like something you'd wear hiking, except for all the lace. "The fire kept going out."

"So they let her go free?"

"Oh no. By then it was a point of pride. They *had* to defeat her."

There was that vague, oppressive *they* again.

"So what did they do?"

"Nothing very exciting. That's the thing about saints. They're like James Bond."

"What?" I almost laughed. This morning was getting weirder by the minute.

"Well, you know. Their enemies are always planning these elaborate, dramatic schemes, and it never works. It's like if someone would just take out a gun and *shoot* James Bond—"

"—we wouldn't have any movies."

"Exactly. The whole point of the saints is to have their cool stories. Whenever the governors or emperors or whoever get annoyed enough to finally just run a sword through somebody, it works. That's what happened to Lucy."

"That's *it*?" It seemed a little anticlimactic.

"Yep."

"But—why would God work so hard to save her from the brothel and the burning and all that, and then just let her bleed to death?"

"I don't know." M was sitting comfortably—in socks but still no shoes—smiling at me. "Mysterious ways and all that, I guess."

Dust is the only Secret—
Death—the only One
You cannot find out all about
In his "native town."

Nobody knew "his Father—"
Never was A Boy—
Had'nt any playmates,
Or "Early history"—

I'd been afraid I wouldn't seem convincingly upset when I talked to the detective. I mean, of course I'm not happy about what happened, but I'm not the kind of shocked everyone else is. Surely he'd notice the difference.

Turns out I had nothing to worry about.

I knocked on the door when they told me to. Ms. Lurie said, "Come in," and my hands began to shake so hard I almost couldn't manage the doorknob.

Ms. Lurie's office is tiny. Her desk and chairs take up most of the available space, but it's rescued from being claustrophobic by all the windows. Even on dreary days, Ms. Lurie's office feels like the focus of all the light in the world.

There was plenty of sunshine on this cruelly bright autumn morning, but still the room had never seemed smaller. I felt as if I were pushing my way into an occupied coffin.

"Hello, Emily," Ms. Lurie said.

Hawthorne isn't the kind of school where you get called in to talk to Ms. Lurie because of misbehavior. She likes to talk to all of us as often as she can—to hear any news we might want to share, or just to say hello.

I don't know if it just *seems* as if I get called in more often than the others, or if Ms. Lurie really is putting out extra effort in response to how hard I'm always pulling away.

It's difficult for even me to act hateable in Ms. Lurie's office. She doesn't seem to know or care that a work desk ought to be separate from food and other messy concerns of everyday life. She reminds me of Miss Temple from *Jane Eyre*, the way she treats her students like guests when we come to her room. Not that there's ever seed-cake—Ms. Lurie doesn't approve of refined flour—but she always offers a little something lovely and special to anyone who comes in: delicate rosewater pastilles, artfully sliced fruit, a cup of fragrant tea.

Apparently the detective preferred coffee.

Had she brought a coffee maker in for him, or had I just never noticed it in there before? But a coffee maker always smells like coffee even when it isn't in use. Kind of like how smokers always smell like cigarettes.

"Emily," Ms. Lurie said again, in an even gentler tone than usual. "Do sit down, dear."

Ms. Lurie's hair is long and straight and silver. Her face is tan and lined from all the time she spends outside.

She was sitting where she always sits, and *he* was near her—a little back, a little apart. Present, but obviously not wanting to seem intrusive.

I couldn't look at him. I thought about that other Emily thinking I'm a writer, and I thought this proved her wrong, because a real writer would have been busy taking in details so she could scribble every stitch of his tired gray suit down in a notebook she kept just for such occasions.

This isn't that kind of notebook.

I didn't quite kick the chair Ms. Lurie nodded for me to take, but there was nothing graceful about how I hooked it with my booted toe and then pulled it into place beneath me with a shove of my ankle.

If I didn't look at the detective, he didn't exist.

Not knowing this, he spoke to me.

"I'm—" and he said a name that I forgot almost before I heard it. I'm usually good with names. I find them easier to manage than faces. But I couldn't hold on to this one, probably because I didn't want to.

I don't want one more name for my collection.

There was a small silence after the detective tried to tell me who he was. If they were waiting for me to fill it, they'd have to wait longer than they could afford to spend on one student.

"This is a difficult morning for all of us," Ms. Lurie said, and I realized I'd clenched my hands so tightly in my lap that they were white around the knuckles and starting to ache from the pressure. It was better than the shaking, though.

"We don't want to make this any harder for you, dear," Ms. Lurie went on, and I thought about how she might be the only person in the world who can say "dear" a hundred times a day and seem to mean it every time. "But if you feel up to answering a few questions, it would be a tremendous help."

"I don't know anything," I said. My voice was a rasp, and I cleared my throat roughly and added, "About what happened. Just what you told us."

"No, of course not," she said, but the detective was speaking, too.

"We're trying to get more information about the victim," he said.

I tried to think about his voice rather than what he was saying. He sounded tired.

Had he been startled awake this morning, too, or was he already on duty when Ms. Lurie called the police?

Are detectives picked at random from whoever happens to be around when something awful happens, or do they get cases based on the sort of work they've done before?

All things considered, I should know more about police procedure.

All things considered, I should remember this particular conversation better.

It's muddled in my head, and that's strange when if I wanted to I could recite, practically word for word, so many scarier conversations.

Of course there's no way of knowing that for sure. Memory is a trickster god, and nothing makes him laugh harder than silly mortals claiming *he* works for *us*. But at least I *feel* as if I still have those conversations caught in my mind.

And then when I try to think about this morning, which was only a few hours ago, it's muddled. Muddy. Blank in places.

I know the detective told me the man's name. Stephen James. Did I know him? Was that name at all familiar?

I shook my head hard. Maybe that looked suspicious, but I couldn't help it. I don't know that many people, and I'd remember that name.

"I didn't know him," I said to Ms. Lurie.

I remember saying that, because it was like that scene in *Great Expectations*, the one I always thought was annoying though I like the rest of the book: the scene where Miss Havisham is asking poor flustered Joe questions, and he keeps directing his answers to Pip because he can't bring himself to speak to a great lady.

I couldn't talk to this detective. Couldn't even look at him.

I don't remember if I told Ms. Pip Lurie that I would have remembered Stephen James's name if I'd heard it before, because I always notice when people have a first name for their family name. I know it's silly, but it catches my attention. It sounds as if someone just started listing names at random while they were filling out a birth certificate.

I don't always like my new last name, but at least it sounds like a regular surname.

I hope I didn't say any of this.

I'm sure I didn't say anything about my new last name, or I'd probably still be in there answering questions.

I remember I didn't want to look at the picture they showed me, but it turned out to be just an ordinary driver's license photo, not how he looks now.

No I didn't know him. No I'd never seen him. Not in town on one of our occasional weekend visits, not at a gallery showcasing his work, not anywhere. I'd never heard of him before today. I didn't know anything about him.

I was asked terrifyingly ordinary questions and I answered them in the negative in what I can only hope was a reasonable tone, context considered.

I was probably only in Ms. Lurie's office a few minutes. If she offered me a sweet or a drink, I didn't accept it.

I'm not good at memorizing poetry, or anything else, but I've read enough Dickinson that lots of it has stuck in my head. It seems to me now that part of the reason I can't remember the detective's questions is that I could barely hear his words over Dickinson's.

I don't like the particular poem that was drowning everything else out. Like all of Dickinson's poems, it doesn't have a title. I think of it as the blood poem. And I don't like it. But there are times it won't leave me alone, and it was practically screaming at me this morning, if Dickinson's words can ever scream.

The detective said, "His name was Stephen James," and at first I was angry that people always do that, always say her name *was* after someone is killed when of course their name still *is*. Your name doesn't end when your life does, or how would they know what to put on your headstone?

My mother's name never changed a bit. Mine did. And which one of us is in the past tense now?

And then I kept hearing, *The name—of it—is "Autumn"—The hue—of it—is Blood.* Just those first two lines, the way sometimes just a few words of a song will start singing in your head over and over until you have to go listen to it all the way through to make it stop.

I tried to "play" the rest of the poem in my head to get rid of it, but I couldn't remember it. Not in order. Just fragments here and there, about Great Globules in the Alleys and An Artery upon the Hill.

I was angry at myself, because the poem isn't really about a blood-soaked town. It certainly isn't about a murder. It's about the leaves turning red in the fall, that's all.

My mother was murdered in October, just like Stephen James, but in southern California the trees don't have calendars and I don't remember seeing any red leaves the day after she died.

———

You cannot fold a Flood—
And put it in a Drawer—
Because the Winds would find it out—
And tell your Cedar Floor—

I'm extremely stupid to be keeping this journal. "Keeping" in both senses: hanging on to what I've already written here, and adding to it now.

Maybe I'm looking for points. Moral credit. If I confess somewhere in the vicinity of Ms. Lurie, it counts and my conscience is clear. The truth is written somewhere in her school. I haven't entirely omitted it from the record.

Oh, please.

Why do people act as if lying by leaving something out isn't as bad as "really" lying by making something up?

If someone says something, it might be a lie. Everyone over the age of two knows that.

It's impossible to look behind silence for all the lies that might be hiding there.

———

Over and over, like a Tune—
The Recollection plays—

I haven't done anything wrong.

There's nothing for me to "confess."

I didn't do anything.

I keep thinking about "The Tell-Tale Heart." That's what it was like, in the office with the detective and trusting, gentle Ms. Lurie. I can't remember what they asked me because I could barely hear over the pounding of my own heart and the urge to scream, to tell— to stop being a walking, talking lie.

Yes, it was me. I didn't kill anyone. I didn't know him. I don't know who did it, or how, or why. But it's me. I'm the one you want.

I answered their questions and I answered them honestly.

I looked right at Ms. Lurie and I lied and lied just by being here.

The truth and nothing but the truth, but not the whole truth.

But what would it help to tell everything?

The police have never managed to find the murderer before. Why should things be any different now?

I'd have to admit I've been lying to Ms. Lurie all along. Using the truth to tell a lie.

I'd have to leave Hawthorne. Even if she didn't make me—and of course she would—I'd have to go. I'd never see this room again. Never sit under a Hawthorne tree and look up at Hawthorne's own particular sky. Never be taken such absolute care of.

Never live this close to closeness again.

And for what?

So the police can continue to fail?

So I can enter solitary confinement a year early?

And, anyway, how can I know this has anything to do with me? Stephen James is a stranger. This could just be some ghastly coincidence.

~~It can't be just a coincidence.~~

And even if it isn't, I'm not going to destroy the little bit of peace I've found here on the off chance that the truth might be able to be of help now when it's never been before.

———

I heard a Fly buzz—when
I died—

We're all in the lounge again. We could be in our rooms, but nobody wants to be alone just now.

Outside, helicopters are circling.

———

My Life had stood—a
Loaded Gun—
In Corners—till a Day
The Owner passed—identified—
And carried Me away—

"Vultures," M said, looking up at the ceiling with a disgusted expression, as if she could glare the helicopters down. "There isn't even anything to see."

She thought about it a minute, then added, "I'm almost tempted to give them something. How good are those news cameras, do you think? Would they see exactly which finger I was pointing at them?"

"If they see anything interesting, they'll just stay longer," Lucy said in a pale echo of her bossy tone from earlier. "And more will come."

"I *am* pretty interesting," M conceded.

"Ms. Lurie wouldn't like it," an anxious girl added.

Ms. Lurie was still in her office, where she had been pretty much since the catastrophe struck, and where it seemed she might be stuck forever. The mentors were keeping a considered, considerate distance from us: close enough to be available if anyone showed signs of wanting them, not so close as to intrude. Bianca Young seemed to want to join our tight circle at one point—either to offer comfort or to take it, I couldn't tell—but Vera whispered something to her and she turned away, looking wistful.

I would have gone back to my room, but it would have looked odd being the only one and of course I couldn't afford to draw attention to myself now.

Yes, all right. I *wanted* to stay. I wanted to be with the group. It felt good to be part of a group, for once. Just once. To be human-adjacent.

And it couldn't do any harm, could it—not when *every*one was there?

Anyway, maybe Stephen James means it doesn't matter what I do anymore.

I don't really believe that. Of course I don't.

I stayed, but I pretended to read, or scribbled the occasional meaningless note.

"What did you think of the detective?" one girl asked nobody and everybody.

"Scary," the anxious girl said promptly.

"I *thought* he'd be scary, but he was actually really nice." That was Natasha. Her last name is something Russian. I remember being surprised that a Natasha could be small and round and timid-looking. She's a playwright, so that part fits her name pretty well, at least.

"Speak for yourself." Anxious again.

"Why? What did he do to *you*? He just asked *me* if I knew anything about the guy or had heard anything last night. Stuff like that. Pretty basic." Natasha looked around, as did I. Everyone else was nodding and shrugging. Apparently only Anxious Girl and I had been alarmed by the detective, and only I had any reason to be.

"*Did* anyone hear anything?" Lucy Holmes, girl detective.

There was a murmur of negatives, almost too low to be heard over the vultures' buzz. I accidentally caught M's eye, and she quirked an inquisitive eyebrow at me: *Well?* I looked down at my book again.

"I mean, *I* wasn't even *awake*," a girl said defensively, as if we'd accused her of the murder.

"Of course not. Nobody was."

"Except Ms. Lurie," Anxious Girl said, in little more than a whisper.

We were all quiet again for a minute. Then:

"What's going to happen now?"

No one had an answer to that.

M looked at me, gravely this time, and I thought about what she'd said about cakes and ale and Hawthorne closing.

"I want to go home."

This voice was so nakedly childish that a few of the girls glanced uneasily at me. I felt a little insulted. Yes, I'm nasty, but I only use it defensively. I don't shoot fish in a barrel.

I wished I could tell that to Madison, who was glaring at me almost eagerly, daring me to give her an excuse to slap me down.

"I don't." That was a girl named Alyssa, speaking in a determined tone.

Alyssa is small and blonde and likes photography. I know her voice because she asked to take my picture once and I asked her if she liked to focus on other people's faces because her own was such a disappointment.

That one got me in trouble. I even had to apologize. She didn't forgive me, though, so it was all right.

"I'm not scared to be here," Alyssa went on. "I mean, sure, this is freaky. But that's just it. It's a freak accident, right?"

"Accident?" Madison's tone was scornful. "You do know the guy was *shot*, right?"

"Yes, I know that," Alyssa said quietly. "I know as much about this as you do, unless you really did see or hear something you should be telling the police."

"I didn't—"

"Then don't talk to me like I'm an idiot," Alyssa said. "I know he was murdered. But he wasn't one of us. He didn't have anything to do with us."

"And he was *here*!"

"Exactly. That's completely random. I'll bet that's even *why* he was brought here. To throw the police off the scent. To make them try to find some connection that isn't there."

Or to make me try to find a connection that was?

Maybe I'd gotten too comfortable. Too simplistic.

Or maybe my assumptions about the rules had been wrong all along.

But why tell me *now*? It had been almost a decade since Zoë and the beginning of my boarding school career. Not exactly pleasant, but at least uneventful. Enough to convince anyone they had gotten the rules down, surely.

Maybe this wasn't meant for me at all.

"But how do you *know*?" Madison asked. She didn't sound angry now. She sounded almost pleading. "How do you know this was just . . . some freaky coincidence?"

"I don't," Alyssa said. "But I don't see any reason to feel any worse about this than I'd feel just knowing a murder had taken place in town. *Anywhere* in town. Because that's all this is. Awful things happen sometimes. Today something awful happened near us. But not *to* us. This is still our school, and I still love it here. I'm in the middle of a great project. I don't want to have to stop. They'd *better* not make me stop just because of some lunatic."

There was a heavy, unconvinced silence. I stared at the floor, not even trying to pretend I was looking at the open book in my lap.

Then M said brightly, "It's a shame no one cares about *our* opinion, isn't it?"

———

Pain—has an Element
of Blank—
It cannot recollect
When it begun—Or if
there were
A Day when it was not—

Would someone please tell me what sense it makes for the helicopters to be here the day after the day after the night a murder was committed? Hanging in the sky, loud and sullen, making sure we can't think of anything but a man none of us knew?

His life was neighbor to ours and his death was inflicted on us and of course we'd still be thinking about him anyway—it's only been a day since his body turned up and we're not terrible people—but yes, it would be nice if our minds were allowed to wander even for a second.

The police are long gone. We're only significant in the past tense. Why keep staring at us?

Poke your own open wounds if you like, but stop clawing at ours.

Maybe it would be easier, today, if Hawthorne were more like an ordinary school. *Never mind all the noise, girls—ten o'clock is math time, same as always.* Even if no one was really listening and no one could concentrate, there would be motions to go through.

As things are now, though, what can Ms. Lurie or any of the mentors say? *Never mind all the noise, girls—learn and grow and think and create!*

So far as I can tell, none of us are even pretending to try to work. We're gathering in silent little groups in the lounge or the library, and going to the dining room long before meal times.

We're quieter than the helicopters, but we're doing the same thing: waiting to see what happens next.

Waiting for another body.

Waiting for the police to solve something.

Waiting for the damned helicopters to get bored and go make someone else miserable.

Waiting to see if Hawthorne lives or dies.

Waiting for all of this to make some kind of sense.

———

Hawthorne appalls—entices.

Alyssa is gone. For good, it sounds like.

She alternated between crying and shouting—on the phone, and then to Ms. Lurie, and then to anyone who would listen—but her parents live not too far away from Hawthorne and they're shaken up, so they came for her and that was that.

"They'd better let me homeschool," she said fiercely when it became clear even to her that she couldn't stay. "I'm not going back to one of those stupid conformity mills and spending all day reading made-up shit about Columbus and the ocean blue. I'm not going to be cooped up in some stupid *classroom*. I'll run away. I mean it."

I should write her an apology and leave it with my will. To Be Sent After My Death.

That only works if I don't outlive her, though, and I seem to outlive everyone.

———

Dare you see a soul at The
"White Heat"?

At breakfast this morning, a round, redheaded, glaringly white girl named Abby said her parents are making her go home tomorrow. "But it's just for a few days," she insisted.

"Why?" M asked bluntly.

"Why what?"

"Why go at all if it's only for a little while? Either they want you out of here or they don't. Tell them to make up their minds."

Everyone was staring at M. She didn't seem to mind. M never seems to mind anything.

"Is that how you talk to *your* parents?" That was Brianna. She's skinny and black and as blunt as M is. Well, almost.

"Yes, actually," M said. "They called me the day it happened and said they were pulling me out of Hawthorne, and I said if they didn't let me stay I'd smash all their windows and then get myself expelled from the next five schools they sent me to."

Even Brianna was impressed by that. "Did they believe you?"

"They know me well enough to take me seriously when I say something like that," M said. "Especially when I started going into detail about exactly what kind of personal best I was looking to set."

"Okay, I'll bite," Brianna said.

M laughed. "I just said if they didn't like me going to a school that made the papers for the wrong reasons, they should try to imagine how they'd feel if the wrong reason was *me*."

There was an uneasy silence at our table.

"That's a pretty creepy thing to say, all things considered," Brianna remarked at last.

"To my parents, you mean? Or just in general?"

"At *all*!" Abby burst in. "God, what is *wrong* with you? How can you joke about something like this?"

M gave her a puzzled look that was, so far as I could tell, sincere. "I wasn't joking. They really were going to pull me out, so I had to bring out the big guns."

"Again with the tactful language," Brianna murmured.

"Excuse me for assuming you'd understand a metaphor," said M.

Abby looked about ready to haul out an actual gun herself. Brianna put a hand over hers. "I'm just saying, maybe now isn't a great time to sound flippant about weapons in general and guns in particular."

"Um, yeah," Abby said. "And maybe it's not a great time to talk like you don't care a man was *killed*."

"Is that what I was talking like?" M said in a dangerously pleasant voice.

"Yes, as a matter of fact," Abby said, voice rising. "It's *exactly* what you were talking like. And it really makes me wonder—"

"Wonder what?" M said, setting her fork down with care. "Wonder if I had anything to do with what happened?"

"Well, now that you mention it—"

"Girls?" Ms. Lurie was standing next to our table now. "Is everything all right?"

Abby pushed herself away from our table, knocking her chair over in the process, and ran toward the bedrooms. Maybe if Hawthorne doesn't work out for her, she can enroll in drama queen school.

Ms. Lurie sighed and started to go after her. "I'll go," Brianna said quickly, standing up. "I was going to help her pack, anyway."

Ms. Lurie nodded. "Thank you, dear," she said. "And tell her— well, never mind. I'll be talking to her soon."

She watched as Brianna caught up with Abby, and then she turned back to the rest of us. Everyone else was staring down at the table except M, who was looking at Ms. Lurie with an expression I couldn't quite read. Ms. Lurie looked back at her expectantly.

"Would anyone care to tell me what just happened?" she asked.

Nobody said anything.

"M?" Ms. Lurie prompted.

M smiled, and I realized she was furious.

"Oh, we were just chatting about current events," she said.

"Meaning?"

"Well, apparently since I'm not curled up in a corner somewhere crying my eyes out, I must be a murderer," M said.

Ms. Lurie looked stern. "Someone said that?"

"Someone was about to."

"I see." Ms. Lurie hesitated for a moment. Then: "I'm sorry, girls," she said. "I haven't managed this situation as well as I should have. There have been so many practical matters to deal with, I haven't given enough thought and time to how you must be feeling about what happened."

No one said anything.

I looked at M. She looked serious, almost fierce. She looked a lot like Violet.

Or maybe I was just imagining that.

"I had hoped to speak to each of you about this later, in more detail, but it can't be said often enough. So let me make it very clear right now," Ms. Lurie said. "We don't yet know why this tragedy was brought to our door, and that uncertainty is every bit as frightening as the fact that a man was murdered. We're all shocked and frightened. It's natural to feel that way. It's also natural to want to point the finger of blame at someone. *Feeling* that way is perfectly valid."

She waited until all of us were looking at her. The dining room was silent, so even though she was supposedly only speaking to our small table, no one could help hearing her.

"*Feelings* are valid," she reiterated. "Acting on them isn't. At least not if those actions take the form of lashing out at the innocent."

Ms. Lurie looked at M and smiled fondly.

"For the record," she said, "being what's popularly known as a smart-ass is not a sign of guilt. At least not when the girl in question has, by all accounts, *always* been headstrong and as stubborn as the proverbial mule."

A muted giggle crossed the room, and Ms. Lurie looked serious again.

"My point is, we need to be pulling together now. Not pushing others away and picking fights. No more unfounded accusations, please. From everything the police have told me, I see no reason to believe that what happened has anything to do with anyone here."

I was glad I'd already eaten enough to get by on for a while, because I wasn't going to be able to take another bite any time soon.

"No matter what I'm doing, I always have time to talk to anyone who needs me," Ms. Lurie said. "You girls have always been my top priority, and that's true now more than ever. Knock on my door. Interrupt me at anything and everything. Wake me up at night—or in the morning, if anyone can get up that early." Another giggle, this one more convincing. "The only thing I absolutely will not tolerate is another scene like this one. I understand that feelings are running high, but that's no excuse for a witch hunt. Understood?"

Ms. Lurie looked around the room. It was a quick glance, but somehow she managed to make it feel as if she'd spared a careful moment for everyone.

I was probably imagining that.

"Thank you, girls," she said. "I'll let you finish breakfast now."

Ms. Lurie sat back down. Bianca Young put a hand on her arm and gave her a soulful glance, and I wondered if she was already thinking up a poem about the morning's events.

M waited until the room's noise level had risen to a subdued chatter, and then she looked around at the diminished population of our table.

"Anyone want to finish the question Abby was asking when she was so rudely interrupted?"

If you offered M the choice between ending world hunger and snarking even once, our world would be a loud and hungry place.

"M, do you even know *how* to shut up?" I said.

For once, no one looked shocked or disapproving at my reflexive rudeness. Instead, they all burst out laughing, M the loudest and longest of the bunch.

Ms. Lurie looked over at our table, startled at the noise. Then she smiled, most of all at me.

I wish I'd been imagining that.

———

It dropped so low—in My
Regard—
I heard it hit the Ground—
And go to pieces on the
Stones   in the Ditch—
At bottom of My Mind—

Another girl left Hawthorne. Hannah. The one who said she wanted to go home.

She got her wish and I guess I don't blame her, but my *God* that girl can shriek. I was in my room when her parents came and from

63

all the noise she was making you'd think she'd just learned *she* was going to be the next corpse.

Well, she's got nothing to fear from me as far as that goes. The only change in my feelings toward her is that I've moved from indifference to dislike.

She's just one more person making it more likely Hawthorne will close.

———

The Bustle in a House
The Morning after
Death

Ten days.

According to the paper, the police are currently speaking with "one or more persons of interest."

(I have never understood why when a person of interest meets another person of interest, they become interesting persons. The rest of us turn into people when we go plural.)

Reading this, I felt a faint stirring of hope. Then I was amazed at my own idiocy.

I'm fairly sure the police talk to interesting people all the time. And murders still go unsolved.

But this time is different. Isn't it? I'm allowed to hope I'll learn something new after something so new has happened.

———

Not all die early,
dying young—
Maturity of Fate
Is Consummated Equally
In Ages, or a Night—

Stephen James lost his whole life—his present and his future, too. He wasn't married, didn't have kids, and he was young enough that people would say "yet" after each of those. He was clearly going to get better known in his field, given the chance.

He lost all those possibilities.

But he also lost his "real" death—the one that had been waiting for him down the road until the murderer pushed him down and stole it.

Maybe that death would have been terrible, too. Maybe Stephen James would have ended up out of his mind with pain, or on life support, or both. Maybe one sunny summer day the doctor would give him six months to live, and tactfully refrain from pointing out how horrible the last half of that time would be.

Maybe, when Stephen James was face-to-face with the end that had been written for him, he would have thought that a bullet to the back of the head wasn't such a bad way to go. Maybe he'd have been willing to make a deal with the devil to have such a swift and painless end, even if it meant leaving a few years early.

But I bet he still would have resented having someone else decide his death for him.

Nothing has happened but loneliness, perhaps too daily to relate.

A rare burst of rain today. It caught Ms. Lurie by surprise, but she laughed it off. Said it was nice to be able to take a shower *out*side for a change.

She's taking walks again. Has been for days now.

M said she can't decide if Ms. Lurie is a portrait of courage or a prisoner of muscle memory, but she sounded admiring so no one yelled at her.

In other local news, the persons in question are no longer of interest to the police and new ones haven't come along to replace them.

———

SOUTH HADLEY SEMINARY

Nov. 2d, 1847

BILL OF FARE

ROAST VEAL

POTATOES

SQUASH

GRAVY

WHEAT AND BROWN BREAD

BUTTER

PEPPER AND SALT

Dessert

APPLE DUMPLING

SAUCE

WATER

Isn't that a dinner fit to set before a king?

There's a book I love about a girl whose family dies of arsenic poisoning while she's safe upstairs, having been sent to bed without her supper for being bad.

It was a novel and the narrator was legitimately insane, but still I think there was a lot of truth in that story.

Not being allowed to eat can be a gift. It can certainly teach you perspective, even if the dinner in question promises not to kill you.

Perspective like *this is no fun but it could be a lot worse.*

And *so many things are out of your control, it's important to be able to control the things you can.*

And let's not forget *being a little hungry doesn't kill people—knives and guns kill people.*

Tonight I sent myself to my room without dinner, not because I'd broken any rules but as a reminder to keep them firmly in mind.

Contrary to popular opinion about boarding school food (which has definitely held true at every other school I've attended), Hawthorne dinners are good. Easily as good as what Dickinson was served at Mount Holyoke, I'll bet. Certainly good enough that missing dinner tonight felt like legitimate punishment, even if it spared me one more meal with everyone either avoiding everyone else's eyes or giving one another Meaningful Looks.

Anyway. I planned to get some work done and think very hard about anything but food and go to bed early. If Ms. Lurie came up to see what was what, I'd tell her so.

It wasn't Ms. Lurie who knocked, though. It was M.

"Hey, writer-girl," she said without waiting for me to answer or open the door. "Put down the quill. It's dinnertime."

I opened my mouth to argue and then closed it again. Anything I said could and most definitely would be used against me.

A pause, and then a *rat-a-tat-tat*, as if she were banging on my door with something metallic. Brass knuckles, probably.

"Come on," she said, and then lowered her voice a bit. "Ms. Lurie has enough to worry about without you being a diva."

I gritted my teeth. I was *not* being a diva, and Ms. Lurie had the opposite of anything to worry about as long as I was shut up in my room.

There was a long silence. I thought maybe she'd left, and felt a surprise that was almost like disappointment. M didn't seem the type to give up so easily.

I'd just clicked on the online random number generator to see which poem I'd try to write an essay about—I like that better than reading Dickinson's work in order, and her poems only have numbers, not titles. Then I heard an odd rustling noise, and turned to see what it was.

A note slid under my door.

No one is weirder than M. Does she think she's at secret-agent academy or something?

If I'd been at my desk, I'd have had to get up to see what it said; but unfortunately I was on my bed in a nest of books and papers, so I could read *Fresh strawberry shortcake* as easy as glancing.

I didn't respond, didn't even move. She was probably listening for the least little anything.

More silence, and then another note. *This* one I could have read from across the room—possibly across the school—since M was kind enough to write in block capitals as big as the moon:

I jumped off my bed, knocking a book to the floor in the process. Picking up both notes, I crumpled them up as loudly as I could as close to the door as possible.

M laughed heartily.

"All right, little princess," she said. "I'll tell Ms. Lurie you're suffering from the vapors and beg to be excused for the evening."

I waited until I heard her footsteps retreat all the way down the hall, and then I returned clumsily to my bed. I was still holding the notes.

M's handwriting was pretty and upright. Even her capitals were elegant.

Had she brought writing materials with her on the suspicion that I wouldn't open the door to her, or does she carry them around as a matter of course?

I do that. So did Dickinson. Her famous white dress had one pocket, on the right-hand side, just the right size for a pencil and a bit of paper.

(I've read this and I understand it would be handy, but it still seems batty to put a pencil in the pocket of a white dress. Granted, Dickinson didn't have to do her own laundry.)

The notes in my hands were opening a bit in spite of my violence toward them, like origami if you don't fold it hard enough.

M had used a fine pen for the first note and what looked like heavy pencil—charcoal?—for the second.

The paper was so thick it had been hard to get much in the way of a satisfactory crunching noise from scrunching it up. It was from a sketch pad, maybe—or would paper this heavy be for painting?

It seemed a shame to waste it on me, at any rate—especially when she had to know it wouldn't work.

And now, with the mention of cake, I was officially starving.

———

It is startling to think that the lips, which are keepers of thoughts so magical, yet at any moment are subject to the seclusion of death.

Last night I went to see Emily Dickinson's house.

I can only dream about it, of course. I guess maybe it shouldn't be "of course"—she's past being hurt, even by me. But I can't help worrying the place might get burned down after my visit, and then I'd feel guilty for the rest of my life.

It's one thing for me to go places I clearly *have* to go, and another to make what's obviously a trip only for fun. Can't risk it. Especially now, after Stephen James.

I've had this dream before. I'm never visiting the house the way it is now—a museum. In my dream Dickinson is still alive, a local legend smiling secretly in her bedroom.

Her home was sort of a tourist attraction even then. The Homestead, it was called—probably the first brick house ever built in the town, later added onto and fancified by Dickinson's father.

People didn't care about the house itself, though. They just wanted to see *her*. Meeting Miss Emily, the myth of Amherst, earned you some serious bragging rights—mostly because it almost never happened.

It hasn't happened to me yet, but I keep hoping.

I knock on the front door and the maid, Maggie, answers. I know it's Maggie and not Emily's sister Lavinia—I've seen the old photographs. In the picture I like best, Maggie stares at the camera, looking half-amused and half-impatient, as if the photographer is a child she's hoping will run along and leave her alone so she can get on with her work, for pity's sake.

I feel a little rude thinking of her as "Maggie." The Dickinsons called her that. So did their friends. But her family called her Margaret, and that seems to be what she called herself when she had any choice in the matter.

Bosses tended to rename the servants back then—to show them who was in charge, I guess, as if that wasn't obvious enough.

To be fair, Margaret didn't seem to mind the nickname that much. She once ended a letter by signing herself Miss Emily's Maggie. And she called Dickinson "Emily" when they spoke, which Dickinson seemed to like very much and which seems quite warm and open for a time when people would usually say Miss or Mister until they'd known each other a hundred years or so.

Fortunately, I don't have to call her anything. She opens the door with an inquiring look and I hand her a card with my name on it— kind of like a business card, but old-fashioned, with just my name and some flowers around the border. A calling card, back when calling meant using your feet rather than your phone.

I ask Maggie/Margaret if she could please send word to Miss Emily that a guest would like to see her, if quite convenient.

Her expression is professionally blank. "It would mean a great deal," I continue in my best imitation of nineteenth-century speak. Nothing I say will work, of course, but I have to try.

She doesn't say anything. She just leads me into the smallish sitting area I recognize from pictures of the house—too wide to be a hallway; too small to be a room.

I seat myself in a hard wooden chair with a strangely curvy seat, and watch as Maggie/Margaret disappears up a dark, narrow flight of stairs.

I may not get to see Miss Emily, but the woman I've already met gave the world Dickinson's poetry every bit as much as anyone else did. Dickinson wrote the words, and her sister pushed for them to be published posthumously, but Margaret Maher, Miss Emily's Maggie, was the one who gave Dickinson almost twenty years of writing time. She took over the hard, unglamorous housework Miss Emily had been stuck doing before Maggie came along. When Dickinson sewed so many of her poems together into dozens of strange, clever booklets, she asked Maggie to keep them in her trunk. And when Dickinson died, Maggie sobbingly handed that poetry over to Lavinia rather than destroying it as Miss Emily had requested.

Without Margaret Maher, there wouldn't even be that one photo of Dickinson you always see on her books and biographies. Dickinson's family didn't think the picture did Emily justice, so they didn't bother keeping it. Maggie did. Not because it would become the only known image of a great American poet. Just because Maggie loved Emily.

Not right away. When Maggie first came to work for the Dickinsons, she found the household so strange, so little like what she was used to—no babies to look after, but they did insist she play with the cats!—she nearly left. Strong, competent Margaret Maher was in demand, and she wanted to accept an offer elsewhere. But her sister Mary was lonely and illiterate and wouldn't hear of Margaret moving miles away. Margaret was fifteen years younger and the only other girl-child in the Maher family to survive to see adulthood. Mary wouldn't part with her, so Miss Emily got to keep her, too.

And Margaret—like Dickinson and very much unlike me—got to have a sister who held tight to her and protected her like a mother might.

I sit and wait for some sort of reply. The house is absolutely silent. It's huge, so I suppose I shouldn't make this sort of assumption, but I feel sure no one else is there.

I don't know exactly what year it is. Maybe the Dickinson parents are already dead. But where is Lavinia? Out on an errand, maybe—*she's* not the one who stays in the house all the time.

It would be nice to meet Lavinia Dickinson, or even one of her cats.

I wait what feels like forever, but one time I woke up from this dream in the middle of waiting and it was only three minutes after I'd fallen asleep, so clearly my mind is playing games with me.

No matter how long I wait, "Miss Emily" never comes down to see me, and she certainly never asks me to come up. Maggie is always forced to deliver the message that she's very sorry, but Miss Emily can see no one today.

When she says this, I always feel the same combination of disappointment and relief. I don't quite know that I'm dreaming, but I have a vague understanding that it's a miracle I'm in this house at all—to have fought so hard and well against all kinds of impossibility, and then not to be able to see her after all!

But if I *had* been granted a visit, what would I say? It's not as if I could exactly count on Dickinson to carry the conversation. She was famously flustered and speechless in person, even with close friends. And what do you say to a genius? "I know you decided never to publish during your lifetime, but I was born a long time after you died and I love your work"?

The first few times I had this dream, Maggie came downstairs with an empty-handed apology. After that, Miss Emily started softening her refusals with a handwritten note. She did that in real life—she hated being intruded on, but sometimes she hated hurting people's feelings even more. So she'd send down a few words, occasionally even a poem if the visitor were really lucky or had offered her something in exchange.

(One lady played the piano and sang so that Dickinson could listen to her from another room; and when she was finished, Dickinson sent Maggie to give her a poem she'd just written about how awful it was to have visitors barging in all the time.)

Last night Miss Emily sent me a note that might have been a poem. It's hard to tell with her letters sometimes.

I decided to believe it was one, and that I'd finally joined the ranks of the lucky few.

I wouldn't have minded if my poem had been a complaint, but it wasn't. At least I don't think it was. It seemed more like an apology.

Usually I can't remember what she writes to me, but this note I remember perfectly. It was wrapped around the stem of a white rose, which Maggie offered me on a tray.

I pick it up, embarrassed by my gloveless hands. I'm never dressed for the nineteenth century in these dreams, and I'm the only one who ever notices or cares.

I feel a little shy of reading the note in front of Maggie, but she seems to understand and whisks her aproned self away, having wasted enough of her busy day on yet another fangirl.

The note is secured with a bit of white thread. Maybe she'd pulled it from the hem of her famous dress—or her nightdress? Surely that would be white, too?—or maybe she'd asked Maggie to fetch her some.

The rose itself is perfect, of course: a silky white bud just beginning to open.

The note unrolled itself as soon as I tugged the thread. It was written in pencil.

> *Silence is the sum*
> *not of too few words*
> *but too many.*

That's not one of Dickinson's real poems. I checked when I woke up. Which means *I* wrote it, sort of.

It's not a bad poem, as bad poems go. Anyway, I'm not interested in being a poet, at least not when I'm awake.

I sit and look at my flower and wish I could take it home with me. A wonderful smell of bread baking has begun to spread through the house. Maggie at work—but didn't she leave the baking to Emily?

If I stayed long enough, maybe one of them would offer me a crust, if only to keep me from passing out from hunger. That would be embarrassing for everyone involved.

Instead I woke up hungry at Hawthorne.

Usually I'm happy to find myself here.

———

then it is all over, as is said of the dead.

what used to be

I have to walk by ^ Alyssa's room to get to the closest bathroom. (I wish there were some way for each of us to have our own, but there's no way Ms. Lurie would agree to that. Sharing common space teaches habits of consideration, and of course makes us appreciate the privacy we *do* have that much more. Which would sound like a preachy way to save a lot of money and earn virtue points in the bargain if she weren't so obviously sincere.)

The door to Alyssa's ex-room keeps surprising me by being open to emptiness. Today that room startled me with an occupant. A girl was standing quietly looking out the window as I hurried by.

Just for a second I thought Alyssa's parents had let her come back. But this girl, though small and blonde like Alyssa, was the wrong height and shape.

I stopped, she turned, and I saw it was M.

She smiled, though her eyes were serious. I didn't say anything, but she answered me anyway.

"I just came in to say hi." She shook her head and pulled one of the dimity curtains closed. "Muscle memory is kind of an idiot."

I didn't know they'd been friends.

"We hung out a little," M went on. Apparently, I wasn't required to talk in order to hold up my side of this conversation. "Her art was—is—really good. Completely different from mine, of course. Well, it would have to be. The whole point of photography is to

76

show you what's there. My pictures are all about what *would* be there if I had my way."

She wasn't smiling now.

"She took a few pictures of me." M laughed a little. "She said I could have one but I said it would only be fair if we traded and I got to draw a picture of *her*. She said yes and then she kept making excuses to get out of it."

M lifted her chin and looked out the window. Now that they've turned the clocks back for fall, the sun starts to set really early.

"I guess I'll never get that picture now."

Her voice was quite steady.

"There was a waiting list to get into Hawthorne when I first applied, did you know that? I had time to get kicked out of two more schools before I finally got to come here." She tried to laugh again but it didn't quite work. "Who'd have guessed that waiting list would start running in the wrong direction?"

"I have to go," I muttered, and hurried down the hall.

I didn't want to hear her start speculating as to who might be at the top of that new waiting list.

I'd only been planning to wash my hands and brush my hair. Instead, I took an extra-long shower and used the last of Madison's deep conditioner. She writes her name on everything she owns with a thick black marker. I'm waiting for her to branch out and add THIS MEANS YOU or I'M NOT EVEN KIDDING.

Which picture did M wish she had now? The one she wanted to draw? Or the one Alyssa took of her?

Anyway. I wish she'd stay in her own room and quit moping around where she doesn't belong.

———

Tell L—when I was a baby father used to take me to mill for my health. I was then in consumption!

One of the big Dickinson biographers says he doesn't think this actually happened. He says nobody else in the family mentions Emily being "in consumption" when she was a baby, or taking any trips to a flour mill, and that's the kind of thing that naturally made its way into diaries and letters.

Also, Dickinson's father was always fussing about her health. If she felt a bit under the weather, or if it was very hot or very cold out, he thought she should stay home and be ladylike. He tended in that direction, anyway, when it came to his wife and daughters.

I don't think Dickinson is lying, but that doesn't mean what she's saying is true.

Once I read a story about a woman whose father gave her a picture book when she was little—some kind of strange fairy tale. Her father read it to her and laughed with her about it. She remembered joking with him all through her childhood about one character in particular they found especially funny.

Then she grew up and decided to read the book again and noticed that it had been published the year after her father died. He'd never read the book at all, to her or to anyone else. He'd never lived long enough to laugh about it.

It was just the kind of book she knew he would have loved, so she'd imagined he'd had the chance to, never realizing she'd made up a story of her own in the process.

I've certainly never done that kind of thing with *my* father. I can't remember him reading to me. I can barely remember a thing about him. I'm afraid to even try.

What if I start making things up without knowing I'm doing it?

People talk about memory like it's a storehouse of everything we've ever heard or seen. Sometimes you have to move a lot of new stuff aside to find what you're looking for, but it's bound to be in there somewhere if you look hard enough.

But really, memory is a thief passing herself off as an eager-to-please shop clerk. You come in looking for something, and she says she doesn't have it in stock. You look disappointed and she says, *Oh, hang on, maybe we have it in the back. Wait right here, I'll check.* She leaves for a few minutes, and then comes back carrying the very thing you were looking for. *Is this all right?* And it's perfect. And you smile, and she smiles, and you pay for it and leave, not knowing that what you're carrying away was stolen—the clerk broke into the shop across the street when no one was looking.

"Memory" makes things up all the time if you push it too hard.

Memory is untrustworthy even when it isn't lying.

I remember finding my mother.

I don't remember why I woke up that night—a bad dream, or maybe I was just thirsty or lonely. But she didn't come when I called, so I went to look for her.

I found her, and I didn't understand what I'd found.

I know this memory is true because even the strangers who wrote about it say it happened. But I don't remember the next morning, when apparently our housekeeper showed up and found us together.

I remember the police, but I don't remember anything they said to me or if I said anything to them.

I do remember something that may not have happened. I remember being in the hospital, being taken care of by very kind nurses. I was surprised, because I wasn't the one who'd been hurt. For a long time, I believed that the reason my mother died was that the wrong person got taken to the hospital.

I remember wishing I knew who to be angry at about that. I remember feeling guilty. And then when I was older I remember thinking that I must have been being treated for shock. That would make sense, given that I'd just spent several hours huddled next to a corpse.

No one else seems to think it happened, though. The newspaper articles don't mention it, and neither do the books. Well, the articles might not have bothered, but the authors of those books were famished for details—and when they couldn't find enough, they were happy to fill in blank space with greedy speculation.

Typhoid Emily was especially excitable in that department. It even had a sequel, *What Ever Happened to Typhoid Emily?*, in which, with no facts to go on, the author ponders whether certain grisly murders could have somehow been me-related. The fact that I'd have had to be in Moscow one day and Lima the next didn't trouble her in the slightest. My murders being so magically brutal and varied makes anything possible, I suppose.

And of course their being so relentlessly unsolved makes them endlessly fascinating to a certain kind of mind, in spite of what *Child* of *Terror* describes as "a surprisingly low body count, considering the level of interest the case continues to inspire."

Well, Lizzie Borden only did or didn't murder two people, and we're still talking about her a hundred years later.

So: given that "level of interest," if I'd been brought to the hospital, surely one of those authors would have mentioned it. They'd have tried to get one of the doctors or nurses or janitors to say something, anything, about my visit. So maybe—likely—it never happened.

(But I remember it.)

Aunt Paulette didn't seem to know about it, either. One night when I was very young and very sick, Aunt Paulette said that if my fever got any higher she'd have to take me to the hospital.

She sounded annoyed rather than worried by that prospect.

At least that's how I remember it.

"Which hospital?" I asked. "The one I went to before?" I hoped so. They'd been nice to me. I'd rather be there than at Aunt Paulette's house any day.

"What are you talking about?" Aunt Paulette asked irritably.

"I don't know the name of it," I said. I didn't want to say when exactly I'd gone there. Aunt Paulette didn't like to talk about that part of my life. It made her even more unpleasant than usual.

I couldn't exactly blame her for not enjoying the subject, but it made things awkward at times. As if we didn't have a hard enough time getting along, back when she could be said to be half trying.

"Well, you've never been to the hospital before, so far as I know," Aunt Paulette said. "Unless you mean when you were born."

"No, not then," I said. "I don't remember that."

Aunt Paulette laughed. "No, you don't," she said, in a tone I considered rather rude. She didn't have to make it sound as if everyone *else* remembered their birthday and only I was stupid enough to have forgotten such an event.

"Why *are* people born in hospitals?" I asked, to change the subject slightly.

"To make sure they're safe," Aunt Paulette said.

"Who? The babies?"

"Everyone."

"But what's not safe about being born?"

"Stop asking ridiculous questions," Aunt Paulette snapped, and she took my temperature again.

Aunt Paulette is certainly in no danger from me.

Maybe she just didn't know I'd been taken to the hospital after what happened to my mother, or maybe she didn't care enough to remember since it hadn't involved Aunt Paulette herself.

(But *I* remember it.)

But Aunt Paulette was the one who took care of me until my father got back from his business trip. If she'd had to pick me up from the hospital, wouldn't it have been stuck in her memory—if only because making that special trip would have given her one more thing to complain about? ("The *parking* there—!")

I don't remember anyone driving me anywhere.

I remember being in the hospital and being scared to be there at first and then being scared to leave; and I remember being at Aunt Paulette's house and not understanding why, since Aunt Paulette hated having her routine broken up by visitors.

I *remember* it.

How can I remember it so well if it didn't really happen?

Why doesn't anyone else remember it if it did?

Ask that lady with the storybook and the dead dad, I guess.

I don't remember my father coming home, but I remember him bringing me back to the house. Our house.

Would he really have done that? Brought me back to where I found her?

Maybe he just didn't know what else to do.

I've read about how important it is for tragedy-kids to have as much routine and normalcy as they can get, but it still seems a bit much to expect me to go back to *that* house. Even after they'd cleaned it.

(I wonder who had to clean it?)

It *feels* real, in my memory. I remember the angle of the sunlight as I stood on the front porch. I remember stiffening up and wanting to scream but not being able to. I *was* able to cling to one of the pillars so fiercely that they couldn't make me go inside no matter how hard they tried. They'd have had to hurt me.

And then I remember being at Aunt Paulette's house and not liking it there since Aunt Paulette so obviously didn't like having me there.

I don't remember the night my father was killed. I don't even remember being told about it. I certainly don't remember who told me.

I just remember knowing.

It feels as if I've always known. As if he was always meant to be a temporary fixture in my life, while my mother's death still comes as a shock almost every day, though I've had more time to get used to the idea.

I don't know why.

Maybe fathers seem like less than "real" parents, at least compared to mothers.

Maybe I just spent less time with him in general, so his absence was less of a shock when it became permanent. He took a lot of business trips. I was in the habit of thinking of him as someone who went away.

Maybe my father had always seemed to be mine conditionally—on loan from the outside world, from the work I didn't understand that took him away so often and so long—while my mother had only ever been mine. If she had a life away from me I never knew it. She was more my home than the house I grew up in ever was. She was my world.

Who can expect to lose that?

———

I can wade Grief—
Whole Pools of it—
I'm used to that—

I've never questioned my life, never burningly wondered who could be doing this to me.

Why should I have? Whatever you grow up with is just how things are.

I learned—I suppose I knew all along—that other people weren't pursued like this. Other people got to have friends and families and homes.

But even that fact of my set-apartness became part of my ordinary. This was just how life was.

I followed the rules set down for me and tried not to think too far ahead.

~~Nothing has changed~~

———

Our share of night to bear—
Our share of morning—

The calmer things get around here, the worse my sleep is.

Not that I've ever been very good at drifting off or whatever it is normal people are supposed to do, but it's never been as bad as this. Even in the come-and-go patches of my life when nightmares are the norm, sleep has always been a given.

Not anymore.

Nowadays—nowanights—I lie in bed trying as patiently as I can to remember how to doze off. All around me, tucked away in their snug beds, my sister-students, as Ms. Lurie calls them, are locked away in slumber.

In the morning, I'm not tired, exactly; I just feel as if I've lost something. And the world seems heavier.

Last night I waited for sleep until 2:30 and then I gave up.

There aren't any rules about when we can be in the common areas—the lounge, the library, the dining room. *Be thoughtful*, Ms. Lurie says. *Hawthorne is a place for you to work when and as you see fit, but please remember your sisters have to live with your choices.*

She must have said something like that approximately eight hundred times a day back when the girl population here was her four daughters. Or maybe only six hundred, since two of the sisters were twins.

I wonder if my room is one of their original bedrooms.

Do twins share a room? It must feel like plenty of space after sharing a womb.

I didn't really feel like working, but I didn't want to stay in my room, either. It takes a lot to make me sick of it in here, and a lot is exactly how much time I've been spending in here lately. Too much. Even for me.

I slipped into the hallway. Everyone else was asleep, of course. All lights were off, at any rate.

I didn't turn any on. I know my way around Hawthorne well enough to find my way in the dark. I like that. If no one can tell where I am, I might not be anywhere at all. Just an unusually restless shadow.

I made my way to the library. It's small—that is, it's a pretty big room as Hawthorne measures things, but it wouldn't be called a library anywhere but here. The books are just books, no labels or special bindings or stamps saying PROPERTY OF HAWTHORNE ACADEMY.

I like to bring my own books and papers and work at one of the long, beat-up tables—more room to spread out than my spindly little desk offers.

Tonight I only had my pen and paper and a few books grabbed at random, and it was just as well I hadn't put together anything more organized or set my heart on getting any real work done because the light was already on and the library was occupied.

Of course it was M.

She looked up from her book quizzically. "Isn't it past your bed-time?" she asked and glanced at the wall clock. "Goodness. Isn't it past mine? I was just wondering why it was so quiet around here."

"What are you *doing*?" I snapped. I just wanted to be able to sleep. If I couldn't, I wanted to work. If I couldn't do *that*, I just wanted to feel safe in safely alone in the library, with the cozy old curtains closed tight against the darkness.

"Knitting a sweater for my pet kangaroo," M said. "What are *you* doing?"

I was noticing that this was the only room in Hawthorne that always smelled just a little musty, and now it smelled lavender-musty. I was wishing there was any sum of money I could offer that would tempt M to just go away. I was deciding that the best thing to do now would be to turn around and go right back to my own room, since I doubted M could be persuaded to return to hers.

And then I looked at the book in her hands. In spite of all my best intentions, I found myself rolling my eyes. "Don't read that," I said.

M raised an eyebrow. "You own the rights to Emily Dickinson, now, do you?"

"No, I mean, don't read *that*," I clarified, gesturing at her book. "If you're going to read Dickinson, at least read the real thing."

She shut the book, not bothering to mark her place, looked at the cover, and touched the name on it. "Looks like Dickinson to me," she said.

"They're allowed to *say* it is," I said.

"Okay, now you're sounding paranoid."

She had a point, but I wasn't ready to admit it. "Open that book again," I said. "Anywhere."

Obediently M turned to the beginning. I rolled my eyes again. "*Not* the introduction, half-wit," I said.

"You said—"

"It's a poetry collection. Obviously I meant a poem."

She shook her head, but flipped a few more pages. "Okay?"

"Now look at the punctuation."

She looked at me as if I were a misplaced question mark, then looked back down at the page. "Looks fine to me."

"Exactly," I said triumphantly. "That's how you know it isn't really Dickinson."

M just stared up at me, waiting. I thumped my books on the table and sat down next to her. "Look," I said. "Here. Wait."

Fortunately, I'd grabbed a good edition of the complete poems. I thumbed through until I found the one M had turned to, and showed it to her in my book.

"See?" I said. "No periods. No commas. No damned semicolons, that's for sure. A *real* Emily Dickinson poem looks like it was written by someone who's never heard of anything but dashes." A bit of an exaggeration, but close enough to the truth to pass for it.

M was glancing quickly back and forth between the supposedly same poems. "'It struck me—every Day—'" she murmured. "Yes, I see what you mean. You have to slow down and really think about what she's saying when it's written like *that*."

"Exactly," I said again. "People who knew her said that's how she talked, too—in little bursts. But quietly."

"She capitalizes like a madwoman," M noted approvingly. "I notice they changed that, too."

"They changed *everything*," I said.

M glanced at me sideways. I thought she was going to ask me who "they" were, and then we'd have been up all night as I struggled to explain how big a lie the usual Dickinson story is.

There was no sweet sheltered girl hiding in her room jotting down secret verses. There was instead a sly, sophisticated poet who was friends with bigwig editors and best-selling writers. There were piles of poems found in her room after her death, true; but dozens of those had been slipped into letters over the years, and booklets of them stowed in her maid's trunk.

Everyone knew she was a genius and a poet. She was a legend in her own time, and she was good at it.

And then after Dickinson died, her married brother's married lover decided that God had chosen her to bring Dickinson's genius to the wider world. She typed and edited and "corrected" the poems—and when this would-be Mrs. Dickinson overstepped her bounds and got her editing role slapped away by the courts, she avenged herself by hiding away a sheaf of Dickinson's poems.

It took decades to sort it all out, and it's about as easy to explain as what started World War I.

But M didn't ask, so I didn't have to answer. Instead, she said, "It's strange that there are different versions of the same poems. I mean, they're in English. They aren't even very old. It's not as if they have to be translated."

"Well—" I hesitated. "Partly, it was because when they first decided to try to publish her, the editors didn't want to turn people off. I mean, Dickinson's poems weren't like *any*one else's. They're still not. They don't have titles. They *do* have all those random capital letters." I don't think they're actually random, but that was another story I didn't feel like telling.

"So the editors didn't want to kill off her audience before she even had one."

I was beginning to think Brianna had a point about M's ever so tactful word choices. "Something like that," I said. "But also—well, here."

I carefully opened my favorite book of all. I love it because it isn't important in the usual way. It isn't all of her poems, or a selection of the best ones. It's just a big collection of photos of the old envelopes Dickinson jotted poetry down on.

That sounds ugly, and I guess in a way it is. They're all scrawled in pencil, which doesn't make her indifferent handwriting any easier to decipher. The envelopes themselves have turned a sort of sickly yellow-brown with age.

But when I want to be mesmerized by Dickinson, this is where I go.

"Here," I said again, turning to a favorite page. "Look at this."

M stared, seeming both impressed and alarmed. "Goodness," she said. "You can *read* this?"

"Not always," I admitted. "Never easily. But never mind that for now. They have the words typed up over here if you need it. Just look at this part."

This is the part of the poem I love—the part where Dickinson refuses to decide which word she likes best.

She writes a phrase: "But nearer to Adore." And then she wonders on the page if "nearer" is the word she really wants.

She doesn't cross it out. She simply stairsteps a list of alternative choices under it, so it looks like this:

But   nearer to

Adore—closer

further

simply

merely

finer

She left a huge space on the page for all those possible words before she started the next line of the poem. She didn't cram them in or write them in the margin.

That staircase is part of the poem.

"*That's* the kind of thing you lose when you read a neat little typed-up book like the one you were looking at," I said. "And you don't even know you're losing anything, because you don't know what it was really like in the first place. You figure if they say, 'Here's a poem she wrote,' that must be what she wrote. It must be *all* she wrote. And it isn't."

"But—all writers do this, don't they?" M asked. "Jot down first drafts?"

"That's different," I said fiercely.

"How?"

"You're talking about authors writing to get published. Then when their stuff's in print, you can see what they ended up deciding to say. Dickinson isn't like that. She wasn't trying to get published. She was just writing. We don't know if she would have changed anything if she'd known other people would be reading her work. This is all we have—what she left behind in her own writing. If she didn't make up her mind about a poem, it's lying for an editor to say she did."

"Lying is a strong word," M said gently.

"It's the right word," I said. "It's the *only* word."

M sat very quietly, her head bowed over the book before her, and I realized I was nearly shouting. I didn't care how that made her feel, but I did worry about waking someone up and having a big scene, so I lowered my voice. A little.

"Look, most of her poetry isn't like this," I said. "But the stuff that is—it's as much like art, visual art, as it is like writing. That stack of words is wild. It isn't neat or tidy or simple. Nobody should pretend it was. Nobody should pretty up her work and try to domesticate her. Especially when she isn't alive to speak for herself."

I was glaring at M now. I realized to my furious terror that I was just plain talking to her about something I love.

And M was smiling, looking amused. Was she laughing at me?

No—good God, she looked *affectionate*.

"I think I understand," she said. Very gently, as if I were one of those tiny hyperactive brown birds that fly frantically away if you so much as look at them. Sparrows.

"It doesn't matter," I muttered, gathering up my books with clumsy haste.

"What doesn't?"

"All of this. Any of this." My heart was racketing like a hummingbird's wings. Does it hurt to flap so fast?

It hurts to be the cage to those wings.

"Please don't go," M said. "I like to hear you tell me things. It's

almost as good as talking myself, and I never thought I'd like anything more than that."

That was supposed to make me laugh, I guess. "I keep telling
you to leave me alone," I said. I was almost shouting again, but this
time I didn't care. "Why won't you listen to me?"

"Emily—"

"Leave me alone! I mean it!"

She didn't try to stop me as I barreled out. Good. I think I would
have hit her if she'd so much as touched my sleeve.

Why the hell was she reading Dickinson, anyway?

If she'd been in the lounge in the middle of the day, or waving
her book in my face at the breakfast table, I could believe she was
just being her usual annoying self; but it was the middle of the night,
and she was obviously surprised to see me.

Can it happen here?

It happened to Stephen James.

—but that was outside, and tidy, and he was a stranger.

Either a coincidence, or a waste of a murder.

———

Your bond to your brother reminds me of mine to my sister—early,
earnest, indissoluble. Without her life were fear, and Paradise a
cowardice, except for her inciting voice.

Dickinson's sister Lavinia took care of everything Emily couldn't or
didn't want to do. Emily did the baking; Lavinia made sure there

was more to eat at the Homestead than bread and cake. Emily wrote poetry; Lavinia wrote notes to the butcher. When Emily withdrew from the world completely, Lavinia offered her own body to be measured by the dressmaker for Emily's dresses.

Emily couldn't have lived the life she did without Lavinia, because Emily was the point, the center, the reason for everything Lavinia did. Every move Lavinia made was an answer to the question, "What does Emily need?" Marriage might have been casual by comparison.

I think of Lavinia a lot—the sister who lived on long after her parents and siblings died, who was beautiful when she was young, who never married in spite of having suitors, who kept cats Emily despised and wrote mediocre poetry of her own after Emily's death even as she recognized her sister's genius and insisted on showing it to the world.

Was she deprived of a life of her own? Or was she one of those people who live for others and prefer it that way?

Her talents were for organizing, socializing, and making the household run smoothly. If she'd been born a hundred years later, she could have gone pro and commanded a terrific salary as someone's personal assistant. Heck, she could have run a company.

No one would have thought she was deprived if she'd lived *that* life. So why is it seen as a sacrifice that she gave her gifts to those around her just because she was born too soon to take them to the market?

She was the one who had faith in Emily's talents, right from the start. It was her determination that metamorphosed sheets and bundles of almost illegible handwriting into published poetry and forced the world to see that her sister had been the great poet of the nation. And it was her cheerful hard work that made the life that allowed her sister to create that poetry in the first place.

No wonder Emily loved her so much.

Did Dickinson ever wonder if she was worthy of such a sister? Did she work so hard in order to prove herself worthy of that gift?

It's hard for me to believe Lavinia was the younger of the two. Only by two years, but still. She seems so much a stereotypical big sister, bustling in and telling everyone what to do.

I can imagine a life where my parents didn't die, but when I try to think of having brothers and sisters, they seem like an alien species. Not unwelcome, exactly; just unnerving.

But I was very young when it happened, and I suppose that means my parents were, too. In a basic biological sense, at least.

There could have been more of us, in time.

What would life have been like if I hadn't been an only child?

Am I the one singled out for this doom, or would a brother or sister have shared it with me?

~~Would I be less alone if~~

But none of it would make sense that way. Considering what the rules were, up until Stephen James.

I followed those rules as soon as I figured out what they were. I never even argued with them.

And still this happened.

Maybe it wasn't about me.

Maybe some deaths just happen.

Maybe people just get shot in the head sometimes.

And are dragged to my school and left at the gate.

God, I'm so tired.

I notice where Death has been introduced, he frequently calls, making it desirable to forestall his advances.

One more girl went home and one's thinking about it.

"I want to stay," she said at lunch. Katia, her name is.

"So stay." Gosh, I wonder what tactful soul said *that*. I don't even have to hear M's voice to know when she's talking—I can just go by her I Am The Boss Of All I See dialogue.

"My parents say it's up to me," Katia went on. She has honey-brown hair and somehow manages to look about ten years older than she really is. "But I can tell they feel weird about my being here. If—" She glanced around and lowered her voice. "If only the police could figure out who did it, you know? I thought they would have by now."

I put my fork down.

"It hasn't been *that* long," another girl said. Then she added, "Has it? I mean, in terms of figuring out that kind of thing? How long does that usually take?"

"I don't know."

"*I* don't know."

"*I* think if they haven't figured it out by now, they're not going to."

"Ever? That's a little dire, isn't it?"

I stared at my plate, wishing there was some way I could go to my room without it being loud and obvious. Unfortunately, we'd only just sat down.

"Well, I don't know anything about *that*," Katia said. "All I know is, my mom offered me a trip to England if I come home. We can leave as soon as I want and stay as long as I want."

"To go to school there?"

"Just to hang out."

"Is that even legal?"

"Sure. We can just say we're homeschooling."

A pause. Then:

"So, when you say you want to stay at Hawthorne," M said, "what you mean is you want to stay at Hawthorne if Ms. Lurie will relocate to London."

Katia smiled, not offended. "That *would* be pretty cool."

M shook her head dismissively. "Too rainy."

"You've been?"

"Of course."

I don't know what's so of coursey about that. *I've* never been to London.

Of course, I've never been much of anywhere.

Still—plenty of the other girls looked a little embarrassed when M said that. M noticed me noticing their expressions, and smiled impishly. God. She can't shut up even when she isn't saying anything.

"How long did you stay?" someone asked.

"Long enough to learn that the food's as bland as everyone says."

"Oh, come on," Katia said. "You went to *London* and all you bothered to notice was boring food?"

"I went to *school* in London," M corrected, "and I noticed the boring food because, trust me, it was the most exciting part of any given day. I got myself kicked out as soon as I could."

I rolled my eyes. *Gosh, what a shock.*

"What did you do?"

"One of the teachers was big on making us take bracing walks in the rain. Right out of *Jane Eyre*, I tell you."

"And?"

"I took her twenty-pound tomcat out for a bracing walk in the rain."

A chorus of kitty-sympathetic *oh*s. I found myself fighting back sudden hysterical giggles, and didn't dare look up for fear of meeting M's eye.

"Oh, lighten up," she went on. "He was a nasty piece of work. Scratched me up good and proper." She sounded a little British as she said that, and I wondered if she'd had to stay at the school long enough to pick up the occasional bit of accent. "And, anyway, he was only out for a minute. I made sure to get caught right away. I didn't want to drown the stupid beast. I just wanted to teach my parents a lesson about shipping me off to places I don't want to be."

If my life were a young adult novel, this would be the part where the nerd-girl becomes best friends with the rebel blonde by telling her about how Emily Dickinson once dropped four kittens into a jarful of pickle brine while the rest of the family was at church.

M would love that story, but she's just going to have to find it for herself. And I happen to know for a fact that the one book that talks about it isn't in Hawthorne's library.

I have it in mine, of course, but she's not exactly welcome to browse there.

"Look, it's your life," M was now saying to Katia. "Do what you want. That's how *I* live, as you may have noticed. But before you decide anything, I think you should check and see if England will still be open for business after you graduate, and then think about how easy it might or might not be to come back to Hawthorne if you leave."

Katia, who's a senior, said nothing, but her face was very thoughtful. She wants to be a poet, and I was sure she was thinking about what a poetry country England is compared to America, but also about how leaving Hawthorne behind would also mean leaving Bianca Young, who's Katia's mentor and who's pretty famous considering she's a poet and alive. Ms. Lurie was lucky to get her. Katia's lucky to be able to work with her.

But to work you have to be able to concentrate, and that may be hard to do with her parents giving her a hard time.

And then there's the memory of a dead man messing with her head, of course. But isn't that the kind of creepy thing poets love to work with?

Maybe Katia wasn't thinking about any of this when M gave her unrequested advice. Maybe she was just hoping someone would change the subject.

I know I was.

———

Did you know there had been a fire here . . . ?

. . . Vinnie came soft as a moccasin, "Don't be afraid, Emily, it is only the fourth of July."

I did not tell that I saw it, for I thought if she felt it best to deceive, it must be that it was.

... Vinnie's "only the fourth of July" I shall always remember. I think she will tell us so when we die, to keep us from being afraid.

Even when nothing but a lucky shift in the wind kept their house from being destroyed by fire, Lavinia was calm and soothing, taking care of Emily. And Emily knew very well what she was doing, and was grateful even when Lavinia lied. Especially when she lied.

I used to think that if I could be allowed to have just one person to be my family, it would be a sister—one who would take care of me. Someone who would stand in for an older sister even if she were younger. Like a parent, but better. Parents are required to die, after all.

———

I never felt at Home—Below—

People think Dickinson was obsessed with death, and in a way she was. Plenty of her poems are about death. Some of them even have the narrator reminiscing about back when he or she died, which is weird to write about even once, let alone multiple times.

What's *really* weird is how cheerful some of those death poems are—jaunty, almost:

> *If I should die—*
> *And you should live—*
> *And time sh'd gurgle on—*

—and then she starts talking about the birds building their nests the same time of day as usual, and the bees "bustling," and she's practically humming and skipping on the page at the thought of dying while a friend lives on.

Or the poem where she really *does* die—the poem-teller does, anyway—and then starts wondering how everyone's doing without her, and which member of the family misses her least, and whether it will bum any of them out at Christmas to think that her stocking hangs too high now "for any Santa Claus to reach." But since that's too gloomy for a proper dead person, she ends the poem cheering herself up with thinking about how one day they'll all come and see her. Because, you know. Death.

Given when and where Dickinson lived, the amazing thing isn't that she went on and on about death, but that she managed to be so happy about it in so much of her writing.

Three of Dickinson's uncles had died before Dickinson was born—one when he was a baby, two in their twenties. Women died during childbirth. So did babies. Teenage girls might be asked to "watch" the sick at night, which meant spending a sleepless night with the terminally ill and hoping they survived until morning. Some of them didn't.

Kids were taught that anyone of any age might die on any given day because that was the simple truth.

That's still the truth, but these days most people can pretend it isn't. Dickinson seemed to take it to heart, at least. She once wrote that she could not spend a week away from home, for fear that someone she loved would die after she left. And that was *years* before she started staying at home all the time.

I think part of the reason I read about Dickinson so much is that I feel more at home in her time. Not that I want to do without plumbing or electricity, and I'd hate to have to wear long dresses every day. Or any dresses ever.

But sometimes I wish I could live somewhere—somewhen—that death was more ordinary.

How I lost everyone I loved would be noteworthy no matter when it happened, but *that* I've racked up so many dead people wouldn't be exceptional in Dickinson's world.

And people would know without my having to say anything. Not just because the story would get around, but because back then your clothing spoke for you, at least on that subject. There were certain things you were supposed to wear for certain amounts of time depending on how close you were to the dead.

I guess I wouldn't have been wearing black anymore anyway. You didn't forever for parents, and I guess you didn't at all for pets or friends.

And of course even in Dickinson's time, there wasn't a mourning dress to show you'd lost a spouse or child by never being allowed to have them at all.

Sunset at Night—is natural—
But Sunset on the Dawn
Reverses Nature—Master—
So Midnight's—due—at Noon—

This murder can't be related to my life. It doesn't play by the rules. This murder can't be unrelated to my life. Either the rules have changed or they weren't what I thought they were. ~~Or there were never any rules and no one is safe anywhere.~~

———

Dreams—are well—but
Waking's better—
If One wake at Morn—

Sleep runs away from me as if it thinks I'm going to hurt it.

Last night I couldn't fall asleep until midnight, and then I opened my eyes at 3:30 and I knew that was all I'd be allowed to have.

This autumn has been unusually warm, so there wasn't even anything cozy about lolling around in bed under piles of blankets.

3:30 doesn't feel like part of night *or* morning. It's kind of a lost time. Nobody sets their alarm to get up at 3:30, and anyone still awake at 3:30 is someone committed to staying up all night.

Waking up to that number felt like wandering into a stranger's party.

I got up and made my bed in the hope that reverse psychology would take over and as soon as my mind saw some proof I *shouldn't* go to sleep, I'd want to.

Of course it didn't work, so I lay on top of my quilt reading until I couldn't stand it anymore.

I grabbed my soft-soled boots and an energy bar and made my quietest way to the front door and out onto the huge, wooden front porch. Much too early to hope for sunrise, but the moon was pretty big.

I sat and looked at it while I ate. It's funny how staring at some things is an activity in and of itself. Watching the moon or the ocean or even the patterns in a stucco ceiling is fine. Looking at a wall or a rock for twenty minutes is a cry for help.

I shoved the empty wrapper into my waistband and walked down the front steps slowly. Hawthorne is set in several acres of unapologetically raw outdoorsiness. Everything grows where it wants to. There's no sense of a fight for survival—or maybe that fight was won and lost before I arrived. At any rate, the hulking trees and inquisitive herbs and occasional wildflowers seem to have settled things to their own satisfaction, and no one interferes with them.

Ms. Lurie tried to keep chickens once, for the eggs, but the stupid creatures kept getting eaten by local fauna.

I've always liked roaming around Hawthorne's grounds, so I know my way well enough that the moonlight was more help than I needed. I was heading over to my favorite tree when Ms. Lurie surprised me, silently seeming to appear out of nowhere.

I suppose it might be more fair to say I surprised her, since I'm not the one who's all about the predawn walks.

She put her finger to her lips and gestured me away from the house and toward the path I had wanted anyway. "Did I wake you, dear?" she asked softly when we were far enough from Hawthorne that even waking ears couldn't have heard us.

I shook my head. "I couldn't sleep, so I thought I'd get some air," I said.

She smiled. "It's beautiful, isn't it? Not quite night and not quite day."

I didn't answer, just breathed in some of the aforementioned atmosphere. It was cool and clean and strangely empty, as if all scents were still asleep. Ms. Lurie slowed to a standstill and I stopped with her, not wanting to be rude. She gazed lovingly up at the moon.

"Gorgeous," she said. And then startled me by adding, "'How much can come, and much can go, and yet abide the world!'"

I stared at her, and she smiled mischievously back. "You're not the only one who loves Dickinson," she said. "She's saved my sanity on any number of occasions."

I felt guilty for being another reason her sanity needed saving, and also for not recognizing the poem she'd quoted.

"It's a relief to come out here and be among so many living things that can't know or care about my petty problems," Ms. Lurie went on. "Sometimes it can seem terrible to see the world going about its business as if nothing had happened. As if what had happened didn't matter. But then to realize that what happened to you didn't stain the whole world—that the sun will still set beautifully if you're willing to wait, and the constellations will rise and dance and sink just as they always have—it can be a comfort. If you learn to let it be one."

She paused. "I didn't always think that, of course. I used to find it infuriating, truth be told."

"You did?" Ms. Lurie could be infuriated?

"Oh, yes. When I was much younger, I used to come out here and storm at the heavens." She laughed. "They stormed back once. That cooled me off. Literally."

The image of a young, angry Ms. Lurie shouting at the sky was so vivid it felt like a shared memory. "What happened?" I asked before I could stop myself.

"The time I got rained on was when one of my daughters was very young and very sick. I was pretty young myself, and terrified. Nothing really bad had ever happened to me, and I guess I'd figured nothing ever would."

"But—did she—"

"She healed up just fine. But having to leave her at the hospital like that—being told there was nothing I could do but wait and hope—it shook me up. And I'm glad. I needed shaking up. Strange as it sounds, I think that frightening night helped me later, when my husband was killed."

"Killed?"

Ms. Lurie looked startled at my yelp, and then her expression became apologetic. "In a car accident, sweetheart," she said quietly. "He died in a car accident. Nobody's fault, just bad weather and bad luck. He wasn't murdered. I'm sorry. I shouldn't have phrased it that way. Especially now."

I couldn't say anything.

"Don't worry, Emily," Ms. Lurie said. "We aren't living in a haunted house. I promise. This is still the home my husband and I built together, the place where we raised our daughters, the place where I try to help bring up other people's daughters. This is still a good place. One evil person can't change that."

"But—" I couldn't manage the rest of the question.

"But?" Ms. Lurie asked encouragingly.

"Are you going to have to close Hawthorne?"

She looked faintly surprised. "I haven't done anything wrong. Keeping Hawthorne open is up to me. There's no 'have to' about it."

"Well—are you going to?"

Ms. Lurie smiled. She made a gesture as if she was about to take my hand, but she knows how I am about physical contact so she clasped her own hands together instead. She looked like she was praying, or sealing a bargain with herself.

"As long as even one girl wants to be here," she said, "Hawthorne will welcome her."

———

Work is a bleak redeemer, but it does redeem.

So that's that.

Ms. Lurie doesn't lie, and she isn't often wrong.

Maybe Hawthorne really isn't going to close, and I'll be able to finish out my last year here. If nothing else goes wrong. If everyone leaves me alone and I return the favor. If that murder really was just one of those terrible things that happens sometimes.

Right.

Well, there's nowhere else for me to go. I'm not eighteen. I wouldn't go back to Aunt Paulette even if she'd have me. And just because I'm emancipated doesn't mean there are a lot of people out there willing to rent a place to a seventeen-year-old.

And that's okay. I don't have to think about it just yet.

~~I don't have to think about~~

I simply have to think about Emily Dickinson and pretend I'm just another Hawthorne student.

I measure Every Grief
I meet

That's one of my favorite poems. The whole thing, I mean—not just those first few words.

I love it so much I learned it by heart—which was tough, because I have a hard time memorizing *any* poem, and this one's really long.

I learned it back when I was still reading Dickinson in a pretty haphazard fashion. I hadn't learned much about her life. I certainly hadn't started to unsnarl the tangled mess of how and when and why her poems were published.

It took a long time to learn that whole poem, and I was proud of myself for doing it. So I was startled and annoyed one day, much later, when I was leafing through a collection I'd grabbed from the library and found a totally different version of the poem I thought I knew.

They got it wrong was my first thought.

My second, when I read this new version again, was *Wait—I got it wrong.*

The new version had ten verses. The one I'd learned only had nine.

It made more sense to assume that some editor had cut a verse than to think someone had added one.

But how? Why? And why were some of the words in this version just plain different from what I'd managed to teach myself?

Why did she measure grief with *analytic* eyes in the poem I'd learned, but *narrow, probing* ones in the poem I'd just found?

That was when I started really studying Dickinson, instead of just reading her.

I went online and ordered all the really pricey editions of her poetry I could find, and when they arrived I learned why they'd cost so much.

There was a huge, ugly-on-the-outside set that turned out to be a careful collection of photos of all those handwritten booklets Dickinson sewed together. There was an elegant, ugly-on-the-inside boxed set that turned out to be a typed-up collection of every poem Dickinson ever wrote, along with a record of every known variation of each poem.

Sometimes there were different versions because Dickinson played around with her poems and then sent them in undated letters to various friends. Sometimes it was more complicated than that.

Last night I was working late in the library again—mercifully alone—with all my books spread out around me.

Sometimes I like to pretend someone bought them for me.

I was frowning over that poem again.

Every editor has messed with it one way or another.

Her first editor—that mistress—made the punctuation and capitalization boring, but she did keep the word changes Dickinson handwrote into her own little booklet version—changes she obviously made after writing out the first draft.

But then the mistress made some word changes of her own, and cut a verse seemingly at random.

The editor I like best is a man who put Dickinson's booklets back together after the mistress pulled them apart and scrambled the order they'd been in.

He kept Dickinson's wild punctuation and strange sprinkles of capital letters and put that missing verse back in, but he left out the word changes she made.

Why?

That's always the question with Dickinson.

She was born. She was a genius. She wrote. She shut herself away from the world. She died.

Nobody knows the *why* of any of that, but plenty of people pretend to. I learned that when I started reading every biography I could get my hands on.

Sometimes what she *didn't* do is stranger than what she did. She could have tried to publish her work. She had the chance to marry a man she loved. She didn't do either of those things.

I looked at the poem again and sighed.

The thing is, I actually kind of like the bit about "narrow, probing eyes." It's creepy.

But is it fair to keep what you like and say that's what the poet wrote when she made a clear revision?

Once you start down that path, wouldn't it be all too easy to start "correcting" the text with, say, words you think would be a better choice?

The mistress did that sometimes.

And then there's the capitalization. Dickinson's handwriting is so tricky, there are plenty of times it's hard to tell whether or not she meant a letter to be capital.

Maybe she didn't care.

The last four words of this poem all look capital to me, but even the editor I like best left them as shorties.

I had a sudden feeling of power.

If I look at her writing and see capital letters, and I can say why I think that (look, this T is taller and the crossbar is on top rather than cutting through the middle, and this M has that special squiggle she uses for the uppercase), my opinion is as valid as anyone else's.

That's the beauty of Dickinson's work: she never published it, so it belongs to everyone.

Including me.

Maybe I'll never be a real scholar with letters after my name, but I can learn as much as anyone else can about her and I can say what I see.

Maybe I can write a book of my own about her. Why not? I could publish it myself if no one else wants to. And if no one wants to read it—well, it's not hurting anyone by existing.

Especially if I don't sign my name to it. That would be a very Dickinson thing to do.

I glanced up, smiling triumphantly at the thought of strangers wondering who this brilliant anonymous literary theorist was.

—and I met the eyes of M, who'd just come in and who seemed to accept my smile as a gift.

———

I cannot see anything to prevent a quiet season. Father takes care of the doors and mother of the windows, and Vinnie and I are secure against all outward attacks. If we can get our hearts "under," I don't have much to fear—I've got all but three feelings down, if I can only keep them!

Dickinson wrote this when she was twenty years old and Lavinia was eighteen. So far as I can tell, her parents weren't afraid of "attacks" from wolves or bears or burglars. They seemed to be locking up against gentlemen callers who might steal their daughters' hearts.

Later in this same letter she describes spending the afternoon visiting friends. When she got home, her mother was weeping and wailing and her father threw a fit about how long she'd been gone and how late she was getting home.

Nine o'clock does not seem terribly late for a twenty-year-old woman to be out visiting her friends. Even a twenty-year-old woman in nineteenth-century New England.

To be fair, *everyone's* parents were a little weird back then, apparently.

I have a copy of the child-rearing manual Dickinson's parents read. There's all sorts of advice about when (not if) you should hit your kid, because keeping your offspring terrified of you was a crucial part of parenting.

It says so in as many words: "Fear is a useful and a necessary principle in family government."

Apparently some parents were known to overdo it on the fear front, because there are also some this-really-happened stories in the manual about children getting so scared they spent the rest of their lives morons, or else they literally died of fright.

Doesn't seem likely, but of course I wasn't there.

In spite of what she said in this letter and some others, I don't think Dickinson was afraid of her father.

One time when her father wanted her to go to church, she just kept saying no. I don't think she'd have done that if she were afraid of him. Certainly she wouldn't have done what she did next, which was to drop the argument, leave the room, and hide until church was over.

They went without her, which seems an odd thing to do when one of your daughters has gone missing; but they did have another daughter to spare, and, anyway, everyone knew Miss Emily had her odd ways and would turn up in her own sweet time. Which she did.

Dickinson most definitely wasn't afraid of her mother. I'm not sure anyone ever was. Even the houseflies probably relaxed when she was the only one in the room—no swatting today, not from such a sickly, weary, faint-voiced worrier as Emily Dickinson, Senior.

I don't remember ever feeling afraid of *my* mother.

Most of my memories are tinges of sweetness—flashes of fun.

Once I picked a dandelion and my mother told me to "blow on it, darling—blow as hard as you can, like a birthday candle!" and then she burst out laughing at the look on my face when the tiny gray cloud burst apart and took to the wind.

Once she found me in the kitchen, crying because a cabinet door was open. I wasn't one of those kids who can't stand it if everything isn't exactly as it should be. I didn't care that a door was open. I'd just never really noticed this one before, and now it was swinging on its hinges in a way that seemed menacing to me. It was low to the ground and I couldn't see all the way to the back, and that made this cabinet seem suddenly full of dark possibilities.

My mother probably wouldn't have been able to understand this even if I'd attempted to put it into words. She didn't try too hard to sort out what the problem was. Instead, she just sat down on the floor with me and made the can of baking powder talk, and then she sprinkled flour on her hair and cried, "Oh no! I'm old!" Then she smelled the bottle of vanilla extract and pretended to faint at the wonderful scent, and made me smell it, too, and watched me faint, and then we beat a little of it into butter and sugar and cut the gritty sweetness into shapes and ate them as if they were cookies when really they were a million times better.

In the memories I have of her, my mother seems more like another child than an authority figure. How could I ever be afraid of her?

I remember *her* being afraid once. I was very little and I must have been moving much too quickly toward much too much traffic. I remember squealing in delight when my mother scooped me up so quickly and so hard that we both nearly went flying. I giggled, and then was puzzled that my mother was hitching with sobs rather than laughter, clutching me hard enough to hurt.

If you wanted a hug that much, you could always just ask for one, I remember thinking, baffled.

Maybe it never happened. There's no one to ask now.

———

Meeting a bird this morning, I began to flee. He saw it and sung.

I ought to be able to calm down a bit now. Hawthorne isn't going to close. The detective hasn't come back demanding to talk to me.

114

The student population of Hawthorne is lower than it was a month ago, but it seems to have leveled off. The ones who stayed are doing a pretty good imitation of their pre-murder selves.

I ought to be able to get some work done, and maybe even sleep now and then.

M, however, is trying to make me as crazy as she is.

She seemed to take my presence in the library that night as some sort of invitation. Which is ridiculous, considering how I spoke to her the *last* time we ran into one another in that room.

And excuse me, but I've been working alone late at night in the library for a lot longer than she's even been at Hawthorne. Probably longer than she spent at the last three schools she went to, wherever *they* are. It's just something I *do*. I'm specifically there to *not* run into people.

It was a million o'clock at night and everyone in the world was asleep and I was obviously only in the library because I wanted to be *alone*, so naturally M strutted in like she owned the damned place.

I glared at her as best I could on short notice.

"Care for a little company?" she asked.

That girl could not take a hint if you carved it into a gold brick and threw it at her head.

"No."

She smiled, surveying the grand, organized mess of propped-open books before me. She was wearing the same white nightgown she had on the night of the alarm, or maybe a lacier cousin.

"'No room! No room!' 'There's *plenty* of room!'" she said in a strange singsong, pulling back a chair.

"Have you been drinking?" I asked coldly.

She laughed. "I'm quoting, silly. Don't you like *Alice in Wonderland*?"

"Never met her," I said, trying to look completely occupied by my books.

"So what are you working on tonight?" she continued.

"Writing."

"Excellent. You've certainly nailed that whole brevity-is-the-soul-of-wit thing."

I tried to catch my train of thought, but it had sped off into the night at the first approach of M's ridiculous chatter. Oblivious to my scowl, she pulled one of my books toward her—the most expensive of the bunch, of course.

"Ooh, more indecipherable handwriting," she said approvingly, leafing through it. I mean, it wasn't as if I could possibly have wanted it open to a particular page, or as if these books were arranged so I could look at them in an order I preferred. I'd just scattered them this way to be decorative.

I didn't bother saying that, much as I wanted to. She would have given me a straight-faced artistic assessment of my arrangement.

Instead, I paper-clipped my loose notes together, put them in one of the books as a page marker, and began closing and stacking the rest of the volumes.

They were of all shapes and sizes, and they resented my efforts to make them neat and portable. It'd taken two trips to lug them all in here in the first place.

"You know, I think I'm starting to get the hang of this," M said, poring over the volume she'd chosen. "I swear I can make out a word or two here and there."

I snorted. "That's her earliest work," I said.

"So?"

"So her handwriting still looks like handwriting. You can tell she's trying really hard to make it neat and pretty." Honesty compelled me to add, "Some of the later stuff is actually even easier to read. It's loopy and weird, but at least it's big and round."

Reluctantly, I showed her an example in a volume heavy enough to break someone's foot and possibly the floor as well. "You'd never know it was the same writer," M said, looking at the page. "It's so different. And strange. It looks—sorry to say this about the great poet—kind of goofy." She glanced back at the volume she'd appropriated, then at mine again. "The letters are *huge*," she said. "Was she having trouble seeing or something?"

"She did have eye problems for a while, when she was younger. But yeah, she might have been having trouble seeing smaller print when she wrote these. I mean, she was in her forties."

"Elderly," M agreed. She looked back at what she now clearly considered to be her very own book and flipped a page or two. "What the *hell*?"

"What?"

"What happened *here*?"

"Here" was a page spread covered with nothing but ruthless black scribbles. The paper the poem had been written on had been torn in two, the pieces then placed carefully back together for the photographer to record.

"Her brother's girlfriend did that," I said.

"Great howler monkeys," M said. "What, did she have anger management issues or something?"

"The brother was married, but he was fooling around with the woman who first typed up the poems," I said. "This was a poem Dickinson wrote about her brother's wife and how wonderful she was. So the girlfriend—mistress—kind of flipped out."

"*Oh*. Well. My goodness. How sordid. And creepy."

We both stared at the mutilated page in silence. "Why didn't she just throw it away?" M asked. "She obviously wanted to get rid of it."

"There were poems on the back she didn't want to lose," I said.

"Wait—how do we know what the poem was about if this chippy crossed it all out?"

I smiled in spite of myself. *Chippy*. "Dickinson had sent a copy of the poem to the wife already," I explained. "And the wife hung on to it her whole life."

"I'll *bet*," M said.

"What do you mean?"

"If a brilliant woman wrote *me* a love poem, I'd get it as a tattoo. And make them copy her handwriting onto my skin while they were at it."

"It wasn't a *love* poem," I protested. "It was just . . ."

"A *like* poem?"

"She talks about her being a *sister*," I said.

"Mmm."

M's utterly unconvinced tone was even more annoying than her voice usually is.

"Look," I snapped. "If someone had the hots for *me*, I'd be pretty pissed if they couldn't think of something a little more romantic than *that* to say."

M looked up at me. Her expression was startled and also something I couldn't figure out. I certainly wasn't about to waste time trying.

I'd wasted enough time tonight.

"Since I obviously can't get any *work* done now," I said, gathering what books I could reach, "I'm going to try to get some sleep. And in case I haven't mentioned it—"

"Wait," M said. "Let me guess." She closed her eyes tightly and pressed her fingers to her temples, as if concentrating. "Should I . . . leave you alone until the end of time?"

"Just fuck *off* already, M," I said. "Don't tell me no one's ever said that to you before."

"I'm usually the one saying it, actually."

"Good. At least you know what the words mean, even if you're not used to hearing them from this angle."

"Emily—"

"No," I said, and went back to my room as quickly as I could, considering how many damned heavy books I was juggling and also considering that no matter how much I wanted or needed to, I couldn't stomp my feet and I certainly couldn't slam my door. Ms. Lurie is very patient, but even she wouldn't put up with me slamming around in the wee hours of the morning.

M still has one of my books, damn it.

~~Why do I always~~

~~Why does she always~~

———

The book you mention, I have not met.

Other than Dickinson, I mostly read junk.

I mean, I like *some* of the smart stuff. I'm not as insane about Shakespeare as Dickinson was, but I like *Othello* and *The Tempest*. I love *Jane Eyre* (which she loved, too) and *Anna Karenina* (which I have no idea if she ever read or not).

I know I'm supposed to like Jane Austen, but she makes me fidget.

I think I like *Wuthering Heights*, but it kind of freaks me out.

But most of what I love to read is just nonsense. Silly books about teenagers with silly problems. Vampire romances. Star Trek novels.

M would mock me endlessly if she knew I'm not even reading them ironically. I want them all to be true.

I want the world to be that place.

I don't need a book to have exquisite prose or make some searing point. I just want it to make me fall in love—with a character, a story, a town; it doesn't matter to me, I just want to get to feel like someone else for a little while.

I read a lot of books that are way too young for me. I love the Ramona books. You know nothing too bad can ever happen on Klickitat Street.

My friends are books, and books are my friends.

Sometimes I jot things down in the margins so I can do some of the talking.

Dickinson thought of books as people, too. Her niece Martha said she talked about characters as if they were neighbors and friends rather than imaginary creatures.

Dickinson also read a lot of junk. I'm not saying that to be mean. I've checked. For every great novel or play she talks about in her letters, there are always two or three she mentions that are out of print because no one cares about them anymore.

I like that. It gives me something in common with a genius.

Her dad had mixed feelings about her reading habits. "He buys me many Books—but begs me not to read them—because he fears they joggle the Mind," she wrote to a friend.

Her brother Austin bought her books, too. He brought home a boring novel called *Kavanagh* once and hid it in the piano, because their dad said Emily couldn't read it.

She did anyway. I'm not sure if she took it out of the piano first, or read it right at the keyboard while pretending to practice her scales.

I read that book to see what all the fuss was about. The copy I got called it "an early lesbian romance."

All I can say is, if lesbianism consists of teenaged girls talking about carrier pigeons and kissing each other on the forehead, it's a lot less exciting than it's been made out to be.

———

For each extatic instant
We must an anguish pay

M didn't even bring my book back to me. She just left it in the library, on the same table I had been working at. Propped open, which is absolutely terrible for the spine.

Oh—and she WROTE in the damned thing.

That's a damned expensive book and it's part of a two-volume set. I'll have to pay for both again to replace it.

At least she used pencil. I think I'd have to stab her in her sleep if she'd marked it up in ink.

And she wrote in the margin, way off to one side.

I didn't even notice right away, because it's the book that's just photos of Dickinson's handwritten pages. A little scribbling off to one side didn't stick out at first, especially since the words were a little like something Dickinson would write.

I don't frighten easily.

I stared at the book, pausing mid-reach.

Then I pulled my hands back and went to my room for a pencil.

She'd left plenty of room under her remark for a reply.

Of course I ~~could~~ should have taken the book to my room, erased her message, and pretended not to have seen it, but that wouldn't exactly be credible—not when she'd practically hung a neon arrow over it. And she was the type to pester me if she didn't get a reply, possibly at the dinner table where it would be more awkward to try to get away from her.

Plus my book was ruined already, so why not go all the way?

My handwriting isn't as pretty as M's, so I printed my words carefully.

What's that supposed to mean?

Then I left the book and left the room and tried to work and failed. Instead I paced and paced and paced.

What was I doing? What was I *doing*?

The hummingbird was trapped inside me again and I couldn't say which one of us was more frantic.

A fragment of a phrase kept going through my head and for once it wasn't Dickinson. It was Shakespeare.

If it were done when 'tis done . . . if it were done when 'tis done . . .

I knew Macbeth kept muttering that to himself but I couldn't remember why, so I sat down long enough to look it up.

It's when he's trying to decide if he should murder someone.

(Spoiler: he does.)

I slammed the book shut and slammed my door open and went back to the library to get my stupid book back.

I was going to just bring it back to the shelf where it belonged, but she'd written an answer.

> *It means that I don't care how nasty you pretend*
> *to be. I'm not some dumb bunny who scampers off*
> *when you say "boo."*

Every rule I'd ever learned fell out of my head as I picked up the pencil again.

> *Geese are the ones you're supposed to say boo to,*
> *not bunnies.*

I dropped the pencil and ran for my room as if chased by ghosts. I don't know how to explain myself, if anyone asks.

I should have stayed in my room all night—and the next day and maybe the next—but I went to dinner at the proper time as if I were a proper person.

She didn't say anything to me, or give any sign of knowing we were having a slow, silent conversation. She was bland and airy and witty, just as usual.

I left the table the second I could and went to take a very long bath.

I should have burned the library down after that—the whole house, even—but of course I went back and looked at the book.

I'll take your word for that, writer-girl. Anyway,
I'm not a goose <u>or</u> a bunny.

I felt a dangerous glow at being called "writer-girl" in print.

This is an expensive book. Stop writing in it.

I went back to my room and went to bed but not to sleep. For once I didn't care.

First thing in the morning, before the sun had even finished rising, I went to the library.

It looked as if she'd hauled out the charcoal pencil again. She'd drawn beautiful 3-D block letters an inch tall:

MAKE ME

I've read about people shouting with laughter, but I've never heard it and I've certainly never done it myself. Before today.

Then sanity returned and my hands started to shake and I felt so cold so suddenly I almost checked behind me to see if someone had thrown ice water.

I slammed the book shut without marking the page.

It's back on my shelf now, sitting next to its innocent partner.

I can't believe I let M mess up my pretty books.

From now on, if I work in the library I'm going to be completely portable. If I can't pick it up and run in one sweep, I'll just have to do without.

God only knows what she'll ruin next if I give her half a chance.

Who could be motherless who has a mother's grave within confiding reach?

I didn't allow myself dinner for two nights after the book incident and I put myself on half rations the rest of the time, which was a good double punishment because being so ravenous made it harder than ever to sleep.

I wanted to make it three nights in a row to make sure I remembered the rules from now on and because three is a good strong number, but at breakfast on the third day Ms. Lurie asked if everything was "all right dear" and I didn't want to risk drawing attention to myself now of all times. So tonight I made myself go to the dining room and load up my plate with everything I like least.

Ms. Lurie has taken one of the smaller tables out of the dining room, so I still can't sit by myself. So even the one possible benefit of the great Hawthorne exodus has been denied me.

"I love my family, but they're driving me nuts," Brianna said. "Every morning and every night, my mom needs to hear my voice. 'Are you okay? Is everything okay?' It's taking everything I've got not to say, 'I was until you asked me for the hundredth time today.'"

"Well, they're worried," Natasha-the-playwright said. "I mean, we can't really blame them for that."

"But could she maybe mix it up a little? Ask how I'm doing, how the painting's coming along, what I think I'd like to work on next. Heck, ask me what I had for dinner. That would be an exciting change."

A few girls snickered. "We can trade parents if you want," Natasha said. "Mine want to hear all about my writing. They're not just checking in—they want a full report. It's getting to the point where I can't get any writing *done* because I'm so busy telling them about it. I can't tell if they're just making an excuse to talk to me five times a day, or if they want to know what I'm working on to make sure I'm not, you know. Traumatized."

Brianna nodded ruefully. "With my mom, it's that terrified tone of voice that's getting to me. It feels like she's not asking *how* I am— she's asking *if* I am. 'Are you dead yet? No? Okay—I'll talk to you in the morning. Unless you're dead, of course.'"

M laughed. The other girls at our table looked shocked. A few at the next one over looked curiously in our direction.

"You're not the one who was scolding me the other day for 'tact-less' language in the wake of a tragedy, are you?" M asked. "And if I may say so, your gorgeous mahogany skin is made even more lovely when you blush."

"I choose you may *not* say so, since you give me the option,"

Brianna said. "And what about *your* folks? Still nagging you to come home? Or just happy to have all the windows in one piece?"

"Oh, they've left me alone about that," M said. "I'd just get in their way now. I think they're planning a trip to Greece. My mother is, anyway."

"Now? And just her? Not even your dad, too?"

"She likes going off without him. It makes her feel powerful. I guess *some*thing has to—he's the one with all the money."

The girls at the table glanced at one another uneasily. "But—she wanted you to come home," Brianna said. "And now she's going off island-hopping like nothing even happened?"

"Oh, she never *wanted* me to come home," M said, without a hint of complaint in her voice. "She doesn't like to have me around. She just knows she *ought* to. Looks good to the neighbors and all that. She's very good at going through the motions."

She glanced up from her whole-grain pasta. "Oh, don't look at me like that," she added. "My mother has *never* liked me. I can't say I blame her. I mean, to be fair, I started it."

"I think I'll stop complaining about my parents now," Brianna said.

"Me first," Natasha said.

I caught M looking at me with inquisitive concern as I stopped even trying to eat and stared down at my plate as if I'd lost something there.

I have to admit, I envy M.

I mean, yes, I'd like to have Brianna's mother fearing for me, or Natasha's parents demanding a verbal book report every day; but what I'd really like is to have the option of thinking of my mother as anything but a saint.

She's my mother. She was murdered. She died when I was very young.

What else *can* she be but perfect?

If my mother had lived, ~~maybe~~ probably she wouldn't be anything special. At least not to the rest of the world. She inherited wealth and then married more of it.

I'll never know what kind of mother she really was, or would be. She's just this vague, angelic, golden-haired memory.

There's no room in my life for the sort of casual irritation Brianna and Natasha and girls in novels feel toward their mothers. I certainly can't go in for M's brand of barbed contempt.

Would I have hated my mother, if I'd had the chance?

———

Won't you tell "the public" that at present I wear a brown dress

I was ~~safe~~ in my room working on a piece I'm trying to write about Dickinson's white dress. It's the one thing people know about her other than the poetry, but they know it wrong.

They like to think of Dickinson as a romantic woman-in-white floating around the attic like a literary ghost.

Certainly there's something glamorous about wearing long white gowns *now*, or M wouldn't go in for it so much.

But Dickinson's gown was actually much less fancy than M's nighties.

M loves wearing things that are frivolous and impractical. She thinks about how she looks all the time.

Dickinson is more like me. She wore her flowing white dress for the same reasons I wear blue jeans.

If something gets on my jeans, it won't show much and it's easy to wash out.

A plain white dress could be boiled and bleached until it was completely clean.

Dickinson's dress wasn't quite as ready-to-throw-on-and-go as my jeans, but it was simple and loose. She could bake or write or even work in the garden, if she put a blanket down first. (She *did* work in the garden for most of her life. She left the house; she just didn't leave the yard.)

Best of all, her dress was considered as casual as a pair of blue jeans is now. She probably didn't even wear a corset under it, which must have been a relief. Her insistence on wearing a very plain dress was a defiant statement to the world: I am *not* at home to visitors.

I want to write something about all of that—about how Dickinson is the opposite of people like M, who dresses herself up like a new painting every day.

I can't think where she gets the energy, either to do it or to deal with people looking at her. M isn't exactly beautiful, but she's striking, especially when she goes all out. Which she generally does.

I was trying to write something about all this. Maybe I can start a blog.

I'd like to have something to think about ~~other than the obvious~~.

I was scribbling random thoughts when there was a knock on my door. I knew it was M even before she spoke.

"Emily?"

I sat absolutely still.

"Can I come in?"

Nothing.

"I'd like to talk, if that's okay." A pause. "Or *you* can do all the talking. You can tell me something weird about Dickinson. I'd like that."

I looked down at my notes and had a sudden urge to throw them all in a fire.

"I'm sorry I didn't answer when you asked the other day; but in case you're still interested, I *do* know how to shut up."

Don't say anything.

As if to demonstrate her claim, M said nothing for a full minute. I could tell she was still there. There's a certain sound that comes along with standing silently.

And then she sighed and walked quietly away.

I wish she'd stomped or stormed or made some catty remark over her shoulder. It would have made things easier.

Now I can't concentrate. Instead of working, I just sit here writing about what I was planning to write about. What I *would* have been writing about, if only someone would let me.

Is M getting any work done, or is she sulking because I don't happen to be in the habit of letting people barge into my room all the time just because they feel like it?

———

The Bee is not Afraid of Me—
I know the Butterfly—

The pretty people in the Woods
Receive Me Cordially—

I was tired of sitting in my room. I couldn't settle down to work—not while I had to wonder if M was going to come tapping at my chamber door.

I put on my boots—thick ones with hard heavy soles, in case of thorns and snakes—and went to take the kind of ramble Dickinson used to enjoy.

One thing I love about Hawthorne is the way that, if I'm facing away from the school, I can feel as if I'm the last person in the world. The only road that leads away from the property is a long, curving driveway, sloping down so it seems like we're in our own private valley. It's hard to tell you're basically playing on the side of a mountain, at least if you keep to the paths I prefer.

I'm glad Ms. Lurie and her husband bought plenty of land back when it was cheap and they had the chance. I'd hate to have close neighbors. As it is, it's easy to avoid the boundaries.

I love wandering around outside partly because it's beautiful and wild and partly because, next to holing myself up in my room, it's the best way to avoid everyone. It's too easy to be in accidental proximity in the library or the lounge. The grounds here are open enough that it's easy to spot other people and avoid them. And of course it's easy for them to avoid *me*. If anyone wants a walk of her own, there are plenty of non-Emily-intensive locations to choose from.

I was wandering no path in particular and paused to look at some poppies and think about something Dickinson said in a letter to her favorite cousins. "The career of flowers differs from ours only in inaudibleness," she insisted.

In other words, their lives are just like ours, only quieter.

I think it would be pretty horrible if flowers had emotional lives. Mother Nature is even meaner to them than She is to people. Mass executions! Beheadings without benefit of trial!

Dickinson seemed to understand this. One of her poems is from the point of view of a guy picking a flower for the girl he loves—but it sounds as if he's kidnapping and possibly planning to rape the flower in question, so the poem is creepy rather than sweet or romantic.

Back before she decided her room was the best place in the world, Dickinson used to love wandering around outside. A friend of Emily's wrote about going with her on a five-mile walk to a mountain, where they gathered specimens for Dickinson's herbarium—a book of dried flowers she put together, complete with labels and proper Latin names.

She mentions flowers in a lot of her poems, but she was pretty scientific when it came to collecting and studying them. And growing them herself. She had quite the green thumb.

I have a black thumb, as I learned when I tried to grow some herbs on my windowsill. Either the light was wrong or the rules that govern my life can even boss around photosynthesis.

I keep planning to learn the proper names of the plants on Hawthorne's grounds.

So far I know poppies, and that's about it. Which isn't even Latin.

Dickinson would not approve.

All this was going through my mind and giving me ideas for the blog I might start and the book I might write, and I was regretting not bringing my notebook to jot down ideas (I always regret it when I don't have it with me on hikes, and then when I have it I never use it), and then I glanced up and there was M, striding right toward me in a blouse the color of the poppies and—wonder to behold—practical, nature-oriented shoes.

This was a million times worse than being cornered in the library. At least inside of Hawthorne there are walls and a roof and thick cozy curtains. Out here I felt pinned and frozen and completely exposed, like one of Dickinson's dried blossoms.

I wanted to run and yet I was afraid to. You don't flee something unimportant, after all.

"I do have to ask what those flowers did to piss you off," M said, so casually that you'd think we were friends who'd just happened to run into one another.

"Excuse me?" We were in a patch of openness surrounded by clumps of dense greenery. Usually that makes me feel gratefully alone.

"You're glaring like they just insulted your grandmother," M explained.

"No, I'm not," I said.

She didn't say anything, so I added, "I guess I don't see the point of flowers."

M looked profoundly amused. *She'd* brought a notebook with her, in a bag with a strap that went across her front as if she were a guerrilla warrior. She pulled out a regular pencil and scribbled a few quick lines, then found a blue colored pencil and did a little shading. "Here you are," she said, tearing the page out and offering it to me.

I looked at it without taking it. It was a drawing of a blue ribbon, the kind an aunt who isn't Aunt Paulette might win at a county fair for Best Cherry Pie.

"Congratulations," M added. "You're the first woman ever to say she doesn't like flowers."

I looked around at everything but her. There was something dangerously interesting about being referred to as a woman. Obviously I know I'm female, and ever since I was officially emancipated "woman" is my legal status, but it's not a word I'm used to applying to myself. Ms. Lurie calls us all her girls, and no one else calls me anything I'd care to repeat.

"I mean, sure," M went on, tucking her notebook back in her bag, "others may have *said* it, but none of them have backed it up with evidence. And here you are out in broad daylight trying to murder one with your laser beam eyes."

I felt my lips twitching against a smile, and made them stop it. "I'm not a killer robot. That's just how I look when I'm thinking."

"Mmm."

"And, anyway, I don't *hate* flowers," I said. "It's just—I know they're the kind of thing I'm *supposed* to like. Everybody says so. The *flowers* say so. They're so blatant, you know? 'Hey, look at me! I'm *pretty*!'"

"So you don't like flowers because you think they're slutty," M said agreeably.

"I didn't say—"

"Sure you did, goth girl."

"I'm *not*—"

"Of course you are. You've got at least six different black blouses that I've counted, and I'll bet the real number is higher than that. It's like your closet has a sign on it saying 'Death Before Pastels.'"

My face felt painfully hot, and I realized to my horror I must be blushing.

She'd been looking at me. Watching me closely enough to notice the difference between Monday's black T-shirt and Tuesday's.

Sure, I've noticed what *she* wears, but that's different. M's clothes are worth looking at, for the same reason her paintings are.

"Anyway, you're right," she said.

"Excuse me?"

"About flowers. They're nature's little sex maniacs. I've never been too big on science, but that's what they are, right—a plant's way of hitting on birds and bees?"

"I guess that's one way of putting it."

"Well, then." M picked a pale purple thistle and stared at it somberly for a minute. "You *tramp*," she whispered.

"And they're only pretty for a little while," I went on. "Then they rot and die."

M dropped the prickly blossom and shook her head, smiling a bit. "So you don't like beautiful slutty flowers because they're not immortal," she said. "No offense, but that sounds like something out of a really emo vampire novel."

"They don't have to live *forever*," I said, blushing again. I couldn't help wondering how hard she'd laugh if she could see some of the stupider books on my shelves. "It would just be nice if they lasted more than twenty minutes."

"They do, actually," M said. "Change their water often enough and they can stay fresh for days."

"That sounds like a lot of work for some soggy petals."

"Well, then, enjoy them while they're in the ground."

M looked around, and I did, too. Undoubtedly for different reasons.

"Look," she said, pointing. She walked down the path a bit, then squatted in front of some drooping flowers.

She was wearing a short skirt. I'd never noticed how tan her legs are. Or maybe her skin is naturally golden. But her face is so fair.

I stared resolutely at the flowers. "Well?"

She smiled up at me. "Chocolate lilies," she said. "Even *you* have to like a flower with a name like that."

They were kind of nice, actually. Their slim necks were a strange shade of purple, and the way they bowed their bell-like heads made them look as if they were embarrassed to be stared at. *Don't mind me. I'm just here to see a friend.*

"They're okay," I admitted, and M grinned.

"I'll have to take this back, then," she said, looking down at the drawing she still held in one hand. "You're giving up your shot at a major award."

"I kind of wasn't planning on accepting it."

"What? After all my hard work?"

"You drew that in ten seconds."

"It's the thought that counts." M stood up and stretched, arms raised to the sky. Her skirt shortened accordingly, and I frowned hard at the purply-brown lilies.

If M weren't there I might have picked one and taken it home to press it. I certainly have enough heavy books to get the job done.

That might be illegal, though. I guess I don't know the rules about wildflowers. But you certainly can't take wild *animals* home, and why should plants be any different?

Better to follow too many rules than too few.

"You know," M said, and I almost jumped. She's soft on her feet even outside, and was standing much closer than I'd noticed her getting.

"Thanks to you," she went on, "every time I walk through a flowery meadow, I'm going to feel like I'm on a porn set."

Dear Friend,—We must be less than Death to be lessened by it, for nothing is irrevocable but ourselves.

Dickinson's letters are incredible works of art. They're always outshone by her poetry, which is strange to me when so many of her letters are like little poems themselves.

Then again, some of her poems are "letters," so maybe she just couldn't stand to be told what to do and wrote whatever she wanted, whenever she wanted to.

Her letters have a lot of death in them just like her poems do, because death was such a frequent visitor. She was always seeking and offering comfort after the loss of friends or family or the family of her friends.

But maybe the strangest loss she suffered was one where she could never be sure if death was the culprit or not. Her uncle went out to go to church one night and was never seen or heard of again.

It bothers me unreasonably that we'll never know what happened to him. It seems as if we ought to be able to do better than that from this end of history.

But detectives can't even solve the things that are in front of them, so I suppose it isn't fair to ask them to take care of the past while they're at it.

At first, Dickinson thought it was awful not to know what had happened to her poor old Uncle Joseph. The first poem she wrote about it was angry and indignant. She calls the silence surrounding his disappearance a thief even crueler than death. She sent that poem to her aunt, the uncle's wife, who could probably be counted on to feel the same way.

And then, a few months later, she changed her mind. At least in verse. She decided that however terrifying our ideas might be, they're "a softer woe" than an immutable fact.

I couldn't understand that at first. Isn't there something cavernously terrifying about never knowing what happened to someone who simply wandered off one day in winter and never returned?

But of course that still offers the possibility of keeping hope alive. Depending on your personality, hope might be the most valuable companion you could have.

I don't know how much hope anyone in Dickinson's family could have had. Her uncle was an elderly man. He'd slipped on some ice and hit his head a few days before he disappeared. What kind of happy ending could there be to that story?

I mean, assuming that anything's better than death, the best-case scenarios seem to be either that he got kidnapped by someone who forgot to ask for ransom, or he changed his name and started a new life somewhere else, leaving his family to wonder for the rest of their lives.

That first idea is unlikely; the second makes him a total jerk.

Which I guess would be better than him being dead, if you prefer hating a living man to loving a dead one.

But maybe hope means being able to believe in magic. Maybe Dickinson just decided she'd rather be able to think, *We don't know what happened to him. He could be all right somehow, somewhere. As long as we don't know, he might be fine.* Which is prettier than, *My uncle disappeared into the cold one winter night, and he almost certainly died, alone and far from the people he loved. The most we can hope is that it was quick and painless.*

No.

I just can't understand not wanting to know for sure what happened, and how—and especially *why*.

Then again, in terms of living in hope:

Let's say I had to live exactly the same life I do now. I'm still at Hawthorne and I still don't have any friends because I lack that crucial warmth most people call a heart. But in *this* life, I don't know where my parents are or why I'm not with them. I don't know if they're alive or dead. I don't know if they left me for selfish reasons or if they're forced to stay away from me.

Would it be any different, any better, if I could live in the painful wonder of hoping to be able to find them someday?

Would there be some comfort in knitting stories night after night about my jet-set parents, my kidnapped parents, my secret-agent parents, my superhero parents, my witness-protection-program parents, my brainwashed-into-a-creepy-charismatic-cult parents?

Wouldn't that be preferable to "My parents were murdered, and I know all about *how* it happened but no one knows why"?

Which is the real point, I guess. I have half a certainty, which is like being given half an apple when you're starving: you're supposed to be grateful, you try to be grateful, but you can't because it just isn't enough and you can't pretend it is.

No one could.

———

+phrase
I found the +words to every
  thought
I ever had—but One—
And that—defies me—
As a Hand did try to
  chalk the Sun

M left a picture taped to my door.

It was a flower. A black rose.

Penciled underneath it, she had written: *For you, Goth Girl—a flower that will never die.*

I knew I should take it down and rip it up and leave the pieces taped on *her* door, but I couldn't.

That frightened me. I can't remember the last time I felt too weak to haul out the requisite sum of nastiness.

But I couldn't destroy that picture.

She made it for me. And it was beautiful.

She'd obviously spent a lot more time on it than she did on that silly blue ribbon, which was actually pretty good for something dashed off on a hike.

And since no one's ever going to read this: I wanted to keep that flower. I wanted to put it away somewhere safe the way girls in silly novels press the flowers from their prom corsages.

But of course I couldn't do that, either.

I didn't know what else to do, so I left it on the door.

If anyone noticed, no one said anything. M didn't act any different. Ms. Lurie seems to be smiling at me more warmly lately, but it's hard to tell with her.

After a day or two, the picture was gone, but another one had been left in its place. It was another black rose, but this one was wilting and droopy. The handwriting beneath this one said: *I told you to change the water, silly girl.*

One of the dark petals had fallen off and lay in a half-crumpled heap near the bottom of the page.

I looked around. The hall was empty. No windows were in sight.

Anyone who could see me in here would have to have magical powers, and if that were the case they'd already know the worst.

I took the wilted flower off my door, quickly, and I brought it into my room and taped it inside this notebook.

It's on a page of its own in the middle, so if I lose my nerve I can always take it out and destroy it without losing any writing or making it obvious something was there.

If there's a rule-maker reading over my shoulder, I'm already screwed.

———

Judge Lord was with us a few days since, and told me that the joy we most revere we profane in taking. I wish that was wrong.

M keeps trying to catch my eye. She hasn't said anything to me at the table or tried to corner me in my room again. But I can tell she's kind of watching me.

I did accidentally meet her gaze once, when she made one of her usual bizarre remarks at lunch. I looked up while everyone was making the kind of noise she provokes, and she was looking right at me.

I guess I would have expected some kind of crudely triumphant expression—*ha! made you take it!*—or something equally crass. Instead, she looked serious. Inquiring. *Earnest*, if that's a word that could ever be associated with M.

She wanted to know what had happened to that second picture, and there was no way I was going to tell her. But I also wasn't up to my usual lies.

I just looked down again, quickly.

I stared at my plate for approximately seven years.

When Brianna started talking to M, I was able to glance up again without feeling too conspicuous. M wasn't looking at me, but there was a shy, pleased smile on her face that had nothing to do with Brianna's remarks.

M was doing a better job than I was of pretending that the conversation in audible words was the only one going on at our table, but I still felt terrified.

Still do.

This isn't how things are supposed to be.

———

Pardon my sanity, Mrs. Holland, in a world insane.

Thinking about M is driving me crazy. *More* crazy, she'd probably say. As if she's some world expert on sanity.

It's really hot today and I don't feel like staying cooped up in my room. I'd like to go for a walk, maybe read under one of the huger Hawthorne trees, but I don't want to risk her following me again.

And, anyway, I've been much too self-indulgent. Slipping up all over the place when I should be reining myself in harder than ever.

I need to focus on working. Focus on Dickinson.

~~Dickinson is safe.~~

Dickinson was a genius from out of nowhere.

Nobody else in her family wrote poetry, or much of anything at all; and then along came Emily and poetry would never be the same.

Sometimes I think about the idea of her father not happening to meet her mother, not proposing a couple of months later, not being as persistent as he needed to be to make that marriage finally happen. Not being in the mood on the night that made *Emily* finally happen.

All those circumstances had to come together just right.

And of course all the earlier twigs on the family tree had to be in just the right place, too.

Thinking about it too hard makes me dizzy. Retroactively terrified. A single slip and the world is lighter by one genius.

I know if that were the case someone else's work would have moved in to fill the vacuum in my life. I wouldn't just sit around moping: "If only there were an Emily. And a Dickinson." I'd find someone else safe to love.

But who? Sure, there are other writers I like, even love, but nobody else has ever given me the sense of kinship I've found in Emily Dickinson. Not just her poetry, but her letters, her life.

She *was* born, against all odds. Everyone played their part, and all's well in my otherwise empty world.

The biographies all start off talking about her grandfather. Biographies *always* start off talking about grandparents, but Dickinson's grandfather would have been famous anyway. He helped found Amherst College and then went bankrupt trying to keep it afloat.

That's very interesting; but when *I* think about her grandparents, I can't help thinking more about his wife Lucretia, aka Grandmother Gunn.

Grandmother Gunn had such a terrible temper that her grand-kids used her as an excuse. You couldn't just run around slamming doors in old New England, no matter how bad a mood you were in. But if you slammed that door and then cried out, "It's not me—it's my Grandmother Gunn!" —well, then you might get a laugh, and then you'd be safe.

After her husband died, none of Grandmother Gunn's children would let her move in with them. Maybe that doesn't sound so odd now, but back then, a widowed granny could expect to find a home with some family member rather than having to live all alone in her old age. Lucretia practically begged to be taken in, but apparently her kids had all had quite enough of her company. They'd survived a childhood with her; they weren't interested in spending their adult years listening to her nagging. They had lives to lead, work to do, children of their own to boss around.

Poor Lucretia. How horrified she'd be to know that she's remembered as the bad-tempered grandmother of a genius who made fun of her.

I have two grandmothers of my own. One of them and her

husband—my mother's parents—moved to New York City right after it all happened.

Whenever I try to drag some kind of memory up, I imagine them as thin, stiff, silent people. That's probably because they used to send me cards now and then—very formal, polite, expensive ones, with only their signatures added to the preprinted greetings inside.

I used to feel bad for them, and then I felt kind of mad at them, and now I try not to think about them at all.

Either they figured out the rules and are following them, or they didn't and just don't want anything to do with me.

Do I pity them? Should I?

Whatever their lives are now, they chose at least some of their loneliness.

My other grandfather died before I was born, which was probably just as well for everyone involved. His wife, my Grandma Jean Louise, moved to Florida to live in the sunshine with other grandmothers. She went there when I was about two years old, which I suppose I could take personally since it does seem as if she didn't want to play with me even when that was a perfectly safe thing to do; but I guess her health had been bad for a while, and she had friends who had moved there and swore she'd have a great time if she joined them.

I *do* pity *her*. For one thing, the only thing sadder than having your son murdered would be having your only surviving child be Aunt Paulette. And also, Grandma Jean Louise always remembers me on birthdays and Christmas and the occasional random holiday.

I would dearly love to know what her reasoning process is in this respect. Sometimes she'll send me a St. Patrick's Day card—but not every year, and we're not even Irish. Once she sent me Fourth of July greetings, which I'm willing to bet are not easy to find.

I find this baffling and overly intriguing.

~~I kind of love her craziness.~~

I don't think she knows the rules, if only because I can't imagine them fitting into her mindset. Not that I know what that *is*, exactly. But she just doesn't seem like the kind of person who could comprehend why I have to live like this.

She certainly doesn't come across as the kind of brave she'd have to be to understand what happens to anyone I care about and still send me presents, which she does every birthday and Christmas. Not actual physical presents, but checks.

When I was much younger, I loved being allowed to cash these and then buy whatever I wanted to, and I always wrote some stupid note back.

When that stopped, Grandma Jean Louise seemed to wonder what she'd done wrong. I think for a while she thought maybe the checks were too impersonal. At any rate, she went through a quiet flurry of sending every kind of gift card imaginable, some of them ridiculously unsuitable for a child. Nothing bad or inappropriate, just—random. Odd. Who gives a ten-year-old a gift certificate from an online tea leaf emporium, or an eleven-year-old a gift code good for one free cactus?

It was as if she gave up on getting me to actually use the cards, and was just hoping for any kind of response at all.

Eventually, she went back to checks. She keeps loyally sending them to me, one every birthday and a slightly larger one for Christmas.

Every May and every December I wonder if this is the year she'll give up on a granddaughter who is obviously rude and ungrateful. I feel kind of awful every time I see the familiar handwriting on yet another envelope, and I also realize how much I'd hate it if she stopped trying.

I try not to even open them, but of course I can't resist.

There's always a bit of a note—a few words hoping I'm well and assuring me she's just fine. Her pen must be one of those thick, felt-tipped ones. The writing's a little hard to read, but I manage.

I hate not being able to accept that money. I mean, I have everything I need, but it would be fun to go shopping with cash somebody else wanted to give me and then write a letter about what I decided to get and how much I liked it.

How does she feel? Does she wonder if this time, maybe, I'll finally start acting like we're actually related and I'm a civilized human being?

Maybe she understands.

But she can't. That would be horrible. I don't want her to have to think about life in those terms. She's been through enough.

But how is it possible to look at everything that's happened and *not* draw the obvious conclusion?

I can't be the one imagining things.

My whole life would be a mistake. Everything I've done. How I treat everyone—it wouldn't be noble and self-sacrificing, or ruthlessly pragmatic. It would be wrong and unnecessary and just plain mean.

That can't be possible.

I may not be a genius like Dickinson, but I'm not an idiot, either.

There's no way I'm wrong about this.

And there's no way my grandmother knows the rules.

Maybe that's just me believing something I want to believe.

But I can't imagine her doing the kind of things I imagine Florida grandmothers doing—going for gentle morning walks, playing cards with friends, gossiping endlessly—and having in the back of her mind the idea that a killer decided for some reason to put me in the center of several extremely thorough murders.

Probably she never even heard about Violet and Zoë.

I want to believe that. I want to think she thinks my mother and father died the way they did because sometimes horrible things just happen, that's all.

I want her to feel safe.

———

To die—takes just a
little while—
They say it does'nt hurt—
It's only fainter—by degrees—
And then—it's out of sight—

I swear I'm going to have to order in supplies and hole up in this room until the year ends. If Ms. Lurie says anything, I'll tell her I'm taking my Dickinson project to the next level.

Not that Dickinson ever refused to come downstairs for meals, but what Ms. Lurie doesn't know won't kill her.

Breakfast today was nothing but Stephen James. What a lovely way to start the morning.

Katia the poet, who is still a Hawthorne girl in spite of her parents' best efforts to lure her to London, brought a copy of the local paper to the table. There already was a let's-get-this-body-in-the-ground funeral for Stephen James, but now a bunch of artists are having some kind of celebration of his life and work.

"We should ask Ms. Lurie if we can go," Lucy said after reading the entire article aloud at a volume that couldn't be escaped. "I think it would be nice."

"I think it would be creepy as hell," Brianna said.

"Amen," M murmured, and she and Brianna exchanged a small, surprised smile.

Lucy's tone shifted from compassion to righteousness. "I just think it would be nice if we had some association with him other than—"

"—the fact that he turned up dead on our doorstep," M finished.

Lucy glared at her. "Well, yes. And if nothing else, I would think a fellow artist would be interested in his work."

"I'm not a fellow artist," M said. "Stephen James was a professional. I haven't sold a single picture. Maybe I never will."

"Don't be so down on yourself," Lucy said encouragingly.

"I'm not," M said. "I'm just not sure the world is worthy of my work."

Brianna went into a loud, coughing recovery from a mixture of laughter and a poorly timed sip of tea, and Lucy retreated into lemon-faced silence.

I thought it was safe to try to eat again, but unfortunately we were sharing a table with Anxious Girl. (Yes, I know her real name, but I'm not going to use it unless she comes up with a more distinguishing characteristic. Anything would do at this point.)

"Maybe we should go, though," she said. "I mean, maybe it would be good for our emotional recovery."

If more than three people at a table roll their eyes at the same time, it's audible. I can put that on my list of Things I Learned At Hawthorne, if I ever decide to make one.

"I'm not sure I'd have phrased it quite like that," Natasha-the-playwright said tactfully. "But I have to admit, I'm interested. I mean, the poor guy had a life. I kind of hate the fact that when I think about him at all, he's just 'that dead guy.'"

"That does apply to an awful lot of people, historically speaking," M agreed.

"I just mean," Natasha began, and then stopped and wasn't able to start again.

"I think you're right," Katia said in a soft, clear voice. "For myself, I'd like to be able to think about his life and his work instead of just his death. And for *his* sake—" She fumbled for a minute and then went on, "I'd hate it if *I* finally managed to get some writing done—some *good* writing—and published it and everything—and then every poem I ever wrote was basically wiped out because of how I died."

Her voice had risen, and so had Ms. Lurie, who appeared next to our table without looking as if she'd hurried.

"Like Sylvia Plath," Katia went on recklessly. "Nobody ever talks about anything she wrote. So many great poems, and nobody even cares! Everyone's just, 'Oh yeah—isn't she the one who killed her-self? Tell me all about how she did it.'"

"Katia," Ms. Lurie said softly.

"It's true!" Katia cried. "I hate that!"

Ms. Young rushed over and knelt next to her. "Hey, hey, okay," she said soothingly; and Katia, who's always seemed to be the picture of tranquil togetherness, buried her face in her shoulder.

I don't know quite what I did then—it can't have been anything too dramatic or Ms. Lurie would have said something. I do know I pushed my chair back a bit. I think I may have made some kind of sound. Fortunately, Katia was now sobbing, quietly but obviously, so everyone was focused on her.

Almost everyone.

"Emily?" M said very softly.

If she had dared make a scene or dropped any kind of hint that I knew her from a hole in the wall, I would have smashed a plate over her head. I shook my head hard and clenched my hands into fists in my lap, and she took the hint and backed off. But I could tell she was still watching me. Worrying.

Katia was quieting down. She sat up straight, wiping her eyes and nodding in reply to a murmured question from Ms. Young. Ms. Lurie looked at her and then around the room.

"There's no right way to feel about this," Ms. Lurie said, to all of us. "I'll be happy to organize a trip into town on the day of the exhibit. Anyone who wants to come is welcome. Anyone who'd like to spend the day shopping or visiting the library rather than looking at Stephen James's work is welcome to do that, too. And of course staying here at Hawthorne is always an option."

She stressed "always" as if it applied to much more than just the day in question. Ordinarily I'd have felt reassured by that.

Today I can't find Hawthorne much of a refuge. Not if everyone won't shut the hell up about corpses.

When I state myself, as the representative of the verse, it does not mean me, but a supposed person.

I'm trying to work, but I want to throw all my books out the window.

Okay, not all of them. Not the ones with Dickinson's actual words. Just the ones that talk about her life.

These biographers are driving me crazy.

I guess I shouldn't blame them. I'm the one who wanted to know about the Emily I'm not really named after. They're just trying to deliver the facts.

Except they're not—not all of them, at least. Plenty of them come across as creepy old gossips.

Psst—did you hear that Emily Dickinson had an abortion? And lesbian love affairs? And lusted after married men? Did you hear she might have committed suicide? Did you hear she might have stayed in her room all the time because she had seasonal affective disorder? No, no—it was because she had uncontrollable diarrhea. Well, I think she wrote her poetry because her father sexually abused her! No way—it was because she had epilepsy!

It's starting to make me sick.

It's like someone held a contest: the biographer who comes up with the weirdest "What if—?" scenario gets a million dollars and a car.

I just wanted to know a little about her life. If a *little* is all anyone can know for certain, that's all right with me.

Of course there are things to wonder about. Those strange, passionate love letters to someone she called "Master," the letters she wrote but never sent—who was she thinking of when she wrote them? Or was she thinking of anyone? Was she playing on paper, spinning a fantasy for her own amusement?

I don't mind not knowing. I think I'd rather *not* know if she was ever in love, and with whom, and how much.

I don't want to read "Wild Nights" and think, *Oh, right—she wrote that because she had the hots for so-and-so.* I just want to go rowing in Eden, even if I don't know exactly what that means.

Sometimes I wish I'd never learned a thing about her.

I started reading her poems because they were so shockingly strange and at the same time so familiar. Of course I knew she wasn't really talking to me or about me, but still it *felt* as if I'd finally met someone who'd known me all my life.

I want that feeling back. I want these poems to have fallen out of the sky. I want to not know everything I know.

I finished writing that sentence and I looked up and M was in my room. Standing there, looking as pleased and expectant as if I'd mailed her an invitation. And then looking startled when I practically jumped out of my skin at the sight of her.

"Do they even have knocking as a *concept* on your planet?" I demanded as soon as I could breathe again.

She looked confused. "I *did* knock," she said. "You said 'Come in.'"

"I did *not*—" I started to say, and then I stopped. M is as straightforward as a door slamming on your hand. She's all kinds of annoying, but she isn't a liar.

Had I said it automatically?

But since when am I in the habit of saying that?

"You must have heard someone else talking," I finished brilliantly.

Now she looked amused. "I think I know what your voice sounds like," she said. "And, anyway, nobody else is making a peep. It's as silent as a tomb around here today."

She looked at my bed. There was barely room on it for me and what may have been every book ever written about Emily Dickinson, but that's not the kind of thing that gets in M's way. She stacked a few on top of one another, murmured, "Mind if I cut in?" and sat down in the space she'd made.

At least she'd left a book between us as a sort of buffer zone.

"Please, sit down," I said.

She smiled. "Don't mind if I do."

There was a small silence that disturbed me because it wasn't awkward at all.

"So," M said at last. "What are you working on?"

"Oh, all kinds of things," I said. "Just now I was trying to decide if I should set all these books on fire or pitch them into the nearest tree."

"Goodness, what's the matter?"

I couldn't explain when it didn't even make sense to me, but I tried anyway. M listened to me bumble on about how some biographers stop being explorers and start believing they own the country they've been wandering. They draw up borders and boundaries and laws and constitutions, all the while assuring themselves and everyone else that they're just representing the wishes of the native inhabitants.

I expected M to laugh at the idea of caring so much about a bunch of words written about someone who wrote a bunch of words. But she sat very quietly and looked thoughtful and waited for me to run out of words myself before she said anything.

"Maybe," she ventured, "there's something more important than pinning down the factual, literal truth. Or maybe the greater truth about a person like Dickinson can't be told by someone who insists there can only be one true story."

I felt comforted and a little sleepy, as if I'd walked a very long way and now I got to rest. Or, less poetically, as if talking so much more than usual had sapped my energy. "What do you mean?" I asked, only half caring about her answer. Mostly I just wanted someone else to be doing the talking.

"I mean . . . well, it's like those saint stories of mine," she said. "The best ones are the ones that never really happened. Like Lucy."

"You don't think she was real?"

"I think she was plenty real," M corrected. "I'm just not sure she ever existed."

"Oh. Well, thanks for clearing *that* up."

M laughed. "Maybe there was someone *named* Lucy," she said. "And maybe she was a Christian back when that was a new, weird thing to be. But all the things they say happened to her? All that amazingness about her eyes and the brothel and the fire and everything? Some of those stories stomp all over each other. If one's true, the others can't be. But that's okay."

"Okay," I repeated.

"They're like Greek myths," M said. "There can be a million different variations on a story, and each one has its own reality. It doesn't matter if they didn't really happen."

"It does if you're Lucy," I said.

"If you're Lucy, you know the truth already," M corrected. "Those stories are for the rest of us. They give us something to think about. Something to aspire to."

She'd said something like that before. In her room, when I got to see her pictures. "You like Lucy because nobody tells her what to do," I recalled.

"Exactly."

"But you're not religious."

"So?"

"Well, if you were, you wouldn't be saying it's no big deal whether Lucy really existed or not."

"I might," M said with her usual maddening calm. "I have an aunt who's Catholic, and she says plenty of the stories are full of crap. Her words. She's my one cool relative."

"It's good you have *one*, anyway," I said. "That must be nice."

M smiled at me, and I felt the same jolt of panic I had when I looked up to find her in my room with no memory of having let asked her in.

She didn't see anything amiss. I was alone with my terror. As always.

"It's very nice," she said.

———

The Soul that hath a
Guest,
Doth seldom go abroad—
Diviner Crowd Within—
Obliterate the need—

"I should go wash up," M said a few minutes before the dinner bell rang.

I didn't answer, and she slipped out as quietly as a cat.

For such an intrusive person, M can be oddly tactful at times. She's never questioned why it's so important for me to be the enemy of the world. She's not going to accept that without a fight, but she's also not going to draw attention to it in front of our sister-students. And being seen leaving my room would raise questions—especially if I wasn't right behind her, hurling insults and maybe a shoe. So she kept an eye on the time and left right before the halls were due to be full of people.

I have to get a grip.

What was I thinking, letting her stay so long? Letting her stay at all?

She was in here for *hours.*

It didn't feel like that long. I have never in the history of ever understood the urge to use phrases like "the time flew by" until today.

I can't remember half of what M and I talked about. Dickinson, of course. And saints. She told me lots of stories about them, most of which involved virginity as an extreme sport.

"This is getting a little repetitive," I said at one point. "Don't women saints ever *do* anything?"

"Of course," M said. "Ursula went on that pilgrimage."

"With eleven thousand virgins," I reminded her. "As a virgin. Because virginity."

"Well, that *was* pretty much the only thing people cared about, so far as women were concerned."

"Great."

"Margaret of Antioch killed a dragon," M said brightly.

"To protect her virginity?"

"Kind of," she admitted. "But she won the fight *after* the dragon ate her. I think she should get extra credit for that."

Apparently M's aunt—the cool one—used to tell her saint stories before bed when M stayed at her house for long summer visits. Which explains a lot about M, if you ask me.

She also told me about how they figure out who's a saint and who isn't. It's all very strange.

She stayed and talked all afternoon and left after what felt, looking back on it, like no more than a few seconds.

This isn't okay.

I can't do this.

She can't do this, but she hasn't once listened to me on that subject.

It's up to me.

———

I can't tell you—but you feel it—
Nor can you tell me—
Saints, with ravished slate and pencil
Solve our April Day!

What is *wrong* with me?

I never loved the whole career-nastiness gig, but I thought at least I'd gotten good at it.

At first I thought I should go all out at the dinner table, but then I realized how suspicious that would look. If I started insulting M out of what would seem like the blue, it would just come across as paying attention to her. Like the stories I read when I was little about boys teasing girls they secretly had a crush on. Overcompensating.

I decided instead to just sit and do my usual imitation of a stale dinner roll—unwanted and a little pathetic, but no big deal as long as you ignore it.

I tried to look hard enough to chip a tooth on.

I thought about some of the saints M had told me about. One was thrown into a fire. Another threw *herself* into a fire. There were brandings and burnings and bone-breakings and tooth-pullings and worse, and the women endured them all—looking, in the paintings of them, calm to the point of stupidity.

Surely I could keep a straight face through a single idiot dinner.

Saint Emily, that's who I'd be. Patron of bitchy teenaged girls. An inspirational figure for generations to come. *Heavenly sister, help me in my hour of need. Damn it all, amen.*

What if there was already a saint by that name?

With my luck, Saint Emily was the guardian of newborn kittens and other terrifyingly cute creatures.

There could be more than one saint with the same name, though. Couldn't there? I seemed to remember that from somewhere.

"Is there a Saint Emily?" I asked without thinking.

159

Every head at my table and several at the others turned toward me in astonishment.

Apparently that's the kind of response you get to a perfectly normal question after you spend several years making it clear that if you can't say something nice, you'll damned well say it anyway.

Ms. Lurie smiled with puzzled pleasure.

Wonderful.

I imagined it hitting the local paper tomorrow: PREVIOUSLY NASTY HAWTHORNE STUDENT ASKS STRANGE BUT INNOCUOUS QUESTION—AUTHORITIES BAFFLED.

All things considered, M held it together pretty well. For just a second she grinned broadly, but then she covered by picking up her glass and spilling some of the contents on the girl next to her, who screamed as if the water were lava straight from the source.

"There are a few," M said to me quietly through all the fuss over (who else but) Madison and her wet sleeve. "But they're not too exciting."

She forced herself to tone down another gleeful smile. "We'll have to work on improving that track record," she added.

"I don't really feel like dying young and horribly," I said, as long as no one was listening and I'd already made an idiot of myself.

"Oh, neither do I," M said. "Don't worry. Not all saints are martyrs."

I don't know if that was meant to be funny or reassuring. Maybe both.

Either way, it didn't work.

———

Of Course—I prayed—
And did God Care?
He cared as much as
on the Air
A Bird—had stamped
her foot—
And cried "Give Me"—

Dickinson believed in God, but she didn't believe in church.

In Dickinson's world, even if you went to church and read the Bible and prayed all over the place, you weren't considered a Christian until you "converted."

Dickinson's mother was always a Christian, but the rest of her family held out. Eventually they all gave in—her sister and her brother and, last of all, her father.

They all believed in a God you weren't allowed to argue with. If he took away your loved ones, well, that was how he wanted things for some reason, and you just had to put up with it. No back talk.

Dickinson couldn't give up arguing with that God. Even when Lavinia urged her to convert, she couldn't. She just couldn't give up her own ideas for someone else's.

M seems to have that same kind of relaxed relationship with religion and God. I don't think she believes *or* disbelieves. She picks the things she likes and doesn't worry about the rest.

I don't know what I think.

No one ever taught me anything about religion, but I found bits and pieces of it here and there. It's all very confusing.

There are so many different religions. It's hard to figure them out on your own, and obviously I couldn't go and have long meaningful chats with a priest or a minister or anyone like that. It would seem especially horrible to get someone killed who was just trying to help people and save souls.

Do I have a soul? Is it worth saving?

I tried praying once for whatever this curse is to be lifted. I didn't know exactly what to say, but I did the best I could, and then I had no idea what to do. How could I know my prayers had worked? And wasn't I praying to the same person who was doing this to me in the first place?

I do know that I don't believe in the God I hear the most about—the one who's all-knowing *and* all-powerful *and* all-good. He just doesn't make sense under my circumstances.

If God were just two out of those three; or maybe if he were *somewhat* powerful—certainly stronger than human beings, but not as Ultimate as everyone wants to give him credit for being—that might make sense.

Would such a god feel shy of all the attention he gets? Embarrassed—maybe even a little annoyed at people insisting he is what he isn't?

Maybe that's why he lashes out sometimes.

I could understand a god like that. I could even kind of like him.

But if he's out there, either he doesn't feel like talking or he can't find my phone number.

They say that "Time
assuages"—
Time never did assuage—
An actual suffering
strengthens
As Sinews do, with Age—

M has backed off a bit, which ought to make things easier, but everyone else is obliviously awful.

That Stephen James event is coming up and no one but M can stop talking about it. Every meal, all breakfast and lunch and dinnertime long: *Are you going? Should* I *go? I don't know if I want to go. I don't know if* any *of us should go. I think* all *of us should go.*

On and on and on, like little songbirds from hell.

I wish I could just stay in my room forever. I'd rather dine on dust and cobwebs than try and fail to eat Hawthorne's lovely repasts while my sister-students chirp on about death and death and death.

But I can't just close my door and shut it all out. Rules are rules. Or, since we're talking about Hawthorne, that one rule is still the rule.

"I'm officially horrible," Brianna said at lunch today. "I think I really want to go now."

M looked at her in mocking, wide-eyed fascination. "Let the sky rain potatoes," she said.

"Please shut up," Brianna explained politely.

"Only if you tell me what brought *this* on."

Brianna sighed. "I'm morbidly curious," she said. "Literally. I want to see what his work's like. I want to know who this guy *is*. Was."

"I don't think that's so horrible," M said. "Give me a dollar and I won't even call you a hypocrite."

"Except I'm also kind of afraid," Brianna said.

"Because . . . ?"

"If he's really good, it'll be that much worse that he's dead, you know? It's a loss to the whole world. But then I'm *really* afraid that—" She lowered her voice and looked around uncomfortably. "What if I think his paintings *suck*?"

"Definitely keep that opinion to yourself," M recommended. "At least until you get back to Hawthorne."

"I do know that much, thank you. I just mean—it'll be depressing to think that this guy never got the chance to be really good."

"It'll be depressing no matter what," M pointed out.

"Yeah." Brianna sighed.

"Don't overthink it," Natasha-the-playwright said. "Go, since you might want to. If you get there and it feels wrong, just spend the day at the library. Or go shopping."

"That seems shallow," Brianna said.

"Shop for something deep and meaningful," M suggested.

Brianna snickered. I hoped hopelessly that the conversation would now turn to local shopping opportunities.

Of course not. Anxious Girl was at the table.

"I'm scared to go," she almost whimpered.

God. Here we go again.

"There's nothing to be *scared* of," Lucy said. As annoying as she can be at times, at least she doesn't indulge in A.G.'s style of stupidity.

"But it's—*him*," Anxious Girl whispered.

"It's not," Lucy said positively. "It's his work. It's his art. His *friends* will be there. There's going to be music and food—"

"I know, I know." Anxious Girl was not convinced by Lucy's forceful optimism. "I know I'm supposed to think about his life. I just—I can't stop thinking about what happened to him."

So none of the rest of us gets to stop thinking about it, either. Thanks.

"You *have* to stop thinking about that," Lucy commanded.

I'd kind of love it if Lucy decided to become a therapist. If anyone can verbally bludgeon the world into a state of timid sanity, it'll be Lucy.

"But—"

"Look," Lucy said, setting her fork down. "First of all, his legacy is what's important now. His—*creations*."

I could practically hear M trying not to gag.

"And second," practical Lucy continued, "if you absolutely *have* to think about it—and you *shouldn't*—you should focus on the fact that his death must have been quick and painless."

She sounded so certain. So scientific. Almost triumphant in her rightness.

I think that was what pushed me over—how fond she was of her own opinion, which she never called that because she was too busy finding room for it on a shelf marked ABSOLUTE TRUTH.

At any rate: one second I was sitting there tying my cloth napkin in knots and wishing I could risk a bite of cinnamon-apple kugel, and the next I was up and shouting.

"How the hell would *you* know?"

I heard a few gasps, and a little muffled shriek. Probably Madison.

Poor Ms. Lurie is getting quite the workout lately, what with constantly leaping to her feet and calming things down at my table.

Lucy was gaping at me.

"Where the hell do you get off saying something like that?" I went on. "How can you *possibly* know—"

"Emily," Ms. Lurie said. She was standing next to me, and even at a moment like that she knew better than to touch me. "You have to calm down. Right now."

M's face was completely white. Her eyes were huge.

I didn't know she could ever look like that about anyone.

"Do you need something to drink?" Ms. Lurie asked. She was speaking softly, but in the absolute silence of the dining room she might as well have been screaming. "Come with me to the kitchen and we'll get some ice water."

I shook my head mutely. My hands were shaking so hard, if it had been anyone else I'd have sworn they were faking it.

"Maybe you should lie down for a little while, then," Ms. Lurie said even more quietly. "All right?" She glanced at my untouched plate. "I'll bring you up a tray in a little while. Something fresh, don't worry. Miss Miller mentioned she'd like to do some baking this afternoon."

Her words were like a spell. I clung to the soothing ordinariness of what she described, to the idea of a quiet world where overexcited young ladies are sent to rest and wait for warm whole-wheat cinnamon rolls to be left outside their doors on covered plates.

I still couldn't talk, but I could breathe again. I could make myself walk past all those gaping girls, past M who looked as if she were clinging to her chair to keep from jumping up to go with me, and to my quiet room. Where I did indeed lie down on my made bed until my hands started to behave themselves and I could write away some of my nerviness.

I can't believe I shouted like that.

But I absolutely *hate* it when people say things they can't know about someone's last moments.

Even a lobster deserves the dignity of deciding for himself if being dropped into a pot of boiling water hurts.

Anyone who wants to argue that point should try it out or shut up.

I feel bad about leaving my dishes. Somebody's going to have to take them in for me.

At Dickinson's boarding school, she had to clear up the knives after breakfast and lunch and then wash and dry them. She said so in a letter.

That seemed like an odd division of chores to me, but apparently all the students did a little something in the way of kitchen chores. That way they didn't have to hire as many servants, so the fees were cheaper.

Fees are not cheap at Hawthorne, but we all bus our own dishes anyway. Ms. Lurie says that's the kind of thing it's important to do for yourself—something about human dignity. We also rinse them off, usually to the tune of an improving lecture about how there shouldn't be any need to "scrape" dishes after a meal since you should never take more food than you plan to eat.

I keep planning to eat, and then everyone keeps talking about Stephen James and my throat closes up.

The worst part of it is, I do still feel hungry. Ravenous. I just can't do anything about it.

Today was supposed to be my turn to wipe the counters in the kitchen after lunch.

Lucy might not believe this, but I feel bad about leaving that for someone else to do.

Maybe she'll volunteer to cover for me. She'd enjoy earning the extra righteousness points.

Ms. Lurie has pretty quilted placemats set out for breakfast and lunch, and then tablecloths are laid for dinner. Every night one girl per table takes off the cloth, shakes it, and then either folds it and puts it on a special shelf in the kitchen linen cupboard or (if it's Friday, or the tablecloth is badly marked with a food spill) tosses it into the kitchen hamper.

I find this all very soothing.

I want to go back to being able to think about those stupid little details of life at Hawthorne.

Instead I have to keep thinking about Stephen James.

Did it hurt?

Just because Lucy can be arrogant and tactless doesn't mean she's always wrong.

A bullet to the back of the head means he never saw it coming in one sense; but was he really surprised? Did the killer tell him to turn around, and use the gun to menace him into doing so?

And whether or not it was a surprise—even if his death was "instantaneous" (another word people like to use when they're not the ones doing the dying), wouldn't there have to be a moment of pain?

My father died from a bullet, too, but it was lower and it took a long time to kill him. The books all agree on that.

My mother's death involved no bullets at all and was much less tidy. It *had* to have hurt.

Was that the point? Not just to make her die, but to make her suffer?

It's the only thing that makes sense. Nobody ends up in that many pieces by accident.

Why? What had she ever done to deserve such a thing?

What did *I* ever do to attract this kind of follower?

I was four when it happened. Almost five, but still. It would have been physically, temporally impossible for me to have done something terrible enough to merit this kind of punishment.

I wish this week were over.

I wish Stephen James would go back to being someone none of us had ever heard of.

———

There has been a menagerie here this week. . . . Almost all the girls went; and I enjoyed the solitude finely.

I couldn't decide if Ms. Lurie would expect me to come to the dinner table and smooth things over, or if she expected me to stay away and give everyone the chance to talk about me, so I went with my own preferences and stayed in my room for the night.

I didn't feel up to pretending to be even my strange shade of normal. And if I *have* to not eat, I'd rather be alone than do it as a spectator sport.

If I'd known I was going to be relying so heavily on the supplies

I could lay in, I'd have shopped a little harder the last time I joined a field trip into town.

At least tonight turned out all right food-wise. Ms. Lurie was as good as her word so far as the baked goods went. Unfortunately, she didn't just want to leave the promised tray outside my door.

I opened the door when she knocked, and she smiled and looked around to see where she could put her burden down. My desk was covered with books and papers, so she set the tray down on my bed.

"Careful," she cautioned. "There are breakables *and* spillables in here."

She lifted the lid of the tray—it was like something you'd see a butler bringing to the indisposed lady of the house. There was a plate covered with all kinds of dainty little baked offerings, a tiny glass cup of artfully whipped butter, a couple of heavy cloth napkins, and a single-serving teapot nesting in a matching cup.

"Miss Miller was feeling inspired," Ms. Lurie said. "She wasn't sure what you'd like, so she went all out. These are orange biscuits, and here are honey-wheat gems, and—I think those are called jam thumbprints."

I was starving and terrified at the same time. "She did all this for *me*?"

"Not exactly," Ms. Lurie said reassuringly. "She felt like baking anyway, as I said. The rest of us will get our share of the spoils, don't worry." Deftly, without spilling a drop, she poured me a cup of tea.

I waited for Ms. Lurie to ask me to apologize to Lucy for shrieking at her. At the very least, I figured she'd insist on hearing what had prompted me to make such a scene.

She didn't. "Eat something," she urged gently, and smiled. "Some of these are still warm. This is the kind of precious moment that has to be seized."

The orange biscuits looked gooey, so I clumsily speared a bite with a fork. My stomach roared approval, and I forgot to feel self-conscious, instead launching an all-out assault on the tray's contents.

While I chewed, Ms. Lurie made small talk about how old the tree just outside my window was and how the winter birds were arriving early this year and she was afraid they'd be disappointed at how much rain we were sure to have soon. It had been too dry for much too long in our state, but the weather prophets were predicting that soon the clouds would finally remember what their job was.

She went on like this for a bit even after I'd demolished Miss Miller's masterpieces. I sat back at last, sipping the tea she'd poured me.

"Sugar?" she asked belatedly.

I shook my head, feeling guilty. I wished she'd brought another teacup. It seemed piggish and antisocial to be drinking tea in front of someone without at least trying to share. But all I had was my toothbrush glass, and I couldn't exactly offer her that.

She'd have been gracious if I did, though.

She was still sitting cozily at the foot of my bed, still murmuring about inconsequentials, and I knew this was about more than just waiting for me to empty the tray so she could bring it back downstairs.

"Okay," I said, in the next pause.

Ms. Lurie smiled. "Okay," she repeated, and then her smile faded. "I know there's been—well, a mixed response to the idea of going to the Stephen James celebration." She looked sad. "There's certainly been a mixed response to calling it a celebration, but it's difficult to find a short way of saying that we'd like to honor his memory and focus on his life and work."

"A tribute?" I suggested.

She smiled again. "That's perfect," she said. "It's too late for them to change the flyers, but that's the word *I'll* be using from now on."

We sat together quietly for a minute. "At any rate," she went on. "I was wondering if you plan on going."

Something in her voice stopped me from giving the blunt, truthful "Good *God*, no" I would have. "Do you want me to?" I asked cautiously instead.

Ms. Lurie hesitated. "Ordinarily, I'd say it's up to you—and of course it is," she amended quickly. "I don't mean I'm going to ask you to do something you don't want to do."

"But?"

She paused again. "I know you don't generally like to go on our field trips into town, even on normal occasions," she began.

Not exactly true, though of course she couldn't know that. The times I *have* gone, I've liked it quite a bit. Or rather I've registered a great deal *to* like—so many things I'd love to like, carelessly, if I were someone who's allowed to enjoy ordinary treats.

As Ms. Lurie has gently pointed out to me, the library in town is significantly bigger than Hawthorne's. And (she adds) I may not be a big shopper, but it can still be fun to poke around now and then, even if only to laugh at the sort of things people can make a living selling to wide-eyed, loose-walleted tourists.

Obviously I can't tell her how terrifying it is for me to be out in the open the way I am in town—even such a small town. I jump a mile at every accidental touch or slight noise.

So I tend to just say, like Dickinson sitting out the menagerie, that I like the quiet when everyone's gone.

Ms. Lurie always smiles a little sadly. "I can understand that," she says. "But really, it's not as if the Hawthorne girls are a terribly loud bunch."

"It's not the volume," I say. "It's—I just like how it feels to be alone now and then." I'm ashamed of how easily the lie comes. Although it's not completely a lie. The school *does* feel different when it's empty of people, and it *is* rather nice.

"I worry about you being cooped up so much," Ms. Lurie went on this time.

"I'm not—" I began, and then thought better of arguing. "I like it here," I said instead. "Hawthorne doesn't feel like a coop."

Ms. Lurie smiled. "I'm glad. It's my own favorite place, as you may have noticed. But—I think it's easier to appreciate a house if you get out of it now and then."

I said nothing because suddenly I wanted more than anything to crawl into her lap and tell her everything and beg her to save me, to make this all stop.

But she can't, and even if she wanted to, she'd probably die trying. So I just kept quiet and wondered when I'd become so weak.

"And there are different ways of being cooped up," Ms. Lurie went on, smoothly enough that we could both pretend she'd paused for breath rather than a response. "It's not just that you spend so much of your time inside. You shut *yourself* away. Your inner self. Your feelings. Your gifts."

I put my cup down in its saucer so I'd have an excuse to look at it.

There was a poem I saw once in a textbook that I had thought must be by Dickinson, but it wasn't. It was by Christina Rossetti, who didn't much approve of Dickinson's writing—not pure and religious enough—but who actually had a lot in common with the poet of Amherst. They were both unmarried and both had beloved brothers who got into big, dramatic trouble with women. And they both wrote poems that can slip effortlessly into your memory.

Some of the lines from that Rossetti poem flickered through my head:

> *All others are outside myself;*
> *I lock my door and bar them out . . .*

> *I lock my door upon myself,*
> *And bar them out; but who shall wall*
> *Self from myself, most loathed of all?*

"—more than ever now," Ms. Lurie said, and I couldn't tell if this was the end of just a single sentence I'd missed, or a whole paragraph.

I did know that I needed her to leave.

"I won't push you to go," she added, "but I think it might be a very good idea."

I tried to nod neutrally—to show I'd heard without coming across as agreeing to her request.

She seemed to get it. "Will you promise me you'll at least think about it?"

I nodded again, harder. "Yes," I whispered.

Please just go.

"Thank you, Emily," she said, and stood up. "Oof. I'm feeling my age. Sit for ten minutes and my legs fall asleep." She smiled at me. "Why don't I take this plate down, and you can bring the tea things later. No rush."

"Thank you." I wasn't sure I was audible; but a minute later I was alone in my room with an almost-empty teapot.

———

Dear Emily,—Are you there, and shall you always stay there, and is it not dear Emily any more, but Mrs. Ford of Connecticut, and must we stay alone, and will you not come back with the birds and the butterflies, when the days grow long and warm?

Dickinson wasn't just single all her life; she was terrified of marriage.

I think she was, and the letters seem to back me up.

I don't blame her. Marriage must have been pretty horrible back then, at least if you were a woman. You signed away so many freedoms. No money of your own. Your time, your whole life, was claimed by someone else—and if that someone was abusive, who was to stop him?

And then there was the fear you might die in childbirth, or survive only to see your children die, at birth or a few years later.

All those things happened to plenty of women Dickinson knew.

People seem to feel sorry for her because she never got married—they pity the old-maid poet, and think of her genius as some kind of consolation prize for a solitary life.

I think the woman who liked to write at three in the morning and stay in her room and not see anyone she didn't feel like seeing—who loved to love children as long as they were other people's children whom she could lavish with treats and loving notes from a safe distance—I think she knew exactly what she was doing. And what she was doing was saying *No, thank you* to a life she didn't want.

She had choices, and she chose to be alone.

She was happy alone.

People can be happy alone.

———

There is a pain—so utter—
It swallows Being up—
Then covers the Abyss with trance—
So Memory can step
Around—Across—upon it—
As One within A Swoon—
Goes steady—where an Open Eye—
Would spill Him—Bone by Bone—

I went to Dickinson's house again last night.

Maggie/Margaret the maid admitted me to the small sitting room, and again I waited an age for some response.

I felt unusually nervous—almost panicked—and I realized I was terrified Dickinson would agree to see me.

I stood up to leave the house before it was too late, but there were already footsteps coming down the stairs.

I was never so relieved to see Maggie's sensible black dress and white apron.

She didn't speak, just offered me the tray—covered this time.

I lifted the lid and there was a flower. A black rose.

It was real, but so beautiful—such a perfect bud, just beginning to open—that if it hadn't been for the perfumy scent I would have sworn it was silk.

Under it was an envelope. It looked to be stuffed with as much paper as it could hold.

Open Me Carefully was written on the envelope.

The handwriting was familiar, but it wasn't Dickinson's.

Maggie watched me expectantly.

I just stood there, staring at those words written in the hand of a girl who was fond of wearing long white gowns but who certainly didn't live in the nineteenth century or write poetry.

"Well, Miss?" Maggie had work to do. She couldn't stand here all day holding a silly tray.

I put the lid of the tray back down on the flower and the unopened letter. I could have sworn they vanished just as I started to lower the lid, but of course there was no way to know that.

"I'm sorry," I whispered, and I ran from the house and woke up in my bed, heart pounding so hard I thought it would jump out of my body.

The autumn nights are cooler now, but my sheets were drenched with sweat.

It felt like a long time before I could stop shaking.

———

The difference between Despair
And fear—is like the One
Between the instant of a Wreck—
And when the Wreck has
been—

Good.
  Good.
  That's done, then.
  Finished. Finally.
  All right.
  It had to happen and I'm glad to have it over with.
  It's over.
  I'll never have to do this again.

———

There is a finished
feeling
Experienced at Graves—
A leisure of the Future—
A Wilderness of Size—

I couldn't sleep after that dream, so I got up and tried to work.

  My room was too damned claustrophobic after I'd spent so many hours there in a row.

  Anyway, I had to air all the bedclothes out properly before I could try to sleep again, and that takes up all available space.

And maybe I knew what had to happen and just wanted to get it over with.

———

Three times—we parted—
Breath—and I—

M came and found me in the library in the middle of the night again.

Maybe anyone but M would have asked how I was feeling after my big blowup and subsequent absence from the dinner table.

Maybe M would have asked after the feelings of anyone but me.

I being me and M being M, she simply sauntered in casual as a cat and said, "You know, one of these days you're going to burn this place down with all your midnight-oil burning."

She looked over my shoulder at my laptop's screen, not even pretending not to stare. "Goodness," she said. "That looks dire."

It was. It was a facsimile I'd found of the Sunday school newsletter Dickinson's uncle gave her a subscription to when she was seven. Even the font looked grim.

"Go away," I said mechanically. Her perfume was new, or at least new to me.

"Or what?"

I opened my mouth to give her detailed instructions on how exactly one can, just for a change of pace, go jump in a lake. Instead I found myself saying, "Or I'll tell you the kind of story Dickinson got to fall asleep to when she was a little girl."

M's eyes gleamed. She sat down in the chair next to mine and curled up, elf-like. "I'll give you five dollars and all my desserts for a month if you read some to me," she said.

———

And if at any time you regret you received me, or I prove a different fabric to that you supposed, you must banish me.

Both my thumbs are covered in tiny red crescents from me digging my fingernails into them.

How could I have done that?

Instead of leaving the library—instead of never being there in the first place—I sat there and told her *stories*. Exactly the kind of stories she loves.

I told M the story—written for little New England children long ago—about a young man standing on the gallows, about to hang for his crimes. As they put the rope around his neck, he begged to speak once more to his mother. When she hugged him, he bit off a piece of her ear and told her that if only she'd raised him better, he wouldn't be about to die.

"It's true," M said when she managed to stop laughing. "If she'd only kept her son tied up in the cellar with nothing but bread and water once a day to sustain him, he'd never have been able to do anything wrong."

And then there was the story about the three-year-old boy who died after falling into a barrel of boiling water.

"Because *that's* the kind of thing you want to have lying around when you've got a toddler on the premises," M said.

"Well, they didn't have washing machines back then," I pointed out.

"She could have sent him to play outside while she did the laundry."

"But then he might have gotten lost or eaten by a lion or something."

M looked at me with polite incredulity. "Yes, the lions of New England are famously ferocious."

"Okay, a bear. Look, that's not the point."

"What *is* the point?"

The point was that this wasn't just any three-year-old boy. All his life—

"*All* his life? All three long years of it?"

"Quit interrupting."

—he'd wanted to be a missionary. But now he was going to die too young to fulfill his dream. He had sixty cents saved up, and with his dying breath he begged his mother to give it to the missionaries. She agreed. He bit the dust.

"That did *not* happen," M said, uncurling herself. She stood up and stood behind me, shoving my hands away from the computer so she could scroll up and down the pages. "This is the kind of story they wrote for little *kids*?"

"You're one to talk," I managed. She'd touched my hands. *Pushed* them, but still. "This was two hundred years ago. Children really did die from that kind of accident. It happened to a kid Dickinson's aunt knew. What's *your* aunt's excuse for terrorizing you at bedtime?"

"She didn't *terrorize* me," M said, still focused on the virtual pages in front of her. She was leaning close to me, but apparently only I noticed. *Her* breathing seemed normal, anyway. "And, anyway, I wasn't *seven* when she told me those stories."

She paused, thinking. "Well, all right, I was. But the stories didn't *scare* me, because they didn't seem *real*."

"You keep saying *these* stories don't seem real."

"Not *now*, no. Back then, they must have scared the cranberries out of those poor kids."

"'Cranberries'?"

"Something else my aunt taught me. She didn't mind the big swear words, but she really hated minor-league ones like 'crap.'" She leaned in still closer to the screen. "Okay, *this* is just awful."

"What?"

"Whatever preacher wrote this is telling little kids that they'd better be good or they're going to hell. And it could be any minute now. Very sweet."

M started reading aloud in a low, stern voice. "'And sometimes too, when you stand by the new made grave of some one of your playmates, and see the coffin let down into that narrow house, and hear the minister warn you to prepare for death—'"

It shouldn't have been enough to drop me off the planet, unless I was already ready to fall.

She didn't notice anything wrong at first. She just broke off, laughing incredulously. "I mean, come on. Pile it on a little heavier, why don't you? The grave of just *one* of your little buddies? Because, you know, of course there'll be plenty of *those* funerals to choose from—"

I think I made some sound. She stopped again, looking at me.

"Emily?" she asked, all laughter gone from her voice.

~~The room was closing in and~~

~~The house was dark and when I tried to find her~~

~~She liked cologne and sweet shampoo but that night she smelled like~~

I remembered myself.

I remembered the rules.

I remembered who M was and what she could be if I let her.

I stood up and shoved M aside. Hard.

I heard her gasp.

I shut the laptop hard enough that I should have been worried I'd shattered the screen, and I picked it up and tucked it under one arm.

M stared at me. She wasn't quite standing up—more leaning against one of the tables. Her expression was bewildered and concerned.

Why couldn't she be angry? Or even just hurt?

Why did she always have to be so damned worried about *me*?

It didn't matter. I was good at this now.

"Shut up," I said very quietly.

She opened her mouth and I said in the same soft tone, "I'm not joking. I'm not bluffing. If you ever say another word to me, I'll leave Hawthorne that same day."

Now her face looked as white and huge-eyed as it had when I'd screamed at Lucy.

"I can do it," I said. "I don't have anyone to tell me not to, or to make me stay. It's up to me. I could walk out right now if I wanted to. If you make me, I will."

M said nothing and stood very still. She looked as if she'd have fallen if the table weren't there to support her.

I thought about saying more, but there wasn't any point. She either got it or she didn't.

So I left the room, and left it at that.

So that's over. That's over with.

I should have done it a long time ago.

I never should have let things get so far in the first place.

———

I had no monarch in my life, and cannot rule myself; and when I try to organize, my little force explodes and leaves me bare and charred.

I almost didn't go down to breakfast this morning, but Ms. Lurie would have said something and, anyway, I have to face it sooner or later. If I'm going to stay here.

Maybe I *should* leave early.

Of course I should. I shouldn't even be here now.

But I'll be eighteen in the spring, and that will make it much easier to find somewhere to live. I assume.

I've been planning to spend the time between my birthday and school letting out for summer looking at my options. Maybe asking one of my executors for help. They're not exactly real estate agents, but still they must know more than I do about the practicalities of getting a little place of my own.

I wouldn't even know where to begin if I left now.

I'll do it if I have to, but I don't think I do. Not just yet. ~~I think it should be safe now.~~

184

~~I want to stay at Hawthorne~~

No, I'll say it. In ink, at least. On hidden pages.

I want to stay at Hawthorne for as long as I can.

If I'm not even allowed to love a *place*, there's no help or hope for me or for the world. I'll have to spend the rest of my life hopping around like a fire walker on an endless bed of coals.

Maybe I'll do that anyway. Once I leave Hawthorne. I can't imagine caring where I live after I leave here.

But I want these last months. I paid for them. They're mine.

M sat at my table at breakfast but she didn't say anything. Not to me, of course—she never does when other people are around anyway—but not to anyone else, either.

And she didn't eat. Didn't even pretend to.

Brianna gave her a concerned look, but didn't say anything.

I'm sure she will soon, if M doesn't start covering her tracks a little better. Brianna doesn't keep things to herself any more than M does.

Maybe she and M can run off and live happily ever after and I'll never have to think about either of them again.

———

The little boy we laid away never fluctuates, and his dim society is companion still. But it is growing damp and I must go in. Memory's fog is rising.

Of all the people Dickinson loved who died toward the end of her life—her parents; two guys the biographers like to say she was in love with; one man she certainly *was* in love with; her writer-friend Helen Hunt Jackson, who knew how brilliant Dickinson was and begged her not to keep her genius to herself—the only one she couldn't bear to lose was her nephew Gib.

Gib was eight years old. He was a caboose baby—much younger than his siblings, born when his poor mother was forty-four years old—and apparently spoiled rotten by everyone in sight.

When Gib was five years old, he bragged at school that he had a beautiful white calf of his very own. It didn't exist in a strictly physical sense, so his conventional teacher tried to set him straight by telling him he'd go to hell for lying if he didn't shape up. When Dickinson heard that this had made Gib cry, she furiously dared the teacher to come and see the calf in question, who was grazing in Dickinson's attic even as they spoke.

When Gib was seven years old, he barged into the room Dickinson was sitting in. "I want something," he insisted. She kissed him and asked him what he'd like. "Oh, everything," he said.

She gave him her everything. She gave him a visit when he was deathly sick and she hadn't been in anyone's house but her own in years.

She gave him her heart, and when he died he took it with him.

Violet looks like Gib to me, but other than the blonde hair I'm not sure anyone else would see it. Anyway, I don't have a picture of her, so maybe the resemblance is all in my head.

Violet was a fierce, tree-climbing sort of girl. Her parents talked afterward about how sweet she was, how gentle with her little brother, and maybe that was true. But nobody in our second grade class would have called her sweet. Most of the kids were terrified of her.

She wasn't a bully—she just knew her own mind. Most

seven-year-olds don't have much mind to know, but Violet was always fiercely purposeful. "We're going to do this now," she'd say, and it didn't matter what anyone else said or wanted—that's what they were going to do.

They didn't *have* to. They could always have played with someone else if they didn't want to do what Violet said. But no one lucky enough to be let into Violet's company ever walked away willingly.

Violet was the first person who made me think things might be all right after my parents were killed.

Aunt Paulette had said in so many words that she'd only taken me in because it would be a disgrace to the family name to have me in foster care. No one at school wanted to play with me. They thought I was weird because of what had happened to my parents, and I wasn't in any position to argue with them.

So when Violet started staring at me in class, I didn't think much of it at first. I'd finished the too-easy addition problems we'd been given and was sitting quietly waiting for something to happen. I sighed and turned my head to look out the window, and that's when I noticed Violet's fierce gaze fixed on me. She didn't look angry, just thoughtful and a little puzzled.

She also didn't look away when I met her gaze, the way the other kids tended to. They seemed to think I was blind and deaf. If they wanted to point and whisper, I couldn't stop them, but it was ridiculous how shocked they looked when I showed any signs of noticing. *You mean her parents were murdered* and *she can hear?*

Idiots.

Violet wasn't like that. When I caught her staring and did a bit of staring back, Violet didn't jump guiltily and pretend to have been looking at something else the whole time, or look quickly down at her worksheet and then glance up again in a few seconds to see if she'd gotten away with it.

Not Violet. She returned my gaze steadily, not the least bit disconcerted. I was the one who finally had to look away, feeling as if I'd lost some sort of contest.

I saw Violet looking at me again while one of the more hateable kids was delivering a book report. A boy who liked to point and laugh on top of staring and whispering.

Even if he'd been nice, it would have been torture listening to him struggle to talk about an idiotic story when I wanted to be home reading *The Lion, the Witch and the Wardrobe*.

I looked out the window at freedom, and then glanced around the room to see how impressed everyone else wasn't with Tommy's report, and that was when I saw Violet staring at me again. She had a faint smile on her face, as if she knew exactly what I was thinking and couldn't have agreed more.

This time when I looked away first, it was to keep from bursting out laughing.

After school that day, I was about to walk home when I noticed Violet standing next to me.

"Let's go to my house and play," she said without preamble.

If it had been anyone else, I'd have thought they were trying to win some kind of bet. *Go be friends with her, I dare you. Oh yeah? Well, I dare you to.* Or else I'd have thought she was trying to impress people. *This is my friend Emily. Her mom and dad were killed all over the place.*

But Violet wasn't like that. She didn't have anything to prove, didn't care about impressing people. She just did what she wanted to do, because she wanted to do it.

And today she wanted to play with me.

"I can't go anywhere without asking first," I said, as if this were the kind of request I fielded all the time.

Violet nodded, unsurprised. "Then let's go to your house today, and tomorrow we can go to mine," she said.

"Don't you have to ask your parents?" I asked.

"I can call them from your house. They won't mind."

We walked together for a minute in silence. Then, as if to get it out of the way: "Your parents were killed, weren't they?"

I nodded.

Violet nodded, too. Her expression was even more fierce than usual. "That's awful," she said.

She didn't have that ooey-gooey tone of voice so many people did when they talked to me. Violet sounded angry.

I nodded again. Maybe *I* should have been angry at the inherent silliness of Violet's statement. Of course what had happened was awful. It was so far beyond awful that there weren't words for it.

But—there weren't words for it, and Violet had tried to find words anyway. And she didn't say anything about how someday I'd feel better, or ask any creepy questions about what any of it had looked like.

And there was something wonderful about Violet being angry about my parents being killed. As if we were already friends, and Violet took what had happened to me as a personal affront.

It seemed quite clear that once Violet was in charge of the world, this sort of thing wouldn't be allowed to happen anymore.

If Violet had been allowed to live, she would have grown up to be president, or possibly queen.

"Do you like the Narnia books?" I asked.

———

We outgrow love, like
other things
And put it in the Drawer—

M isn't going to the Stephen James tribute tomorrow, so I have to.

Ms. Lurie was pleased when I said I'd go, but she knows something's happened. I've noticed some concerned glances at M as well as at me.

It doesn't matter.

This is no different from how things were before.

She's known me for a long time. She should be relieved I'm getting back to normal.

———

Called back.

Was able to stand up long enough to wash my face this morning.

Ms. Lurie says not to worry or try to hurry and everything will be fine.

———

The show is not the show,
But they that go.
Menagerie to me
My neighbor be.

Dr. Gray came by today and says I'm fine. A little dehydrated. Nothing worse.

Mrs. Weston (*Call me Ruth, honey*) is sitting with me on the porch. She doesn't try to make me talk. She has her knitting and I have my notebook.

Mostly I've just been looking at nothing.

———

Doom is the House without
the Door—
'Tis Entered from the Sun—
And then the Ladder's
thrown away,
Because Escape—is done—

Back in my own room. Finally.

I barely knew Hawthorne even *had* an infirmary, and now I've memorized every nonexistent crack in its walls.

I'm stronger, but I'm not strong enough to leave. I'm not sure I ever will be. I can't imagine it.

Leave Hawthorne? I can't even leave my room.

I don't know what can happen now.

―――

It struck me—Every Day—
The Lightning was as new
As if the Cloud that instant
slit
And let the Fire Through—

"I don't understand what happened to the sun."

"What do you mean?"

"It was so bright. I've never seen anything like it. It was like—the opposite of an eclipse. Double sunlight." I looked at her hopefully. "That's why I got such a bad headache. That's what started it."

Ms. Lurie smiled at me sadly. "There was nothing wrong with the sun that day, Emily. There barely *was* any sunlight. They were even worried they'd have to reschedule because of the weather—so much of the celebration was supposed to take place outside—but in the end it didn't rain. There were just a lot of clouds feeling sociable."

―――

Forever—is Composed of Nows—

I still don't remember it all, which is fine with me considering what I *do* remember.

No matter what Ms. Lurie says, the sun really ~~was~~ seemed to be mercilessly bright. I remember thinking this was what it would be like to live on a planet in orbit around Sirius.

Even in the car it was bad, and I was in the back and not next to a window.

I remember getting to town and being afraid to get out of the car. Even with the roof and the doors, it was already so bright in there— terrifying, merciless light. As soon as I stepped outside, I knew I would be utterly exposed, and I was. It was as if there was no shade in all the world, no shelter. The sun was a spotlight I couldn't get away from.

No one else seemed to notice anything amiss. I think that was the worst part of that moment. Feeling singled out by the light. Surrounded and alone.

I did manage to stand up. I got out of the car by myself and I stood and waited for whatever would come next.

There was a terrible sound and it went all through me. I thought it was drums—those huge ones you have to hammer with mallets as big as axes. I thought how awful it was going to be to have to listen to whoever's idea of music this was.

But it wasn't music. It was my heart, pounding so hard I thought everyone must be hearing it.

I'm having a heart attack, I remember thinking very distinctly. And then: *but I'm only seventeen.*

But since when was that enough to save anyone?

I remember Brianna saying, "Well, let's get this over with," and then, "Hey—are you okay?"

I remember nodding and hoping that my hand resting on the car for support looked casual.

I remember thinking *just let it be quick* and not being sure what "it" was and not much caring.

I remember Ms. Lurie asking me something, and me trying to stand up and walk normally, and then everything is like a deck of cards that's been shuffled once too often.

It feels as if first I was in the car being sped back to Hawthorne and then I was on the ground surrounded by a crowd of people.

No order, no reason to any of it.

Lucy's voice was shrill and distant, and there was a man with hippie hair and a grave, compassionate face helping me with something. Giving me something?

Brianna said, "I can call so she knows to expect you."

There was a door that opened and a door that closed, but I'm not sure they were the same one.

———

Of our greatest acts we are ignorant. You were not aware that you saved my life.

"What did that man give me?"

Ms. Lurie looked tired and anxious. She's worried I'm not eating enough and I guess maybe I'm not, but it isn't my fault. I do feel very hungry. I want to eat. It's just that I'll suddenly get a specific food in mind, and then that's all I feel I can eat.

My stomach has turned into a toddler.

It's sad because Miss Miller has apparently taken my illness or ailment or whatever we're calling it as a challenge. I hope everyone else at Hawthorne is getting fair shares of what are undoubtedly wonderful soups—bowls of which it must be a pain for Ms. Lurie to keep lugging up to my room.

Unfortunately I've never been that fond of soup, and I like it less than ever now. Too hot. Too salty.

All I feel like eating today is ice cream, but that's not something we ever have at Hawthorne. All that refined sugar, and, anyway, I doubt it would survive the drive from town.

"What man?" Ms. Lurie asked.

"The big one with all the hair."

"I'm sorry, sweetheart," she said. "I don't remember anyone giving you anything."

I nodded, picking up a piece of bread experimentally. Could I have some? Just a little? Bread is nice. Everyone likes bread.

My stomach sneered, and I put the bread down and stirred a little more sugar into my tea.

Sweet was all I wanted these days, and that bread had cheese baked into its crust.

Ms. Lurie sighed. I imagined how horrified she'd look if I asked her for some chocolate milk instead.

And cinnamon toast. On white bread.

"He did," I said. But I didn't argue any more, because just then I remembered what that man had given me.

Everyone in the world had swooped in when I'd fallen, but he'd been the one who kept them away when there wasn't room for me to breathe, when I wasn't even sure I remembered how. He'd said something, and they'd all stepped back a bit.

And then he said something to me. Told me to look at his shirt, which was huge, just like he was.

Now tell me what color it is.

I could feel Ms. Lurie nearby, but I couldn't see her.

How do you spell that color?

I couldn't talk, but I could think, and I could certainly wonder what kind of idiot this man thought I was.

His eyes were still grave, but he smiled a little. Had he heard me? I don't think I was talking, but maybe I was.

Now spell it backwards.

That was harder than it should have been. Everything was too bright. (It *was*, Ms. Lurie.)

How many two-letter words can you make with those letters?

Ow.

Lo.

Ye.

Oy, if that counts as a word for people who aren't Jewish.

Wo? Dickinson spelled it that way once in a poem, but I don't know if that was because they really spelled it like that back then or if she was just a bad speller.

I don't remember getting back in the car, so I don't know if he really picked me up and eased me into the front seat. It seems to me as if he did, and weirdly I don't think I minded.

I do remember puzzling out the three-letter words I could use those letters for, and then the four-letter words, and I felt dimly annoyed that he hadn't worn an orange shirt so I'd have more letters to work with.

What he gave me was small and impossible to see but it was everything.

He gave me something to think about other than terror and pain.

Eight Saturday noons ago, I was making a loaf of cake with Maggie,
when I saw a great darkness coming and knew no more until late at
night.

I don't remember falling, but I must have. Why else would I have
been on the ground?

Ms. Lurie shrieked, but I didn't know what she was saying at
first and then I wasn't sure she meant me.

There are a lot of Emilys in this world.

Men do not call the surgeon to commend the bone, but to set it, sir,
and fracture within is more critical.

Mrs. Weston checks on me every day, though I don't know why she
bothers.

I'm exactly the same as ever.

I'm making a lot of work for her. This job was like retirement for
her before I came along.

Maybe it *was* retirement. She and Ms. Lurie are old friends;
maybe Ms. Lurie offered her this post so she could relax and put her
feet up and always have time for a chat when Ms. Lurie has a few
minutes free.

Mrs. Weston's a nurse practitioner, which I guess is something halfway between a nurse and a doctor. It's certainly more than sufficient for Hawthorne's quiet needs.

Before I fell, all Mrs. Weston had to worry about was coddling seasonal allergies, monthly cramps, and occasional minor injuries. There was a sprained wrist my first year here, and pretty much nothing interesting since.

Maybe Mrs. Weston's secretly been bored out of her mind all these years, and checking my pulse and temperature is the highlight of her day.

I don't know who she thinks she's helping, but if it makes her happy she's welcome to try.

———

The doctor calls it "revenge of the nerves"; but who but Death had wronged them?

Dr. Gray came by to see me today, and just in case anyone's listening she is *not* welcome to come poking and prodding in my room.

I don't need one more person worrying over me.

I certainly don't need someone to "talk things over with," and I'd appreciate it if Dr. Gray stopped sprinkling therapists' business cards all over my bed when I've just made it.

"I'm fine," I said. "I'm working." I waved at the books and papers I'd scattered artfully around my bed and desk.

"Ms. Lurie says you don't go out."

"If I'd known I could get free room service just by staying in my room all day, I'd have started a long time ago."

"Speaking of room service, she also says you aren't eating."

"I eat sometimes." My toddler-stomach tends to sleep through breakfast. Or maybe it just doesn't mind porridge.

"Sometimes is a start. But from what Ms. Lurie says, you're not having nearly enough."

"I'm fine," I repeated. "In fact, I'm so well, I'm worried I'll get *too* healthy if I eat all the food they serve around here."

"Emily."

"It's true. Nothing but whole grains and vegetables as far as the eye can see. Haven't you ever heard of too much of a good thing? I'd be taking my life in my hands if I tried to live on that without some cake to balance it out. Or cookies. Or cinnamon rolls."

Dr. Gray looked half amused and half as if she was looking for loopholes in the "do no harm" part of that oath she'd taken. "I don't remember learning anything like that in medical school."

"Maybe you missed that day."

———

Thank you for the delightful cake, and the heart adjacent.

"Emily." Ms. Lurie sounded fondly exasperated, as if I were a kitten who'd just clawed her favorite sweater. "For heaven's sake, why didn't you just *tell* me what you wanted to eat?"

I put my fork down, but only because there was nothing more for it to do.

I'd been planning at first to ignore the strawberries that came along with the shortcake and whipped cream she'd brought me, on the grounds that fruit is still health food no matter how heavily disguised it is, but Miss Miller had drizzled them with chocolate.

"You *hate* junk food," I pointed out. "You're always saying how terrible it is for us, and how Americans eat more sugar in a month than some countries have in a decade."

"As a rule, yes, that's true," Ms. Lurie said. "I absolutely don't think sugar and fat are things we should consume in great quantities on a regular basis, the way too many people in this country do. People who know better and who can afford to be rational eaters. I know I can get a bit evangelical on that point."

I didn't know how to answer that.

"But there's a time and a place for everything, Emily. Moderation in all things, including moderation. Especially if you didn't feel as if you *can* eat anything else. We all have times like that."

That doctor is pretty sharp. I'll have to write her a thank-you note and add it to the mail-this-after-I-die pile.

"And I do believe in listening to cravings," Ms. Lurie went on. "If your body is shouting for something, there's usually a reason. A good one."

She looked as if she'd like to speechify some more, but I was half-unconscious from the relief of being full for once, so she cut it short and picked up my empty plate. "Would you like some more?"

I shook my head.

"Something else, maybe?"

"Not now, thanks."

"Emily."

I opened my eyes all the way.

"I wish you'd tell me what's troubling you."

I looked down again, wishing I'd stopped a bite or two earlier.

"But what I wish more than anything is that you'd talk to *some-one*. Anyone you feel comfortable with." She smiled a little. "All right, maybe not some strange man at a bus stop, but someone safe. Someone trustworthy. We really do have a lot of someones like that at Hawthorne."

I didn't say anything.

"And if you'd feel better talking to someone who *isn't* part of Hawthorne—"

"No."

"There's no shame in calling a doctor when you're sick, Emily. And there's no shame in seeing a therapist when—"

"*No.*"

She was quiet for a minute. Then she went on, "You may not believe this, but the girls are very concerned about you. Brianna has asked after you, and so have Natasha and Chloe."

Chloe? Anxious Girl was worried about *me?*

"Lucy," Ms. Lurie went on, "has practically demanded to be allowed to come and see you, and when I told her that wasn't a good idea just now, she grilled me quite thoroughly on your eating, sleeping, and work habits."

"Don't tell her about *that*," I warned, gesturing at my plate. "She'll call the sugar police."

Ms. Lurie smiled. "I'm very interested to see where life takes that girl, or rather where she takes life. I have the feeling Hawthorne may be hatching its first CEO."

She became serious again. "I haven't wanted to bring this up—"

Don't.

"—but I know that M is very worried about you."

She waited.

"There's no reason for her to be," I said when I couldn't stand the silence any longer.

———

This is the Hour of Lead—
Remembered, if outlived,
As freezing persons, recollect
the Snow—
First Chill—then Stupor—then
the letting go—

I genuinely thought pushing M away would take things back to where they've always been.

It's not just that I knew I had to do it. I believed the hard part would be finding the strength for that push. And then after, I'd simply curl up into my usual cold ball of nastiness and get on with my old life.

It turns out there's all the difference in the world between renouncing the *idea* of companionship, and giving a specific someone up.

She's hurt, I guess, but she'll get over it. She has other chances. I don't.

———

Afraid! Of whom am
I afraid?

I tried to go to the dining room to have breakfast this morning and I couldn't.

I'm not *afraid*, any more than I'm afraid to fly to the sun. I just can't.

Do they think I'm just being stubborn?

Now I know how vampires feel when they don't have an invitation. Only they can't get in, and I can't get out. And neither of us can even bring ourselves to touch the door.

———

I reason, Earth is short—
And Anguish—absolute—
And many hurt
But, what of that?

Maybe someone wants me to be willing to sacrifice myself—to offer my own life. "No, not her—take me instead." *Boom!* The curse is lifted and the fairy tale ends.

But no one's ever given me the chance. The killings go on and no one consults me.

Unless the murderer is waiting for me to commit suicide.

That's a pretty roundabout way to kill someone. Not to mention inefficient.

But it would work, wouldn't it?

Even if it didn't end the murders, I couldn't be to blame for them anymore. And I wouldn't have to see them.

I enjoy much with a precious fly, during sister's absence, not one of your blue monsters, but a timid creature, that hops from pane to pane of her white house, so very cheerfully, and hums and thrums, a sort of speck piano. Tell Vinnie I'll kill him the day she comes, for I sha'n't need him any more, and she don't mind flies!

There are no flies in my room. I do see a spider now and then, which probably accounts for the lack of insects.

I can't remember where I read about prisoners making friends with bugs and spiders. I hope it was just a story. Even *I'm* not ~~crazy~~ desperate enough to try that.

Of course, a pet I don't care about would be ideal under the circumstances, but it does seem to defeat the whole point of having a pet. Surely there ought to be more to it than simply being conscious in the same room as another conscious creature.

Assuming spiders and flies even count as conscious.

I guess the fact that we even have to ask says a lot right there.

I wouldn't mind trying to keep a mouse as a pet. That might work. It's an animal most people see as a pest, and it's a survivor, and it's much more companionable than a housefly.

But a cage of any kind would be a dead giveaway: someone I care about lives in here.

Maybe I could just let it wander free? Surely even my watcher wouldn't notice a free-range mouse.

That wouldn't exactly be a pet, though. I might as well let rats infest my house.

People used to get cats just to keep that kind of vermin under control. It's not as if Ma and Pa Ingalls went shopping for cat food. Find a rat or go hungry was the rule for cats back then.

I wonder if Lavinia Dickinson fed her cats or just let them catch their dinners.

Considering the names she gave them—Tabby, Drummydoodles, Buffy, and Tootsie—I have a hard time imagining them as blood-thirsty hunters.

Of the two of them—solid, practical Lavinia and dreamy, poetic Emily—you'd think Emily would have been the crazy cat lady. But she hated cats. Emily was pro-dog, pro-bird, and pro-mouse. Cats had no place in her universe, other than a destructive one.

She didn't keep any animals as pets except one dog. Carlo. Her father got him for her, hoping he would make her feel safe, and he did.

Dickinson named her dog Carlo after a dog in *Jane Eyre*. She was okay going out and about when she had him with her. She went for long rambles, and even took him on visits with her. He shows up in her poetry.

And then he died and her life curved completely inward.

———

My life closed twice before its close

She was already named Zoë when Aunt Paulette brought her home. I don't remember it being a holiday, or any particular day at all. I just remember Aunt Paulette saying she hoped I'd stop moping around now, for God's sake.

Violet was gone and I don't know if I was finally starting to get the hint. It wouldn't have mattered much either way, since no one near my age wanted anything to do with me now, not even to make fun of me. But I couldn't have understood completely, because I was overjoyed to be given Zoë.

And either Aunt Paulette didn't understand the rules yet or she thought there was some kind of loophole for animals. I think the first one. Aunt Paulette wouldn't accept the idea of a universe she's not the center of.

Sometimes I wonder how it was clear to my watcher that Aunt Paulette was nowhere near enough to even my poor desperate heart to be in danger. She did take me in. She took care of me. And she even did non-required things like giving me a dog.

But it was all with a great air of impatience and annoyance. Even bringing Zoë home was clearly not an *oh that poor child—she needs somebody to love who'll love her right back* moment. It was more like *if that kid doesn't stop moping around my beautiful house I swear I'll kick her out into the streets and there's not a jury of my peers that will convict me.*

I was a kid. Kids like dogs. Aunt Paulette liked being right, and being left alone. Bringing home a dog would give her a little of each.

Aunt Paulette is going to die of extra old age.

"You can choose a new name for her, if you want," Aunt Paulette had said as Zoë shyly licked my hand and then my face. Aunt

Paulette made it sound as if she were granting me a huge favor. But I didn't think it was right to rename someone who'd already had a name long enough to get used to it. She was a dog, not a doll. Anyway, Zoë was a cute name.

Zoë was a beagle, which surprised me since she didn't look anything like Snoopy, even allowing for artistic license.

"You have to walk her a *lot*," Aunt Paulette warned me. "Not just to let her go to the bathroom, but for exercise. She needs a lot of exercise. Two or three long walks a day, and let her run around in the backyard off her leash, too. And you have to clean up after her when she does her business. I got you some special bags. You have to tell me when you're running low, so I can get more. Don't wait and then tell me when you're already out of them," she warned, since she thought I was a certified idiot. "Tell me when you still have a few left."

Zoë's fur was pretty short, but she shed a lot, so Aunt Paulette was always complaining about hair all over the place. Which was totally unfair. The housekeeper, Jonella, adored Zoë, and Jonella was the one who had to do all the extra vacuuming.

Zoë also smelled very doggy, which meant that I began to, too. More for Aunt Paulette to complain about. I was baffled by that. I liked to hug Zoë just for a whiff of her scent.

On the plus side, Zoë was small enough to not be in the way when she was inside, but not so small that she was easy to trip over. Aunt Paulette turned this into a fault anyway, calling Zoë a sneak and a thief.

It was true that Zoë ate anything she could find, and she could find a lot. She sniffed out treats Aunt Paulette thought she'd tucked away securely. Aunt Paulette accused me of feeding Zoë on the sly until Zoë devoured an entire loaf of bread that Aunt Paulette had left on a counter while I was at school.

After that, Aunt Paulette stopped blaming me for the disappearing food. She also started keeping Zoë out in the backyard when I wasn't home.

I got up an hour early every school morning so I could take Zoë for a long walk, and then I walked her as soon as I got home. I hated having to leave her for so many hours, but there was no getting around it. They wouldn't let me take her to school, and they wouldn't let me not go.

Jonella would take Zoë inside for a few hours every day while I was gone. She liked Zoë, and Zoë liked her. And Zoë barked a lot if she was outside alone for too long. It was sad to hear, and the neighbors complained.

Sometimes Jonella would even take Zoë for a walk "to get her jitters out." She couldn't do it often, though, because Aunt Paulette would grumble that Jonella wasn't getting paid to do any such thing. That made me furious. The house was still as clean as ever, and Jonella was doing extra just to be nice. If anything, she should have been paid more—or at least thanked. Instead, Aunt Paulette made it sound as if Jonella was dodging work, when anyone with half an eye could see that Jonella was the only one at Aunt Paulette's house who did any work.

Jonella was home sick one day with a bad cold, so Aunt Paulette left Zoë in the backyard the whole day while I was in school.

Jonella would have known what to do when Zoë got bored and restless and loud enough to be a nuisance, but Aunt Paulette's dog expertise seemed to begin and end at bossing everyone else around.

Zoë was out there unattended long enough that she could have chewed *through* our little fence if that had been the only way for her to escape. But she was a jumper, a climber, and a digger—all of which Aunt Paulette could have known from the beagle research she spent so much time bragging about, or from her attempts to keep Zoë away from the food they both adored.

At any rate, Aunt Paulette didn't pay any attention when Zoë kept barking and barking, and then she didn't give it a thought when she wasn't barking anymore—other than to be glad that she'd finally stopped making all that damned noise.

They told me it must have been a car, but one of the lovelier kids at school left a newspaper article on my desk. It went into a lot of detail about how Zoë looked when they found her, and warned local dog owners to keep a closer-than-usual eye on their pets until the perpetrator was found.

It's hard for me to remember the order of events because it all happened at about the same time, but Jonella left and Aunt Paulette stopped talking to me and I was handed a new name and sent to boarding school.

I've dropped my Brain—
My Soul is Numb—
The Veins that used to run
Stop palsied—'tis Paralysis
Done perfecter in Stone—

People think Dickinson stayed inside all the time after she came home from boarding school, but that's not quite right. She just didn't leave her father's property. Not after Carlo died.

She still loved to garden. Sometimes she'd do it at night, so she could be sure nosy neighbors wouldn't bother her. Word got around, though, and they'd look for the light of the lantern she brought with her, whispering excitedly if they saw it. It was almost as good as catching a glimpse of her.

Is that what's going to happen to me? Will I become the myth of Hawthorne, with Ms. Lurie my Lavinia and my Maggie all in one?

I can't risk that.

But I also can't do anything about it just now.

The movements that used to come so easily to me are completely out of my power. Gone as if by amputation, and I don't even have phantom limb syndrome.

I remember being able to walk down the hall and sit in the lounge or the dining room with other people—a dozen or two!—but I don't remember how it felt and I definitely don't miss it.

I just keep wondering if it really could have been me doing all that.

I suppose in a way it wasn't.

I can't even imagine leaving Hawthorne, so what's going to happen when I have to?

They'll have to put me outside, and then nothing. A statue, life-size in marble.

"Heaven"—is what I cannot
reach!

Fluttered around in the hall a bit this morning after I heard Ms. Lurie go out for her walk.

Most people wait until they die before they start haunting a house.

Time is a Test of
Trouble—
But not a Remedy—
If such it prove, it
prove too
There was no Malady—

I keep waiting for Ms. Lurie to say something. Something about all this room service she keeps offering me, for instance, which I don't remember seeing anything about in the breakdown of Hawthorne's tuition fees.

She doesn't. She just keeps bringing me soft, simple, sweet food and rich whole milk. Strong tea in the morning; chamomile at night. And a vitamin pill once a day so I don't get scurvy.

Every day she also brings me a small bowl of soup. I force a few spoonsful down until I can't hide the effort and she gently moves the bowl away, telling me it's supposed to be an option, not a punishment.

(It's a new kind of soup every day. Miss Miller must be losing her mind trying to concoct a bowl I'll enjoy. Apparently soup is beneficial to the ailing and that's all there is to it.)

Then, while I'm eating something that actually tastes good, Ms. Lurie sits and talks quietly on soothing subjects. She brings me little finds from her walks—a leaf or a blossom or an herb—and tells me stories about them.

It's lovely and terrifying.

~~What if someone is watching closely enough to see~~

I can't stop thinking and when I'm able to sleep at all I've started to have quiet, bloody nightmares on the subject, but there's nothing more I can do right now. Nothing more than the nothing I'm spending my days trapped in. I can't chase Ms. Lurie away ~~the way I chased M~~ and I can't run away myself. Not yet.

But I will. I have to, so I will.

I'll leave as soon as I can and then Ms. Lurie will be safe.

I'll get stronger and keep her safe and that's as much as I can bear to think about the future just now.

Today as she was about to sit down on the foot of my bed, she picked up a piece of paper that was sitting there. She was just moving it aside, but I grabbed it out of her hands and crumpled it up. "That's just junk," I muttered, pitching it into the wastebasket.

"Emily, you know I never tell you girls what to do," Ms. Lurie began.

"Good."

"Emily."

"Okay, okay. But?"

"*But* I'm a firm believer in never throwing away first drafts, no matter how hopeless they may appear."

"It's not like that," I said quickly, before she could get too far into the story of how Robert Louis Stevenson burned his first try at writing *Dr. Jekyll and Mr. Hyde* and we've all regretted it ever since. "It wasn't writing, exactly. I mean, it was *writing*, but it wasn't creative. It was just copying."

Ms. Lurie looked amused. "Given the lack of tests at Hawthorne, I'm surprised you're feeling any need to plagiarize. I'm glad you're admitting it so readily, though."

"Not *that* kind of copying."

"Of course not, Emily. I was just being silly."

"I was playing around with an idea—a project I want to do with Dickinson's writing," I said. "I mean the writing itself—how it looks, not just what it says. Kind of an art project. But I can't get it to look right. It never comes out the way I see it in my head. I need to be an artist to do this right, and I'm not."

There was a long pause while neither of us said the name of the person we were both thinking about.

Then Ms. Lurie said carefully, "I think many artists feel the kind of frustration you're talking about—of being unable to capture the image that inspired them."

I didn't answer. I didn't want to sound as if I were begging for compliments or asking for encouragement on the artistic path. Also, there's a difference between not liking the image you create because it isn't quite right, and rejecting something you've produced because it looks entirely stupid.

Ms. Lurie was looking at me.

"I'm getting stronger," I said, just to say something.

She smiled. "I'm glad," she said. "But there's no timetable, Emily. You have as long as you need."

I've always hated phrasing like that. Like if someone says, "Have as much cake as you want!" But what if you want *all* the cake? What if you want more cake than there even *is*?

I didn't say any of this, but it must have shown in my expression. "How*ever* long you need," Ms. Lurie said again, emphatically. "If you want to stay a decade at Hawthorne, you're welcome to."

I've always stayed holidays here, and she's never asked why I have to. I used to wonder if she knew more than I'd told her, but she would never have let me stay at Hawthorne at all if that were the case.

Maybe she thinks I'm Harry Potter.

Ms. Lurie took a deep breath. "I'm not bringing this up to pressure you," she said. "I want you to know your options, that's all. So let me just say very quickly that the minute you feel up to talking, *really* talking—"

"Ms. Lurie—"

"—I can find someone kind and helpful who'll come here on your own terms. No questions, no pressure, no judgment. Someone safe."

"I don't—"

"And if money is any kind of issue—well, it isn't. I promise. Don't even think along those lines."

I shook my head, unable to speak.

I haven't been able to cry in a long time, which is just as well, but now I felt a sort of background possibility of tears. Furious tears, if that makes sense.

Oh, Ms. Lurie.

Money problems are the only problems I *don't* have.

———

Heaven is large—is it not? Life is short too, isn't it? Then when one is done, is there not another, and—and—

When early death was more common, belief in a joyful afterlife was widespread. And those who saw no hope for happiness in this life—the desperately poor, the slaves who wouldn't be freed until Dickinson was thirty-five years old and even then they didn't exactly have a great time—pinned all their hopes on the ever after.

Sometimes I think I should do that. Wouldn't it be easier to accept the coldness of this life if it were the preface to an eternity of warmth?

But that's assuming I can make myself believe any such thing. And belief doesn't seem to be available for the asking. Not for me, at least.

Anyway, that consolation prize seems too vague, too far away. I can't let myself think along those lines too often, because instead of feeling more resigned to my joyless, solitary state, I feel angry.

I don't want Heaven.

I want *life*.

———

I noticed people disappeared,
When but a little child,—

I was lying on my bed in a pleasant daze of milk and honeybuns for dinner, reading a little and thinking nothing at all, when I heard stealthy footsteps, and then a quiet rustling.

No.

I didn't look for a minute. If I waited long enough, maybe whatever it was would be swallowed up in silence and disappear.

But the note that had just been pushed under my door was still there when I finally managed to move enough to pick it up.

If giving you this counts as a violation of terms,
<u>I'll</u> be the one to leave Hawthorne. Don't let that
thought worry you, either. I'd be delighted to ruin
my parents' holiday plans by showing up under the
tree, like something Krampus dropped.

Is it getting close to the holidays? I haven't been keeping track.

At any rate—I <u>have</u> to talk to you. In person. I
wouldn't say this if it weren't absolutely crucial.
And then I'll leave, if that's what you need. Or I'll
stay and never speak again. Word of honor.

I'm not saying this so I can plead my case or fight for
visitation rights or anything like that. And I wouldn't
be saying <u>anything</u> if it weren't important. I promise.

I'll tap on your door later. If you don't want to talk
in your room, I'll wait for you in the library.

I know you don't want to do this, and I know you're
not doing very well right now. That's actually part
of why I think it's important that I say what I need
to say. I think it might help.

Also, I'm terrified of waking up one morning and
learning you've been shipped off to a sanatorium or
something. Ms. Lurie won't tell us <u>anything</u> except
that you're not to be disturbed as long as you're in
your room and if you <u>do</u> come out, we can't make a
big deal out of it or she'll tie us to a tree and leave us
for the wolves to eat.

I'm pretty sure Ms. Lurie didn't say it like that.

Please, Emily.

Don't say that. Don't plead with me.

I don't want to hear her pleading, and in spite of what she promised, I'm sure that's what she's going to do.

If that isn't what she wants—I honestly don't want to hear whatever she thinks is so important.

I don't mean I don't want to see her and hear her because yes of
course I do. I want it more than anything.

I just don't think I'm up to this, whatever *this* is.

Can I tell her to please wait until at least tomorrow? Maybe a
few more tomorrows than that?

Of course I can. I can tell her whatever I want to. She can't force me to do anything.

If I'm so powerful, why am I sitting here trying to remember how to move?

———

So I pull my
Stockings off
Wading in the
Water
For the Disobedience'
Sake

I don't want to talk to her in here. I absolutely can't do that.

It's easier not to, anyway. She'll knock and I won't answer and then she'll wander off to wait for me. Simple.

And if we're in the library and she says something I don't want to hear, I can just leave. Easier than trying to boot her out of my room.

But then I have to go all the way to the library.

What if someone wakes up and sees me?

What if I get halfway there and freeze?

If I need to lie down in there, there's only the floor—and I feel so tired so much of the time these days.

It's exhausting existing.

This morning I had to rest between brushing my teeth and washing my face. Ridiculous.

But I can't let her in here. I *can't*.

If I don't say *Come in* and I don't follow her down the hall, this doesn't happen. It's up to me.

None of this is up to me.

———

My will endeavors for its word
And fails

~~This can't be~~
    ~~This isn't possible~~
    ~~She can't~~

———

My Heart opon a
little Plate
Her Palate to Delight

She told me everything.

    In here. Not in the library.

    Why not in here?

    Everything is out of my control now. It always was, really.

    I might as well throw a tea party for the world.

———

I should
not dare to
be so sad
So many
years again—
A Load is
first impossible
When we
have put it
down—

I couldn't speak when she knocked on the door, but I could open it and so I did.

Her face spoke whole paragraphs—first startled surprise, almost shyness (*M*, shy?), and seriousness mixed with uncertainty; and then shock and dismay as she took in my appearance.

"Emily," she tried, just managing to keep her voice down. "Oh sweet Saint Lucy, you look *awful*."

"I do?" Ms. Lurie hadn't mentioned that, but of course she wouldn't. And it's not the kind of thing I'd notice about myself.

"You look as if you've never even *heard* of the sun."

"I'm always pale. You know that." It was my turn to be startled, this time at how easy it was to talk to her now that it was actually happening.

"Not like this, you're not. And you're creepy skinny, too. You look like the madwoman in the attic if she'd been living on rats the whole time."

"Well, I haven't," I said. "It's been like breakfast the day Stephen

James died three times a day in here. Haven't you seen the things Miss Miller's been baking for me?"

M shook her head, and I was amazed to see she was blinking back tears. I never thought I'd live to see the day, as Jonella would say.

"I think maybe she always wanted to be a pastry chef," I said. "I don't know what the rest of you have been living on, but when she cooks for *me*, it's like butter and sugar are the only things she's ever even heard of." I forced my voice to be brusque. "And I'm fine. I would have asked Ms. Lurie to tell you that if I'd known you were so interested. Could have saved us both a lot of trouble."

M looked at me, very steadily now. "No," she said. "No more of that. No more playing games. That's what I came to talk to you about."

She stepped all the way inside my room and closed the door quietly behind her, and then she said a name I haven't heard in a long time. One that's always in the back of my mind, but that I never thought I'd hear from anyone else again.

"It's you, isn't it?" she asked.

———

Think Emily lost her wits—

I'd been standing near my bed as she spoke, so I managed to sit on that rather than falling down completely.

It felt like falling, though, and maybe it looked it too because suddenly M was right next to me, looking worried but determined. "Emily," she said. She picked up my pillow and tried to put it behind me, but I grabbed it and clutched it in my lap, drawing away from her. I needed something to hold. I needed something between us.

We both stared at each other for a minute. I can only guess how I must have looked.

And then at the same time, we both said, "Does Ms. Lurie know?"

She dealt her pretty
words—like Blades—

M smiled a little. "*I* haven't told her," she said. "I take it you haven't, either."

I shook my head numbly. What a stupid question.

"I kind of figured you hadn't," she said. "She does tend to see below the surface, though."

I shook my head again. Ms. Lurie is sweet and good and caring, but even she has a sense of self-preservation. And she certainly has a stated duty to preserve the other selves who live here.

Speaking of which:

"Why?" I managed.

M was looking at me much too calmly. "Why what?"

I didn't know where to start. "Why . . . why are you here? Why are you telling me this?"

Why are you stupid enough to be alone with me if you even suspect who and what I am? Why aren't you running off to tell everyone and rid the premises of this threat?

Now M looked perplexed. "Why *wouldn't* I tell you? I mean, how couldn't I? Once I knew. Or thought I knew, at least."

My heart gave a little drop, which shouldn't have hurt considering it was only going back where it belonged. "Of course," I said. "You had to be sure."

"Sure? Emily, why are you talking like that?" She looked around, almost in exasperation. "Look, can I sit down, please?" She clearly wanted to sit next to me, but instead she pulled the chair away from my desk and close to my bed. "All right?"

I said nothing.

"Emily," she said. "Look, you know I'm a crap liar."

I just waited.

"I didn't know right away," she went on. "Obviously I would have mentioned it. But—"

"How?"

She sighed. She was fully dressed in spite of the late hour, and now she looked down and pleated some of the colorful fabric of her long skirt between her fingers.

"I think a lot of things just added up after a while," she said. "Not any one thing in particular, just—everything. Things you've said. The way you talk. The way you push everyone away. How you acted—and how you didn't act—when Stephen James showed up. There was nothing *wrong* with any of it," she added quickly. "You didn't do anything wrong. I mean, sure, you're an awards-caliber bitch to everyone but me and Ms. Lurie when you're not pretending to be made of marble—"

"Yeah, I've been adorable to you," I said. The idea of *that* being anywhere near true shocked me as much as anything that had happened tonight.

She laughed a little. "As a matter of fact, you have."

"Look, can we just get to the point?" I said. "How do you know who I am?" And what are you planning to do now?

"It was your face," she said quietly. "When they brought you back from—you know."

Sweet of her to be worried about saying something that might upset me.

"Your eyes were huge," she said. "It made you look ten years younger. And your hair was kind of ruffled and mussed up. It was curling around your face—you don't usually let it do that. And I realized it looked familiar. I've always had a good eye for faces, and all of a sudden yours looked just like it did when you were little."

I think I must have dropped away for a second—from consciousness, from the planet—because then she was sitting right next to me, clutching one of my hands urgently. "Emily!"

"You knew me?" I couldn't recognize my voice, couldn't even make out the words.

Neither could M, apparently. "What? Emily, please, breathe. Talk to me. Do you need some water? I can get—"

"How do you know what my face used to look like?" I tried again. "Were you—have we—"

She understood me this time, thank God. "No, no, Emily, we've never met. Not before Hawthorne, I mean. I just—I saw a picture of you once. One from when you were little."

I shook my head, baffled.

"It was in a book," M said. "My mother had one of those true-crime books about—what happened to you. What happened *around* you." She took a deep breath. "God, I'm sorry. She's an idiot. And I was just a kid myself."

We both sat silently for a minute. I realized dimly that she was still holding on to my hand.

"I saw your face in a photograph," she said again. "I think it stuck so hard in my mind because before that, the whole story seemed so—God, just so over-the-top horrible—I couldn't believe it was real. And then I saw that picture and, no, really, this is the girl it happened to, this really did happen—"

"Which one was it?" For some reason I felt a little calmer now. Maybe because M was starting to lose *her* self-control. We couldn't *both* go into hysterics. Not at the same time.

"Which picture?"

"Which book."

"Oh." Now it was M's turn to calm down a bit and think about it. "There was more than one?"

I gave a cough that might pass for a laugh. "Was it the one where the writer thinks my aunt did it, or the one where they think there are really three different murderers, or the one where they say my father—"

"Oh. God. The first one. With the thing about your aunt, I mean. Yes, that must have been the one because I remember being terrified—which wasn't something I felt very often, believe me— thinking about a real little girl having to live with someone who—"

"It wasn't her," I said. "Trust me. Aunt Paulette is all kinds of awful, but she didn't do it. She adored my father, and she hated having to take care of me after he died."

"Oh, Emily."

"At least I didn't have to live with her all *that* long. Not my whole life or anything, I mean. And I never have to go back to her now. I never have to see her again."

"Good." M squeezed my hand.

"That hurts."

"Sorry." But she didn't let go.

Could you believe me without? I had no portrait, now, but am small, like the wren; and my hair is bold, like the chestnut burr; and my eyes, like the sherry in the glass that the guest leaves.

Dickinson was lying when she wrote that letter. She *did* have a photograph of herself, taken when she was about my age. She just didn't feel like sharing it.

It's the only for-sure photo of Dickinson that exists, so all the biographies and poetry collections use it on their covers.

Her hair is pulled tightly away from her face, with a part in the middle. You'd never know looking at it that she was a redhead. Her nose is broad and her lips are thick with just a hint of a smile, and her eyes are a mystery to me. Sometimes they seem frightened. Sometimes she looks mischievous, almost daring. Sometimes she looks frighteningly human—young and serious, trying hard to get this pose right and get it over with.

The biographers figured out a while ago that this picture of Dickinson was taken by some traveling photographer, but they used to think it was taken while she was at boarding school. One of the other girls there wrote in her diary about how excited everyone was to sit for their pictures.

Hawthorne doesn't have any "school picture" nonsense. It was always ridiculous at my other schools. They made me have them taken, but they couldn't make me keep them.

And they didn't know who I really was, so the official record of images of me ends with whatever picture M looked at with such terror.

I knew the books were out there and I hated the people who wrote them, but I never thought about the people who read them. Or rather I thought of them as a great faceless mass, or a wake of vultures eager to make a feast of my grief.

People like M's mother.

I never thought of anyone reading my story with terrified sympathy at the thought of all this happening to another girl, a girl her own age, a girl still alive somewhere.

She thought I was trapped in a gingerbread cottage with my bloodthirsty aunt, waiting to be oven-baked and eaten.

My face—my picture stayed in her mind.

Did she ever dream about me?

———

I incur the peril.

We sat side by side on my bed, me clutching a pillow and M holding my hand.

"So," I said. "Now what?"

"I have no idea." We both sounded absurdly calm. "I just needed you to know that I knew. I thought—"

"What?"

"I don't know. Like I said in my note. I thought maybe it would help if you knew you weren't alone with this."

I stared at her. "You're absolutely crazy," I said.

"I guess I am."

"When are you going to tell Ms. Lurie?"

"What?" She sat up, looking at me indignantly. "I'm not going to tell *any*one. Not unless you want to, of course, and you've made it pretty clear you don't."

"But—"

"What?"

"What *are* you going to do?"

"You keep asking that," M said. "And I keep not knowing what you mean. I don't plan to *do* anything. I've already done it. I needed to tell you. Now I have."

I shook my head. "And then what? We just—stay here?"

"Where else?"

"You're crazy," I explained again, since she seemed to have forgotten. "We just stay here, pretending to be normal—"

"Neither of us has ever done that, my lovely Emily."

That pushed the breath right out of me for a minute. I got it back and managed, "Staying here like nothing's changed, both of us knowing who I really am—"

"Why does that change anything? It's only one more person than knew about you a week ago. And it stops here. I'm not going to betray you, and no one else is paying the kind of attention it would take to figure it out. They're not even looking."

I shook my head.

I couldn't speak.

It was going to happen again.

"Emily?"

It was going to happen again, and this time I knew enough to expect it. This time it would *really* be my fault. This time—

"Emily."

M was kneeling awkwardly in front of me on the bed. She was holding my hands with one of her hands and smoothing my hair with the other.

No one's allowed to touch me.

"Emily. Listen to me."

I had to leave. Tonight. Now.

I could barely breathe, I didn't even know if I could walk, but I had to—

"Emily." Her voice pushed aside the roaring in my head. "You've been very strong and very practical for a long time, and I need you to be both now, all right? I need you to try to breathe and be calm."

I need you.

Oh, God.

"Listen to me, Emily," M said. Her voice was strong and calm and instructive, as if she were explaining another saint's origin story to me. "You're not alone anymore. I'm not letting you be alone."

I stared at her. "You don't know what you're talking about."

"I do."

"You could get hurt. You don't understand—"

"I do. I told you. I read that book. Whoever did—all those terrible things—doesn't want you to have anyone to care about."

"Then you know—"

"I don't know any such thing. I only know I'm not leaving you."

She lowered her head slightly and kissed my clenched hands. "We're in this together."

———

Impossibility, like Wine
Exhilarates the Man
Who tastes it

She's insane.

She genuinely thinks we can be together. Somehow. Somewhere.

She knows every aspect of my curse, and she sees it as just another challenge to be overcome, a new geography to navigate.

Lunatic. *Lunatic.*

———

I heard a well-known rap, and a friend I love so dearly came and asked me to ride in the woods, the sweet, still woods,—and I wanted to exceedingly—

Dickinson doesn't say who she wanted to go riding off into the woods with that afternoon when she was nineteen. She does say that he stayed a long time arguing against her refusals. "He said I *could*, and *should* go," she boasts. But she wouldn't.

She cried after he left, but she wouldn't ride with him.

She felt as if she couldn't go with him, but she doesn't say why.

I don't really care much who she might or might not have loved, but I often wonder about the young man who loved *her*. He must have been someone out of the ordinary himself, to fall for such an unconventional woman as Emily Dickinson.

Who was the man captivated by her strange, fierce, brilliant face, and by her way of saying baffling things in breathless little bursts?

Who was the beloved friend who came so often to see this otherworldly teenager that his knock was "a well-known rap"?

———

From all the jails the boys and girls
Ecstatically leap—

"How?"

"'How' isn't important right now. What's important is 'that.'"

"There can't be any 'that' until we figure out *how*."

"Says who?"

"We've been dating for thirty seconds and you're already driving me crazy."

She kissed my hands again, lingeringly this time. "I'm very talented."

———

The Soul selects her own Society—
Then—shuts the Door—

Dickinson shut her door on so many people. She let just a few in—literally, once she started staying in her room—and kept even those she loved at a sort of distance. Letters aplenty, flowers and poems for those who might need or enjoy them; but a glimpse, a touch, a visit? Too much. Don't ask it.

She was lucky to have so many people who loved her enough that they were willing to abide by any terms she set just to be a tiny part of her life.

M is beautiful and strong and gets whatever she wants. She could have anyone. She could have *every*one.

But she wants me.

"Just tell me why," I said. "Give me one reason I'd be worth the work even if my life were normal."

"I can't," M said. "How I feel has nothing to do with reason."

"Right. You saw me across a crowded room and knew I was your happily ever after."

"Something like that."

"M, for once in your life, be serious."

She looked me in the eye. "I saw you in the hallway that night when the alarm went off. All the other girls were buzzing around like bees without a queen, and you were just standing there, calm and strong and purposeful. You looked like you could climb a mountain or run fifty miles and you were just waiting to hear which was needed."

"M—"

"And then, in the lounge, while everyone else was weeping and whispering and setting their collective hair on fire, you sat like the Rock of Gibraltar. Utterly still and composed. You weren't like anyone else I'd ever seen, and I wanted to know if you were like that all the way down. I gave you the kind of smiles that used to get all my algebra problems done for me without even a 'please,' and they bounced off you like stones skipping across a lake."

I shook my head speechlessly.

"I was used to being able to charm the socks off people first try, and for all you noticed I could have been on another planet."

"So you liked me because I wasn't impressed by you."

"I liked you because you were hot," she corrected. "I kept after you because I wanted to see if I *could* impress you."

"M!"

"You asked."

M could have someone beautiful and tender and safe. But she wants me; and if that means giving up the world and everyone else in it, she'll do it.

"You're insane," I said.

"Flatterer."

"I'm serious. You have no idea what you're talking about. What you'll have to give up."

"Even if that were true, ignorance isn't the same as insanity."

"Will you stop it?"

"Stop what?"

I've spent my life being vicious because I have to, but this is the first time I can remember actually wanting to slap some sense into someone. "You're bandying semantics while I'm trying to talk about reality."

"You know I've never let anyone tell me what to do."

"This isn't about me not being the boss of you, idiot! This is about life and death!"

M smiled into my eyes. "You've got them in the right order, anyway. That's a start."

"M—"

"No," she said in a voice that was both immovable object and irresistible force. "Facts of death later. Fact of life first."

I stared at her. "M—we *can't*." I could barely whisper all of a sudden. "We really, *really* can't."

"We can, and what's more, we will. We have to. This is one night we *know* we have, one night we've been given. We're taking it. And then no matter what happens, no one can ever take this away from us."

She paused and then added, "Think of it this way. If this really is risky behavior, we've already pushed our luck too far. Just my being here. Just me doing this"—she swooped in for a swift kiss on my cheek—"and you not punching my lights out for it. Right?"

I couldn't answer.

"Whatever's going to happen would have happened anyway. So—" she grabbed the pillow out of my clenched hands and tossed it across the room "—let's get some beautiful memories out of this, if we can't get anything else."

———

Is it that words are suddenly small, or that we are suddenly large, that they cease to suffice us . . .?

Dickinson could have married if she wanted to.

She was asked. She loved and was loved. But she said no when he asked.

For whatever reason, she preferred love letters to lovemaking.

Of course, marriage for her would have meant death—maybe not death from childbirth, since she was old enough to feel safely past any such risk by the time the proposal came along, but a death of the life she'd built so carefully, death of her quiet uninterrupted days, death maybe even of her poetry-writing.

So she kept her passion on the page and said yes to life and no to marriage.

There were rumors later that she was caught once on her drawing-room sofa in the passionate embrace of the man who'd proposed to her, and that she was very happy to be there.

I hope those rumors are true.

————

Tell Him night finished before we finished

"Have you really never touched anyone?"

"Of course I haven't!"

M smiled. "Not even someone you really didn't like?"

————

Come slowly, Eden!

"You're rich," she said. "And I will be, one of these days. My parents would never cut me off without a cent. People Would Talk. They can only stand that when *they're* the ones doing the Talking."

"What does money have to do with anything?"

"It means we can afford all the bodyguards in the world. Millions of them." She smiled. "So many that the entire population of our town would be us and the people we've hired to keep us safe."

"It's not about keeping *us* safe. *I'm* not the one who'll need a bodyguard."

"More for me, then."

"And, anyway, how do we know we could trust them? How can we trust *any*one?"

"Then we'll have alarm systems. A house like a stone castle. A moat."

"Oh, come *on*. A moat?"

"Why not? People used to have them because they used to need them. We need one now. Kind of a silly time to be worried what the neighbors will think."

"There's nothing silly about any of this. And I'm not worrying about the neighbors. We can't *have* neighbors, remember? And all the moats in the world won't keep out a bullet."

M's expression grew serious. "Shooting from a distance doesn't seem your murderer's style," she said.

It was dizzying how calmly she could talk about this.

I'd been trying to shake that calm all night. I'd spelled out the rules of terror. I'd catechized her on the insistent brutality I grew up with, and she'd answered with unblinking serenity.

Where did she learn that kind of courage? Or is there a certain brand of audacity some people are just born with?

"You're forgetting Stephen James," I said.

"That wasn't from a distance," she reminded me. "Anyway, we still don't know that was connected to everything else."

"How could it not be? How can this not *all* be tied together somehow?"

"If it is, maybe that's good news."

"*Good?*"

"The world is full of random death. If the rules, as you call them, have changed that much, your life isn't any different from anyone else's."

I gave that the look it deserved. "No different at all? Other than the body count, you mean?"

"Well—you're rich enough to *really* overpay our cleaning lady."

———

I bring an unaccustomed wine
To lips long parching
—Next to mine—

I'm tired of wishing for the ones who were taken from me, and the ones who were never allowed to be. I'm sick of wanting someone to take care of me.

I want to take care of someone now.

Not the way I've always ~~tried~~ had to—by pushing away before they can get close enough to get hurt. I want to care the way other people get to.

I want to draw someone close to me and shield her from harm.

I want to draw her very close indeed and never even think of harm.

But how?

———

"Come unto me."
Beloved commandment! The darling obeyed it.

In a pause between dreaming and fighting, we heard the front door softly open and shut.

"Ms. Lurie," I said. "I didn't know it was that late."

M smiled. "Not late," she said. "Early."

If the whole English language had only three words, M would use two of them to argue with the third.

"How long does she usually stay out?" she asked.

"At least an hour. It takes time to really understand a morning, she says."

"Our lovely Ms. Lurie." M stretched. "We have one more hour, then."

"Not quite. You have to go before she gets back. We can't risk her seeing you leave."

"She wouldn't tell anyone."

"M, please. Don't fight me on this."

She sighed. "Forty-five minutes, then."

"Half an hour."

"Thirty-seven minutes, and that's my last offer."

It ended up being fifty-two.

To thank you would profane you—there are moments when even gratitude is a desecration.

Ms. Lurie brought me breakfast at nine o'clock. I didn't know I was famished until I saw the food. It was simpler than usual—just bread, but a beautiful rich egg bread next to tiny glass dishes of butter and honey and jam.

"Are you all right?" Ms. Lurie asked.

I tried to slow down a bit. "Sorry," I muttered around too big a bite.

She laughed. "No need to apologize," she said. "I'm just glad to see you have an appetite."

I was glad I could pretend to be too busy chewing to answer that.

"Did you sleep well?" she asked.

I had to remind myself that she asks that *every* morning. I shook my head vigorously. "Not a wink," I said. "I'm going to crash any minute now."

Ms. Lurie looked surprised and concerned. "Really? Do you feel well? Do you need me to call—"

"I'm fine," I said. "I just—I think I might sleep through lunch, if that's all right."

Now she looked really worried. "I'll leave something outside your door, if you like," she said. "That way I won't disturb you if you're sleeping, and you don't have to starve if you're not."

"Thank you." I wanted to say a lot more than that, but of course I couldn't. "Thank you, Ms. Lurie."

She smiled, a little puzzled. "Of course, dear."

———

We often say "how beautiful!" But when we mean it, we can mean no more.
A dream personified.

Of course I couldn't sleep. Of course I can't now.

Half of me can't believe last night happened—any of it, all of it—and the other half is too terrified *not* to believe it.

———

"Give me thine heart" is too peremptory a courtship for earth, however irresistible in Heaven.

Can M possibly be right?

Will we—can we—be different?

Can knowing what we're up against be enough?

Of course we don't really know.

We know what *has* happened, and so we know what threatens to happen next; but we don't know why, and we obviously don't know who.

We could never have anything like a normal life.

M insists she didn't want one even before she met me.

But she ought to be able to do the kind of normal things even outlandish M might want to do. She ought to be able to go to college. Her art is brilliant, and she ought to be able to learn from the best so she can get even better.

She ought to be able to travel, like they did in the olden days, when young men would wander moodily around Europe looking at Great Art and learning that they really weren't so Great themselves after all.

Except M *is* great. Or will be, anyway.

Unless she never gets the chance to be.

How can she have a career if she's in a permanent state of hiding?

And where could we hide, really, that would be secure? A bomb shelter? A prison cell? An airplane that never has to land? Antarctica?

How could I look at her every day knowing what she was giving up for me?

Not for you. For me.

You know what I mean.

I don't. I'm not giving up anything. I'm taking what I want. That's all I ever do. Stop pretending you're so special.

When she was here insisting she had all the answers, I almost believed we might be possible; but now I'm alone and the truth keeps beating its way in.

This can't work.

The only important thing now is protecting her, assuming that's still possible.

———

Danger is not at first, for then we are unconscious, but in the after, slower days.

This time I went inside Dickinson's house without bothering to knock.

I knew there was no one to answer anyway.

When I put my hand to the knob, I saw that the door was already open. Swinging just a bit ajar.

I pushed. It was heavier than I'd expected, but I got it open and went into the foyer.

I didn't bother shutting the front door behind me.

The little sitting room was empty.

No visitors. No friends. No family.

I stood for a minute, thinking.

I would have liked to see the kitchen, but there was no scent of cakes baking or bread rising.

There was nowhere, nothing for me on this floor.

I went to the stairs Maggie always climbed to ask Miss Emily if she would see a visitor.

Dark and narrow, and steeper than I'd expected.

I started up. Slowly—my boots were hard-soled and would have rung out against the wood like the angel of death himself if I wasn't careful.

Dark, dark steps, curving around a bit as I reached the top—and then the last step was light, and the floor before me a warm, light-colored wood.

There was a door to my right, but I passed it without pausing. I knew my way.

The second door—*that* was hers. Off-white wood interrupting the white-patterned wallpaper on either side.

I paused.

If I knocked, would she call for me to come in, thinking I was Maggie?

But no—she knew every sound that had a rightful place in this house. She would know the knock of a stranger.

Knocking wasn't the point now.

I put my hand on the white doorknob. Then I stood and listened.

A musical voice murmured behind that door.

Was someone there with her already? Had I come too late?

No—she was alone. I knew it, the way we always know things in dreams.

Maybe she was singing to herself. Or trying a line of poetry aloud.

Maybe she was talking to a mouse, or the tree outside her window.

Now laughter rippled out to me.

Her friends and family said her voice was soft and low and often breathless, but that laugh was silvery and strong.

I wanted to hear her voice for myself, without any barrier between us.

I wanted to see the red hair the coroner was so surprised by— hair without a single strand of silver, though she was in her fifties when she died.

I wanted to see if she really did wear that white dress every day.

As if in reply to my thoughts, her voice sang out—so loud and clear it almost knocked me down.

I'm "wife"—I've finished that—
That other state—
I'm Czar—I'm "Woman" now—

The one poem of Dickinson's I've never liked because I'm so sick of all the arguing over whether she had the right to say any such thing, whether she was actually talking about someone else being a wife, whether it meant she was having an affair or mocking the married or ironically celebrating her own perpetual spinsterhood.

Hearing her now, I knew there was no bitterness, no sarcasm intended. Not just now, anyway.

This was the open rejoicing of someone claiming and being claimed.

This was a love song.

And if I opened the door between us, I would destroy the singer.

As if in agreement, the paint on that door slipped silently from the virginal white it had been a moment ago to a black that matched the stairs.

I turned and fled, not caring about the noise I might make, only caring that I didn't fall.

I reached the front door and ran outside into what was now night.

———

A death-blow is a life-blow to some

Dear M:

First: will you please make sure Ms. Lurie gets the note on my desk—the one that says I'm leaving Hawthorne of my own free will, and asking her to give my things to charity?

I would have gotten rid of them myself, but there wasn't time.

I hope that covers the legal aspect of things. I don't want to get her into any kind of trouble. She's had to deal with too much already on my account.

I hope that makes sure she doesn't have anything else to worry about so far as I'm concerned. I hope I'm protecting her as well as you.

I'd tell you not to grab a keepsake while you're in here, but that doesn't seem your style anyway.

Go ahead and tell everyone who I am, or rather who I was. I'm nobody now.

I will never touch another penny of the money that was left to me. I have the clothes on my back and the boots on my feet and a lot less hair on my head than I did the last time you saw me.

I'm hoping all this will make me pretty damned hard to keep an eye on.

This isn't just about saving you. God knows it's that. But it's saving me, too. It's being honest, finally.

If I have to live loveless and alone, I'm going to stop pretending that I'm just another eccentric millionaire being a bitch to the world because I can afford to.

I've had to act for so many years like someone who enjoys being mean. Putting people off so that it wouldn't show if I cared about someone, and no one would be tempted to care about me.

I'm tired. I'm so tired. I can't do it anymore.

We both know what will happen if I don't.

I can end this now by doing what I should have done a long time ago. Becoming just another filthy, faceless wanderer that no one cares about and everyone's a little afraid of.

There are other endings I could aim for. But as tired as I am, I don't want that. Even if I did, I wouldn't do that to you. But maybe you'll be glad to hear I don't want to do that to me, either.

Becoming nobody is my only escape and I'm taking it.

Yes, M, I love you and you know very well that's why I have to leave. And yes, I *do* know how that's making you feel. I've had the ones I love torn away from me all my life.

The only reason I would ever do this to you is that I can't stand the thought of what will happen if I don't. I'm asking you to imagine how *I'm* feeling now, and ask yourself how you'd feel if our positions were reversed.

You're not a reasonable person and that's part of why I love you, but even you have to admit I'm right about this.

Or don't. I can't tell you what to do.

I can tell you this: I want you to live and be happy, but I'd rather you lived and were unhappy than spent one more blissful day with me and then met the kind of end I know will be waiting for you if we stay together. Even if the latter meant that, technically, you were happy your whole life. I'm not a philosopher, or some kind of emotional mathematician. Given the little choice I have in the matter, I'd rather you were long-lived and miserable.

Do you understand that?

I wandered out of my bedroom one night when I was four years old. I was looking for my mother. You know what I found.

You know I can't let that happen again.

I want you to be happy, but I need you to *be*.

NOTEBOOK 2

Enough Dickinson quotes. I can speak for myself now.

———

Okay, I didn't say I could do it all at once.

———

"It's . . . fireworks," I guessed. "In December, so everyone's surprised to see them."

M took her picture out of my hands long enough to roll it up loosely and smack me over the head with it. "It's a *plant*," she said, unrolling it and handing it back. "A local one. You might have seen it yourself, if you could be bothered to look at the slutty flowers once in a while. Look. The stems grow in red clusters, and then there are tiny yellow blossoms right at the top—see?"

"That was my next guess," I said.

"The common name is live-forever," she said. "They sprout up in dead, gray, rocky places where nothing should be able to survive."

"So, not a metaphor or anything."

There was a rap at the door. "Come in," I said.

M tugged the picture out of my hands again, dropped it on the bed next to me, and threw her arms around me in a dramatic embrace that was all show and minimal contact. "Kiss me, you fool," she said loudly, just as Ms. Lurie opened the door.

"Hello, girls," she said.

"Ms. Lurie, make her stop," I said.

"M, kindly try to control yourself."

M laid a delicate hand on her heart and widened her eyes, a perfect portrait of innocent indignation.

"Oh, please," I said. "There have to be sexual harassment laws in place for times like this."

"There are, as a matter of fact," Ms. Lurie said. "I'm happy to say I've never had to enforce them."

"First time for everything," M said as Ms. Lurie nudged her gently aside and sat down on the edge of my bed. She looked at me intently for a minute, and then put her hand on my forehead and smoothed my hair back from my face.

"How do you feel, dear?"

———

I want to write what happened in order, neatly and accurately. I keep trying and I can't. It won't come out that way. Everything keeps clamoring to be told all at once.

I'm just going to write whatever screams the loudest and worry about the order later.

———

Ms. Lurie says I need to spend a lot more time *knowing* I'm safe before I can feel convinced I really am. "Time really will help," she said yesterday. "I know it's a ridiculous oversimplification to say 'time heals all wounds,' but there *is* a reason we have that saying."

"They say that 'Time assuages,'" I muttered. "Time never did assuage—"

"Emily," Ms. Lurie said. "You told me you were working on using your *own* words now. No more hiding behind someone else's, remember?"

"I know."

She put her hand on mine and I took a deep breath and reminded myself that was all right now, I didn't have to wrench away and I certainly didn't have to spit an insult at her.

"Old habits die hard," she said gently.

———

It shouldn't have been so cold—it's southern California and it doesn't get that cold here, does it, even in the mountains, tell someone from Minnesota or New York how cold it was that night and listen to them laugh—but it *was* cold, I know it was, I felt it.

Sometimes I think I'll never be warm again, especially at night.

Ms. Lurie gave me her heating pad and her hot-water bottle and permission to flip a finger at the drought and spend as much time in a tub full of hot water as I need, whenever I need to. She calls it that: *need*, not want, and that helps. A little.

I still feel guilty, though.

Not just about the water. Everything.

M must have been so much colder. She only had a nightgown on.

And boots. At least she put on boots.

"Don't forget the flashlight," she said.

"You weren't wearing a flashlight."

"You know what I mean. I didn't just run out after you. I'm a lot more practical than you give me credit for."

"All right," I said. "I think you are fully ten percent practical."

"Which is nine percent more practical than you thought I was before?"

"More like twenty."

Cold. Cold.

We were sitting very still and the ground was damp and the cold seeped into our bones and replaced them.

"They found her," she told me, but it didn't seem true, it couldn't be.

"You're safe," she said, and that couldn't be true either.

"Emily, I promise."

"Hey," Brianna said.

"Oh. Hi."

I was on the porch, bundled against the pale winter sunlight. After a minute, Brianna sat down next to me on the step. Not too close. Just on the same step.

"Hey," she said again.

I think it was okay not to know what to say in reply. Anyway, she didn't seem to blame me.

"So, you're staying at Hawthorne for Christmas," she said.

I nodded. It still felt terrifyingly strange not to come back with something sharp and cutting, but it was hard to find the energy even to nod.

"I kind of—well. Here." She put a small, brightly wrapped package between us.

"It's just something stupid," she said. "You don't have to like it or anything."

"Good," I tried to say. I'm not sure I managed. My heart was pounding so hard it sounded to me like it was firing bullets.

"You okay?"

I shook my head. I tried to smile, but it probably looked pretty weird. "Not for a while now, no."

That came out, anyway. "Yeah," Brianna said. "I get that."

We sat together quietly for a minute, waiting for the terror to pass.

"I—" I started, and then tried again. "I didn't. You know. Get you anything or anything."

Brianna laughed just a little. "I kind of wasn't expecting you to."

"Good." That came out right this time, and she laughed again.

"You owe me *two* gifts next year, though," she said.

———

She didn't ask why or what. None of them have. They just know something happened and I'm different now.

That's enough. Enough for me, but even enough for them, so far as I can tell.

I'm not used to enough.

———

I hadn't gotten far.

It was weird o'clock in the morning—too late for anyone to still be awake, too early for Ms. Lurie to be out on her walk yet.

I hadn't gone far. I was still getting used to walking. And being outside. It had been so long.

It was very dark and very cold and the road was smooth under my boots but I couldn't use much of it. There's no such thing as sidewalk in this part of the mountains, and just enough room on the road for cars. There's a bit of space pretending to care about bicyclists, but I know enough not to trust it. Cyclists are killed in broad daylight around here.

Maybe I should have been hoping to be sent tumbling down the side of the mountain by a car, but I wasn't. I wasn't thinking about dying. I wasn't afraid of death, but I wasn't looking for it, either.

I was just moving.

And then I stopped.

———

"This isn't about school anymore, Emily," Ms. Lurie said.

We were sitting in her office, and I couldn't help thinking about the last time we were here and who had been with us.

I'm through with detectives now. That's something.

They've all been very kind and I know they're doing the best they can, but I'm glad to be finished talking to them.

"This isn't about 'Oh, it's June, time for you to graduate and get out of my house,'" she went on. "Hawthorne has never been an ordinary school, and I take great pride in knowing that its students are *far* from ordinary."

She caught my expression and smiled ruefully. "I know that's a bit of an understatement in this case."

I didn't say anything.

"My point is, we've always been able to stretch for our students, to work with whatever their needs are. There are girls who have spent five years here instead of four. Or they came here for their senior year of high school and then stayed on another year after that, because what they were working on didn't fit neatly into the usual chronology. Whether they called those last twelve months a gap year or an internship, we were happy to have them, and proud to be part of that crucial aspect of their development."

I gazed at my teacup. It was beautiful without seeming frighteningly fragile.

"At any rate. I want this to be said in so many words so we don't have to worry about it later. This is your home now, Emily. Not just for the rest of the school year. For however long you want it to be.

"Easy," she added. "I'm sorry, dear. I didn't think that would come as a shock. Surely I've made it clear—"

"How can you possibly want me here?" I said. "How can you ever want to see me again?"

It was her turn to look startled, and saddened. "Why wouldn't I?" she asked. "Do you imagine I blame you for what's happened to you?"

"Maybe not blame, exactly, but—"

"Associate," Ms. Lurie finished for me. "No, Emily. I don't. If I were the kind of person who did that, I would have sold this house after my husband died. Or closed Hawthorne when Stephen James was killed."

I flinched.

"I don't blame others for how they feel," she said. "I only ask that my own feelings be respected. And I'm sorry to disappoint you, Emily"—and her smile was anything but disappointed—"but the sight of you has no negative connotations for these old eyes. None whatsoever."

In response to my face, which must have looked like The Portrait Of A Doubting Lady, she asked, "Am I assuming too much? Maybe Hawthorne has terrible associations for *you*?"

"No," I said. "No, of course not."

She waited.

"I'm just—not really used to having this kind of conversation."

Ms. Lurie smiled.

I hadn't seen or heard anything, but I stopped anyway.

Which was stupid, I suppose.

But someone was there, where no one was supposed to be, and I could either face that or keep going with God only knew what behind me.

I don't know why it's so important, but I want the record to state that I stopped and turned around *before* I heard my name spoken.

———

"You smoke."

"I wasn't smoking."

"No, but you *have*. You're a smoker. I could smell it."

A smile in the dark. "Well. I guess that makes me an official bad guy, doesn't it?"

———

"Even if you go on to university—and I know it's a lot to think about now, but I hope at some point you'll consider it—this will be your home. This is the place you can come back to."

"Home is the place where, when you have to go there, they have to take you in."

"Emily." Ms. Lurie looked at me sternly.

"That wasn't Dickinson."

"I want to hear what *you* think, not Robert Frost. Especially not Robert Frost being bitter and sarcastic." She paused. "Do you remember the rest of it? What the wife says in reply?"

I shook my head. I hadn't even known it was Frost. I thought it was just a saying, something to put on inspirational postcards.

"'I should have called it something you somehow haven't to deserve.'"

———

"Emily."

The winding road up to Hawthorne isn't lit. I guess they figure anyone out on it at night knows what they're doing. Or maybe it's just too hard to put lights in on steep curves like that. Too risky for the people doing the work.

There was a scrap of moon, but it was on its way down.

Of course I hoped it was M behind me.

Of course it wasn't.

"Emily," the voice said again. "It *is* you, isn't it?"

———

I guess I've been terrified—terrorized—for so long that I couldn't feel afraid anymore.

———

It didn't happen all that long ago and still it's a fight to go back and find what I was really feeling. Not what I should have felt, or what I guess I must have felt, but the truth.

I keep thinking about it exactly when I don't want to, and then not being able to pin it down when I do.

———

"Why didn't you wake me up?"

M looked miserable. "Because I read somewhere that people only remember dreams when they wake up in the middle of them," she said. "That the kindest thing anyone can do is *not* wake someone up when they're having a nightmare."

I thought about that. She'd been in my room with me when I fell asleep, but had had to leave soon after. Rules.

"Did it work?" she asked anxiously.

I nodded. "I don't remember any of my dreams from last night," I said. "Just the one I had right before I woke up."

"What was *that* one about?"

"A tidal wave," I said.

"Oh."

"That's new for me, actually."

"Oh." She paused. "Well, I guess it's good you're branching out."

———

I guess I was afraid. Not so much emotionally as reflexively. Intellectually. Knowing that whatever was happening couldn't be good.

But honestly, I think what I really *felt* was anger.

No—anger is too strong. Annoyance. Irritation. Agitated resignation. *Let's get this over with, already.*

I think that's true.

———

"It's not fair that Ms. Lurie doesn't let us room together."

I didn't say anything, but I smiled over my toast.

I'm back on normal food, mostly. Miss Miller still sends plenty of treats my way, but they're not the main course anymore. Ms. Lurie just smiles. I know she still thinks white flour is out to kill us all, but she also knows how to pick her battles.

I'm still not quite up to facing the dining room, but Ms. Lurie lets M and me have our meals in her office, or sometimes on the porch.

"I mean, I'll be eighteen soon. So will you. And we're *going* to live together." A pause. "Aren't we?"

I pretended I had to think about that.

She rapped me on the knuckle with a teaspoon, hard enough to sting. It was worth it to see her fret.

I'm a little relieved that Ms. Lurie is being the bossy grown-up and gently but firmly insisting that There's Plenty Of Time For That When We're Older And We're Too Young To Make A Commitment Now.

"You got *married* young," M muttered rebelliously. "How old were you, anyway?"

"Twenty-two," Ms. Lurie said, smiling. "Not exactly a child bride, but yes, very young."

M pouted. I'm sure she was hoping Ms. Lurie had been eighteen years and one day old the day she popped a veil on her head and slipped on the plain gold band she still wears.

"It was a different time," Ms. Lurie went on. "And yes, it was hard to wait even that long. But I'm glad I did. And I certainly don't think it would have been a good idea for us to have moved in together at the tender age of seventeen."

I tried to imagine Ms. Lurie as an eager teenager. It wasn't hard, actually.

"I'm not being a prude, M," Ms. Lurie said. "And so far as your personalities are concerned, I think you two are exceptionally well suited for one another. But you have your whole lives ahead of you. There's no need to rush into anything. And frankly, I think you'll appreciate each other that much more if you have to wait a little while."

She looked at me inquiringly, and I smiled.

M noticed and punched me on the arm. "Traitor."

"M," Ms. Lurie said severely, but I just smiled a bit more.

M may never understand how rich it feels to be allowed to take my time at this.

———

"Of course it's you. I knew it would be someday."

I couldn't speak.

"I guess I'm surprised you didn't come out sooner. Alone, I mean. Like this."

She stepped closer. In the mostly dark, her hair contrasted sharply with her pale skin.

"Oh, Emily," she said. "How you've grown."

I tell M that the nightmares I've been having are about my family, but really it's a little more complicated than that.

Each one is just a bit different than the others when it comes to the specifics, but the basic idea is the same.

It's simple: I'm very young. I'm in a house. It's always a bright day, and the light pours in through the windows. I'm coloring or playing or holding a fresh-baked cookie someone's given me, with extra napkins so I don't ruin my clothes.

Everything is very clean and light and comfortable. The floor is polished wood, and I'm sitting on a bright-colored, braided rug.

I'm alone in the room, but I know there's someone nearby. A mother will come soon and shake her head over the mess I've made. Or a car will pull into the driveway—who? Mother, father, sister, cousin?

Everything is fine, everything is warm and peaceful and very dull, and I'm trying not to panic. But I know I need to hide.

It's not supposed to be like this.

Someone is standing just outside the door, touching the knob gently. About to come in. Any second now.

This isn't mine. This doesn't belong to me.

The door opens and I'm still sitting there, frozen.

I used to have this dream quite often, and I always woke up just as the door began to open. I never got to see who was coming in.

I do now.

———

"I've thought about this moment so often," she said. "Gone over every detail in my mind. How you'd look. What I'd say. Real life is never quite how you expect it to be, is it?"

We stood facing one another in the night.

There's only so much adjusting your eyes can do in that kind of darkness. She had to have been as blind as I was, but she seemed perfectly at ease.

"Well." She held something up and I flinched, but it was just a cell phone. She touched it and a light sprang out, shining right into my eyes.

"Come on," she said, ignoring my cry of pain. She turned the light away toward the downward slope of the mountain at our side.

"Come and sit with me," she said. "Down here. We have a *lot* to talk about, and with my luck the only waking soul in town will bring their car right here and interrupt our visit."

She held the light so it showed the earth and rock and trees, and turned herself sideways and began to edge her way down. "Come on," she repeated.

I didn't move. "Who are you?" I said.

It was barely a whisper, but in these silent hills it carried like a shout.

She stopped and turned the light so it was shining on her. Not right in her face, but a little across it.

She smiled.

"Emily," she said.

"Oh, there's a resemblance," she said. "A little more light and you'd see it just fine." She laughed. "Or maybe you don't remember her face well enough."

"I remember."

She shrugged as if it weren't terribly important and started making her way down the slope again. "Maybe I look more like my father, then. Come on. Carefully. Just a little way, and then we can sit down and we won't have to worry about anyone bothering us."

———

I can't say she forced me.

If she had a weapon, I couldn't see it. And she certainly didn't threaten me.

But I couldn't run from her any more than I could stop hearing when she spoke to me.

She'd only have gone back to waiting for me.

And she was right: I had to come out sooner or later.

———

"There you are." M sat down next to me as I huddled, knees to chin, against a tree. "Hey."

I nodded.

"Are you cold? You look cold."

I shook my head.

"Are you okay? You look okay."

I smiled a little. "Just okay?"

"Well, I'm biased."

We sat in silence. I wanted to close my eyes but I was afraid it would seem rude.

After a minute, M said, "I grew you something."

"Excuse me?"

She handed me a small sheaf of greenery with a few purple fuzzy spots on the ends. "Lavender," she said proudly. "Don't worry, there's plenty more where this came from. It grows better if you pick some now and then. Ms. Lurie made me promise to keep it in a pot because otherwise it'll take over the whole world, but I can put it outside sometimes to get sunshine, as long as it behaves itself."

Dickinson used to do that. Babysit her plants. Bring them inside when she worried they'd be too cold. In New England, that was a regular possibility.

M said, "It's supposed to have healing properties."

I gave her a skeptical look.

She exhaled loudly. "Fine. It's pretty and it smells good. All right?"

I smiled. "Thank you."

We were quiet again, and then: "Do you want to be alone? It's okay if you want me to go. I won't be hurt. Shattered, but not hurt."

"No, it's okay. I'm just not up to talking much right now."

"Well, *that's* a relief. I have to admit, the nonstop chatter was really starting to get to me."

I nodded.

"That was sarcasm, in case you—"

"M, I love you. Now could you please shut up for a minute?"

"Of course."

I put up with her anxious, watchful, resolute silence as long as I could stand it. "M—"

"Look, I'm *worried* about you, all right?"

"I know. But I'm really okay."

"Well, *I'm* not. I've never worried about anyone but myself before. It's exhausting."

I leaned back against the tree, shifting against the roots. I was getting a little stiff and uncomfortable, but I didn't want her to think I was going inside to get away from her.

She paused and added, "That was my way of saying I've never been in love before. Just in case you were wondering."

———

"Where to start?"

The light was between us, closer to her.

Her hair was lighter than mine, but much darker than my mother's.

"This is as much your story as it is mine. So, tell me: What have you always wanted to know? What have you wondered about the most?"

"Why."

She looked at me. "You're lying."

"I'm not!"

"Of course you are. You've always wondered *who*."

"It's the same thing."

"It is and it isn't. But there's something else you've always wondered, and you're afraid to admit it. You don't want to sound like a coward."

It was ridiculous how much that stung. As though this were the time to feel insulted.

"All right," I said. "I wondered why not me. Why, since you—whoever you were—obviously hated me so much, why you didn't just kill me and get it over with."

"I see. And of course that would go hand in hand with wondering why I hated you so much in the first place."

I didn't answer.

"Oh, my dear Emily. I wish there had been some way to talk to you sooner. I could have told you that you were the only one I *didn't* hate."

I've read about people feeling physically ill—feeling like throwing up—for purely emotional reasons. I always thought it was just an exaggeration.

But the way she looked at me just then made me very glad I hadn't eaten anything recently.

In that strange spot of light in the darkness, she gave me a look that was pure warmth. Her smile was one of deepest affection.

"Emily. My little namesake."

Don't call me that.

"You're the only one I loved."

Stop.

"You always have been."

———

"Don't apologize, dear. Please. I need you to stop apologizing for something you didn't do."

"I lied. I lied to you, and then to that detective. I lied to everyone."

"I'm not sure lying is the word I'd choose. 'Lying' sounds malicious. You didn't have a great deal of choice, did you? You were afraid, and very much alone." She smiled, and gently smoothed what was left of my hair. "Not to mention young."

"What if I'd told you the truth? Told you my real name before? What would you have done?"

Ms. Lurie paused. "I have to admit, I don't know. It's hard to say now, after the fact. I can think of a few possibilities. But none of them include closing the door on a girl who needed this place more than anyone ever has."

———

"I don't see any reason to think she was lying to me. What she said checked out, and the things I couldn't check were plausible. They fit in with everything else she'd told me."

She shook her head in the darkness, as if arguing with herself.

"She was perfectly honest as long as she was talking. It was only her silences that lied."

———

M picked up Brianna's package. "Aren't you *ever* going to open this stupid thing?"

"It isn't Christmas yet."

"You'll have plenty to open on Christmas. I promise. And I don't want any competition. Come on. Let's see what's in here."

She was about to start tearing off the ribbon and paper herself. I took the package out of her hands. "Stop that. It's mine."

"Then *open* it."

"When I'm ready."

"Emily, for heaven's sake—Santa isn't going to get mad at you if you jump the gun on this one. I promise. If he were that strict, I'd have been put on an all-coal diet years ago."

I looked at her. "Are you jealous?"

"Don't be ridiculous."

"You *are* jealous."

"Well, of *course* I'm jealous! Somebody smart and gorgeous gave you a present, and now you're treating it like some kind of holy relic."

"I'm not. It's just—kind of a first."

M looked mortified. "Oh. Right. Crap. I'm sorry."

"It's fine."

"Except now I'm *really* jealous."

I smiled. "Don't be."

"Should I return some of the stuff I got you? I got you a lot of stuff. Is that—is it all going to be too much?"

"Probably."

"Oh."

"M, I'm kidding. I'm just—don't be mad if I'm bad at this kind of thing at first, okay?"

"Don't worry about it. And, anyway, I can pace myself. I can give you some of the gifts on Christmas, and some on New Year's, and some on Valentine's Day, and some on your birthday, and some on Arbor Day . . ."

———

Did my father ever know?

Did she tell him who she was, at the end?

I don't know. I was afraid to ask.

———

Ms. Lurie still wants me to see a therapist.

She says I shouldn't have to deal with "all this" by myself; and when I say I don't, she softens and says that's true, dear, but sometimes there's all the difference in the world between a caring friend and someone who knows how to help.

I know *she* wants to help. I'm sure she's probably right.

But I'm just so tired of talking about all this. Even on paper. This story exhausts me. I'm tired of telling it. I'm tired of *being* it.

Maybe I could just sit in companionable silence with a trained professional who would occasionally say, "I know, right?" and "So, *that* happened," in a meaningful voice.

I don't think therapy works that way, though.

———

"She was really young. Younger than you are now.

"She didn't want an abortion and she didn't want to marry the guy. She wouldn't even say who he was. I think once she knew she was pregnant, he became kind of beside the point.

"She'd never gotten along with her parents. They didn't fight or anything—not before this happened, anyway. They just kind of lived their separate lives.

"They didn't have anything in common, she and her parents. I think they must have been baffled by her. They were stuffy and stodgy and conventional, and she was kind of spiky and fearless and rebellious. Used to be, anyway.

"She said she felt like a changeling. She couldn't even honestly hate them—she just didn't understand them. And they didn't understand *her*, though I'm sure they thought they loved her in their own meaningless way.

"Having a baby would mean having a *real* family at last."

———

M's worried sick and terrified because I said I needed to be alone for a while today. I promised her I was just going to walk around a bit and then go back to my room and read something silly, but the fact that I wasn't doing anything special only made her feel worse.

"I'll be quiet."

"It isn't that. I just need to be by myself a little."

I could have said that I wanted to do some secret online shopping, but these days I'm a terrible liar.

Now that it's something I can choose, solitude has lost its terror. It feels precious, even.

Maybe I'm the kind of person who just naturally likes being alone, but I never had the chance to figure that out for myself.

———

"She didn't tell anyone for a long time. Months. She was practically showing by the time she said anything. She said at first she wanted to be sure, and then she wanted to be sure they couldn't even try to make her end it. She thought after that it would all be up to her.

"She thought she had it all figured out. They couldn't kick her out right away because she was too young. They could cut her off without a penny once she turned eighteen, of course, but by then she'd already have had her baby. The worst of it would be over. She'd already have embarrassed them in front of the neighbors. If they kicked her out, along with their infant grandchild, they'd only be drawing attention to themselves, and they'd make themselves look terrible.

"Sure, people would whisper about her—maybe a lot more than whisper—but most everyone would have time to get used to the idea that This Kind Of Thing happens even in the best families.

"That was one thing she and her parents had in common. They all agreed their family moved in the Best Circles. Maybe she had a little different idea of what 'best' meant, or ought to mean, but in plenty of ways she had a lot in common with them.

"She never said that, of course. I figured out a lot for myself."

The holiday break starts in a few days. We'll have earned the quiet after all this giggling and packing and begging Ms. Lurie for trips into town for last-minute shopping.

My goal is to eat in the dining room the day before they leave.

I think I can do it. And that way if it feels too weird, I don't have to worry about how they'll react to not seeing me the next day.

———

"She kind of knew they wouldn't really throw her out. Her mistake was thinking that was the worst they could do. That that was all she'd have to deal with.

"She figured if it came down to that, she'd call their bluff. Oh, you want me to leave with my helpless child? Fine. I'll go. Proudly. Saying goodbye at every house along the way. Explaining why I'm leaving.

"Or, heck, if they weren't nice to her she could threaten to leave while she was still pregnant. Walking out the door looking all the more pitiful with that baby bump. Probably thought Prince Charming would be standing outside getting his horse repaired, and he'd take one look at her and she'd be set for life.

"She was used to things being like that—always working out for her. She was little and cute. Kind of like an elf—well, *you* remember. She made people want to take care of her.

"So she was pampered and soft. She'd been sheltered by money and family and she had no idea what real life was like. That was something other people had to deal with.

"She didn't have any muscles, figurative or literal.

"So when they found out she was pregnant and really started in on her, she didn't stand a chance."

———

"It was late enough that when they couldn't start their car, they figured, well, why not just stay over and sort it all out in the morning. My mother was seriously pissed because the cottage was barely big enough for *us* by her standards, but of course she couldn't say anything like that in front of our friends.

"We never stayed somewhere that small again, which was too bad. I loved it. Right next to the ocean in what felt like a hut, compared to our regular life. It was an adventure. But my mother hates adventures if they're inconvenient, which is kind of the definition of adventure.

"Anyway. Their son was my age, so he and I were tossed into my room with strict instructions to Go Right To Sleep. We were six, so fat chance of that happening. But we did quiet down after my mother came in and gave us what I'm sure she thought was a jolly little talking-to.

"There were millions of blankets and we made a fort, except we called it a house. Even with the window shut we could hear the ocean, so we pretended it was Neverland and we fought over who got to be Peter Pan.

"Of course I won.

"We pretended my mother was Captain Hook *and* the crocodile and we had to be very quiet or we'd be eaten. But then I decided we also had to rescue someone, so we tiptoed around our island and finally managed to save . . . Who was it? A baby mermaid, I think. He hated that part, so I threw in a wolf, too.

"And then we were tired enough that we actually wanted to sleep, though we hated to admit it. It felt like losing a war. I tried to talk him into sleeping *under* our bed so we could terrify our parents when they came looking for us in the morning, but he was too scared.

"So we bundled up in what had been our roof and lay very still listening to the waves. He fell asleep right away, so far as I could tell, but I stayed awake for a long time thinking about how good it was to have someone so warm and near while I slept. In case I had a bad dream, or just because. I was Pan and he was my minion and that was how it should be.

"That was the nicest night I ever had but one."

M looked at me inquiringly. "Is that the kind of story you wanted? I didn't exactly have a normal childhood, sorry."

———

"She couldn't hold out against them. She was used to winning arguments, but those were about minor things. They didn't care *that* much about what she wore or what kind of music she listened to or even what kind of people she hung around with, at least up to a certain point. That was the kind of thing they could complain about with other parents. It was part of being in the club.

"This wasn't. This was the kind of thing that would turn their family into a cautionary tale, the kind of things their friends would congratulate themselves on not having happened to *them*.

"And when she'd daydreamed about fleeing into the wild with her pregnancy, she hadn't considered the possibility that maybe she wouldn't feel up to running away because she'd be spending every minute either wanting to sleep or trying not to throw up.

"Everything was on their side. Even the timing. School was just letting out for the summer, and needless to say she'd done a crappy job on her finals.

"So it wasn't conspicuous at all for them to send her away on a long trip and tell everyone she was doing some enrichment program in Europe.

"Just like the bad old days. Girls Who Got In Trouble would go away for a few months and come back skinny and quiet."

———

"You're not defined by what somebody did to you."

M keeps getting mad at me. Especially when I answer that kind of statement by saying, "I kind of am, though."

"That isn't all you are. It isn't all you *can* be, or you *have* to be."

No matter how quietly I sigh at that point, she hears it and it sets her off like a rocket.

I know she's right, in a way. There's a sort of core person, the one I'd call "me" no matter what my life had been like. The one who loves books and cake and hates flowers (sorry, M). I know M wants me to believe that's the only "me" that counts.

But I'm also the person all those terrible things happened to.

Those events *are* me. At least in the sense that they'll be the first thing mentioned in my obituary. And more than that. They shaped me.

So, yes, M, I *am* defined by what other people did.

I can try to make a life I want, a life I can love.

I think I have a chance, especially with M to ~~push~~ help me.

But maybe the fact that I'll have to try so hard proves my point.

———

"She didn't tell anybody afterward. She was a different person by that point. Defeated. She'd never had to do something she didn't want to do. She'd never had to give anything up.

"She had a lot of friends but no one she was really close to, and she'd already broken up with the guy so there was nothing to explain there.

"Having a baby would have been one thing. She could have bragged about that. That would have been the ultimate coup against the big bad grown-ups, and never mind that it was also the kind of thing that *made* you one of the grown-ups.

"Except of course she'd *never* be the kind of parent her mother and father had been." She snickered mirthlessly. "No one ever is.

"But having a baby and being forced to give it up? That's not the kind of thing a prom queen wants to brag about.

"Not that our mother was ever prom queen. She just loved knowing she could have been."

———

The dining room was okay. Not great, but bearable.

I guess this should be the part of the story where Madison and I become best friends forever. She still doesn't like me, though.

Lucy looked really disappointed when M and I came in and sat down at the last two seats at a different table. Not that we were avoiding her or anything—her table was already full, too. I didn't know if she might still be mad about me screaming at her, but then I remembered Ms. Lurie saying how Lucy had been asking about me after the Stephen James memorial. There was nothing even remotely normal to do or say under the circumstances, so I met her eyes and gave her an awkward little wave. I had to look away then, but when I glanced back up, she looked stunned.

The other girls obviously feel bad for me and also kind of puzzled. Naturally.

They were awkward, especially at my table, because they had no idea what to say or how to act.

I didn't, either, which helped. If no one knows what to do, it's harder to do something wrong.

It helped a bit when Brianna said hi and I couldn't say anything so I just smiled a little and nodded and then she said, "Dibs on your dessert," and I was able to decently imitate a laugh.

The others kind of looked at each other, taking this all in and making sure everyone else had seen and heard it, too.

Everyone was very quiet for a minute, and then Katia the poet made a valiant effort and said she and her family were going to England for the holidays and was it true M and I were staying at Hawthorne? I nodded and M said that Ms. Lurie and Miss Miller had promised to make us an authentic plum pudding and Katia said, oh, that was perfect, she'd be having one, too, what with it being England and Christmas and all.

We all laughed a bit at that. M squeezed my hand under the table but I was fine, I really was. I couldn't eat much but it was just because everyone was looking at me. I don't blame them. It just made it hard to chew.

So did catching a quick look at Madison's face, which looked as if she'd bitten a large piece of lemon and then decided to keep it in her mouth for a while and see if it tasted any better after an hour or two.

I think Madison and I wouldn't particularly like each other even if I hadn't spent so much time being actively horrible. And if the word around school weren't that I'd had some kind of breakdown and was currently rebuilding, it would have been fine for her not to adore me. But as it is, I must make her feel all kinds of mean. I make her the person who doesn't like a poor little mentally ill girl. Which makes her dislike me even more.

I wish I could just go up to her and say, "Look, it's okay that you don't like me. I'm not crazy about you, either. No offense. And none taken, by the way."

If I could say that, things might be better. It might even break some of the ice between us. Maybe we could manage to be irony buddies. Our greeting could be a raised eyebrow and a curled lip and a rueful sort of "well, what can you do?" expression before we gratefully looked at someone, anyone else.

But I don't feel ready to talk like that, even if it might help. And it might not, after all. As much as Madison hates me, she might be deeply affronted that I don't secretly worship her.

So I'll just have to try to enjoy the novelty of being surface-polite to someone I don't particularly like.

———

I keep wanting to copy out relevant quotes from Emily Dickinson. It would be so much easier. Everything I want to say, she's already said perfectly. Even knowing nothing about me, she summed up my life better than I ever could.

That doesn't count, though. It doesn't get me where I need to be in terms of sorting things out.

I don't need Ms. Lurie to tell me that.

———

I was in the front room and it was dark except for one light and Ms. Lurie was holding me and saying, "It's all right, Emily, everything's all right, you're safe."

I still don't know how I got there but I'm very glad the other girls had already gone home for their holiday.

———

"It took her a long time to feel like a person again, she told me. She didn't feel real. Nothing felt real. It was like she was sleepwalking, or playacting. Or like she was the only one who wasn't.

"She went through the motions. She didn't really want to go to college, but at least it was a way to get away from her parents.

"She'd been very artistic before it all happened. She was really good, as far as I could tell. It wasn't just doodling or copying, and it wasn't just cute. She hung on to a couple of her old sketchbooks, and she showed me one with some drawings she'd done when she realized she was pregnant with me.

"I think she thought I'd look at those pictures and everything would be perfect between us."

———

"Are you going to leave? Is that what you want?"

"What are you talking about?"

"I just thought—maybe that's what you really want. Subconsciously. Or not so subconsciously, and you just don't want to hurt my feelings."

"Don't be an idiot, M."

"Last night—"

"Are you blaming me for sleepwalking?"

"I'm not blaming you for anything. I'm trying to figure things out. And you weren't sleepwalking. You were pounding on the front door, screaming."

Ms. Lurie hadn't told me that. Maybe she thought I already knew.

"Last night, maybe I was trying to save you again."

"Oh." She paused, and then she took my hand. "Well, don't. All right? I promise if there's any saving to do, I can do it myself."

"I know."

———

Last night, maybe I was trying to get away from *her*. Again.

"Her parents thought she was finally growing up and being practical. Probably the first time anyone's ever called becoming an English major practical, but I gather they used to worry she'd run off and become an artist and live in a garret, or something to that effect.

"Sometimes I think that would have humiliated them even more than I did.

"I've thought of asking them, but I despise them as much as she did.

"Nice to have one thing in common with her, anyway."

"I haven't been able to work."

"Really? M says you've been writing a great deal."

"But it isn't—work. I mean, it isn't fun, but it isn't, you know, school stuff. It's just whatever I think of."

"What's wrong with that? It sounds like exactly what you need to be doing right now."

"But what about later?"

"What *about* later?"

"I just don't feel like I'll ever feel like working again."

"Emily." Ms. Lurie put down the Christmas cards she'd been arranging on a table and came to place her hands on my shoulders. "Here's the part where I give you a long, tedious lecture about

284

understanding that how you feel right now—right after you've suffered a serious shock—shouldn't be taken to stand for how you'll feel forever."

"Is this the part where I nod and look serious and only roll my eyes when you're not looking?"

"Exactly." She beamed at me, smoothing my hair away from my face. "You need to give yourself time. A lot of it."

"But—what if I really *don't* ever feel like working again? Not just on my Dickinson project—and I'm not even sure what that *is* anymore—but on anything?"

"You're allowed to not do anything, Emily."

———

"So she went to college. She went through the motions. She didn't care much about the work and she wasn't exactly brilliant, but she did pretty well. It wasn't as if there was anything else she wanted to be doing.

"Everyone expected her to do the usual and meet some eligible bachelor and get married, but she wasn't interested. She graduated and started some stupid job she hated and went to the kind of parties her parents wanted her to go to and did the kind of volunteer work they approved of.

"They thought she'd grown up. She said she felt like she was just waiting to die. Or waiting for someone to notice she already had."

———

"I can't just sit around my whole life."

"You won't. Trust me." Ms. Lurie looked amused. "Especially if you spend your life with M."

———

"No."

"No?" She smiled at me.

"That can't be right. Why would she have married him if she didn't love him?"

I don't know why I felt so betrayed by that idea. Why it seemed so cruel to my father.

He'd already been forgotten by his own daughter and murdered by someone else's, and now I learned he hadn't even been important to the person he should have been everything to.

"She didn't have to marry anyone if she didn't want to," I said.

"She didn't *have* to, no," she agreed. "Nobody was holding a gun to her head."

I closed my eyes tight for a minute, but the darkness there was worse than the night.

"But there are other reasons she might have wanted to get married," she went on. "Reasons other than love, that is. She might have been tired of being alone. She might have wanted to get her parents off her back. Those are all things she hinted at, when she told me that part of her story."

"She said that he was safe, and he made her feel safe. That he seemed to love her, and she kind of liked the fact that she didn't exactly love him. It made her feel strong. Powerful. In control. For once."

Freezing cold. Not the weather: just me.

M thinks I'm mad at her because I spent all day in the bathtub. I wasn't avoiding her. It was just the only place I could feel almost warm. Warm enough not to feel numb.

I guess I wouldn't have minded her visiting, if she really wanted to sit there while I turned into a human prune, but Ms. Lurie wouldn't approve—not after all her talks about Leaving Ourselves Something To Look Forward To.

Anyway, I couldn't really talk, and that only would have worried her more.

"God, you're an idiot," M said.

I don't usually show her this journal, but I'm still having a hard time talking and it was easier than trying to explain.

"Set the record straight, please, writer-girl," she went on, standing up and smacking my notebook down on the bed next to me. "I'm *not* afraid of you getting angry at me. You can scream at me all day, if that's what you want to do. Throw something while you're at it. Something light, at least."

"Okay," I said carefully. I meant about the me-being-angry bit, not the part about throwing things, but she didn't give me time to explain.

"I'm not even afraid you'll break up with me. No," she said, catching my expression. "I'm not. If that were really what you wanted. If you were getting tired of my brand of craziness. Or if you wanted to explore the possibilities now that you're free. I could hardly blame you for *that*. I'd be miserable and enraged and probably throw some things myself, but I'd survive. I'm good at that."

She sat down next to me, hard.

"Get it right," she said. "What I'm worried about is you just kind of slipping away. Not leaving me. Just leaving. I know what to do when someone breaks up with me. I don't know what to do when you're right there but you're not really there."

She smiled a little, reminiscently. "I think I liked it better when you were screaming at me to leave you the hell alone all the time."

"The good old days."

———

"She swore to me you were an accident. Maybe you were. She certainly waited long enough to have you.

"I think she was lying. Just that once, she lied to me. I'm sure she told herself she was protecting my feelings. Really she was protecting herself.

"I think really she was desperate to have another baby, one nobody could ever take away from her.

"Why else would she have named you after me?"

———

"She says she thought about me all the time, and she did but in a way

288

she didn't. She thought about the baby who was taken away from her. She didn't think of me as someone who could ever grow up.

"I think she got the shock of her life when I got in touch with her. I'd been such an abstract idea. The Baby. The child she hadn't been allowed to keep. Now, all of a sudden, here I was. A person. Someone who could walk and talk and ask her questions.

"Of course she said she was thrilled to see me."

———

"Why *Emily*?"

Everybody's name has a story behind it. Emily Dickinson was named after her mother. Her sister Lavinia was named after an aunt. Even when a name is brand-new for that family, there's a reason for it. It's a favorite character in a book or a movie. It's a politician or a war hero. Sometimes it's a place. (Some places are better than others. Madison, okay. Minneapolis, not so much.) Sometimes it's completely made up, because the mom wants to make sure no one else in the world has that name.

"I don't know," my sister said. "I never thought to ask." She smiled at me.

She smiled at me every time I asked her a question. Fondly. Proudly, even—*look at that smart little girl over there.*

It made me sick, but she was the only one I could ask anything.

"I guess she just liked it," she said. "She liked it enough to keep using it, anyway."

———

"I'm not avoiding you, and I'm not going all True Love Waits. I just feel like I'm never going to be warm again."

"Oh, Emily."

She put her arms around me, and all I could feel was a wish that she'd brought a heavy blanket with her while she was at it.

"My hands are freezing, and my feet have been a little numb since—since we got back that night."

"Tell Ms. Lurie. Maybe you should talk to the doctor again."

I shook my head. "She said I'm fine. Ms. Lurie says so, too. Physically, I mean. Here. Feel." I pushed one of her sleeves up and put my hands on her bare arm.

M frowned. "They're not cold. Not even a little."

"I know. I'm perfectly warm. Perfectly normal, temperature-wise. I just can't feel it."

———

"We had—dates. I don't know how else to put it." She laughed jaggedly. "When I got in touch with her, I expected—I don't know what I expected, exactly. I just knew this wasn't it. This wasn't how it was supposed to be."

———

"She called me by my name and she cried.

"It felt like such an act. Not like she was faking it, but like she was excited that she could finally play the role she'd been waiting to perform for so long."

How much of it was true?

Maybe it's not fair for me to question anything she told me. She's the one who was there. And she knew my mother better than I did, in a way. Maybe in a lot of ways.

I spent more time with her, but I wasn't exactly gathering information. I was just alive. And not old enough to be particularly aware.

She had conversations with her. That's more than I ever got to do.

I can't believe I'm sitting here feeling guilty about doubting the truthfulness of a murderer.

And I *really* can't believe I find myself feeling sorry for her sometimes.

When I'm not busy having nightmares that she's still alive.

"So you blackmailed her."

She just stared through the darkness at me.

Don't make her angry, a sensible voice that wasn't my own whispered silently.

"It wasn't blackmail. She gave me money because she wanted to. A *lot* of money. She's the one who offered in the first place. She said it was my birthright.

"She loved that part, I think. Taking money she'd inherited from her parents and giving it to the child they'd made her give up. The child who would have shamed them by her very existence.

"So, no, it wasn't blackmail. If anything, it was *her* trying to control *me*. She thought we'd have an understanding. 'I've given you so much. I love you so much. It wasn't my fault they took you away from me. So let's just keep you our little secret, shall we?'"

Her eyes gleamed in the tiny glare of light she kept such careful control over.

"She's the one who wanted the lies, the secrecy. Not me.

"Sure, it all started with her parents. But she didn't *have* to go along with what they wanted. This wasn't the 1950s. She had choices. She was just too much of a coward to make the ones that would have kept me in her life.

"Then I gave her a second chance, and she still said no."

———

"Emily, she's gone. I promise."

Ms. Lurie was holding my hands tightly, and all the lights were on. It hurt my eyes, but I still wanted more.

"I wouldn't lie to you, and I'm not mistaken. Believe me. The news report was quite specific.

"You're going to have to live with what she's done. I can't take that away from you, no matter how much I'd like to. But she's never going to do anything else, to you or to anyone.

"You need to believe that, Emily. She isn't some kind of revenant.

She was a terribly hurt, terribly angry person who destroyed a lot of lives, and now her own life is over and you need to live yours."

I know.

"Can I keep the light on when you go?" Ms. Lurie hates wasting electricity.

Ms. Lurie smiled. "I'm not going anywhere."

"No, I want you to. It's supposed to rain tomorrow. You should walk while you can."

"Would you like to come with me?"

I thought about that. It was four in the morning, but it wasn't as if I'd be getting more sleep any time soon. I didn't even want to.

We're the ones having them and we're the ones who make them, so why are nightmares so terrible? Why do we hurt ourselves like this?

It doesn't make sense.

My sister torturing *other* people doesn't make sense to me, and I'll bet she never had a bad dream in her life.

Maybe that isn't fair. Maybe it was all a nightmare for her, too.

Still she haunts me, phantomwise . . .

She said that at one point. To me. About me.

I know it's from a poem but I don't know which one. I don't want to.

It better not be Dickinson, that's all.

"Emily?"

"Yes," I said, and then, "Do we have to talk?"

She gave my hands a parting squeeze and then stood up, dropping a swift kiss on my forehead. "No, and you don't have to brush your hair first. Just don't forget your boots, please."

———

"She kept telling me how complicated it all was. She wanted to have a relationship with me—she'd always wanted that. She'd never stopped missing me. She celebrated my birthday every year, she said. She got coffee and a fancy pastry at the priciest bakery she could find, and then she bought a piece of jewelry she imagined I might like. Never wore it, either. Just set it aside."

I don't remember my mother wearing any jewelry. Was I just too young to notice? I seem to remember thinking she was so pretty that she didn't *need* to wear jewelry, but maybe I only thought that later. Her wedding ring was always on her hand, but it seemed as much a part of her as her hair.

"She kept it in a box she never showed anyone, and she gave it all to me the first time we met. She had great taste, I'll give her that much. Must have been those frustrated artistic impulses coming to the surface.

"And she spent a small fortune. If she hadn't given me all that money, I could have survived a long time anyway on what I would have made selling the jewelry."

I looked for a gleam of gold around her neck or in her ears. She noticed and smiled, holding her hand into the light. A pretty ring, gold with a single pearl.

"Happy birthday," she said. "Sweet sixteen."

"What's a revenant?"

It was much too early and dark and cold even for Ms. Lurie to be out, but we were stumbling along anyway, bundled up in hasty layers, looking like mummies who didn't own mirrors. M would have been appalled.

"Someone who returns from the dead," Ms. Lurie said. "Usually someone whose life was misspent, and who comes back to haunt her family."

"So far as she was concerned, the damage had already been done. The chance for her to be my mother in any meaningful sense had been lost a long time ago.

"She'd never told her husband about me. But explaining to *him* would have been a piece of cake compared to trying to tell *you* the good news."

She could have. She could have told me.

When you're that young, the world is completely insane anyway. *Nothing* makes sense. So why not add a little more weirdness to the mix?

I'd been terrified by an open cupboard door, for hell's sake. I probably would have handled something *really* strange just fine.

Guess what, honey? You have a sister!

Parents have to say that kind of thing all the time. They're just usually talking about a *younger* sibling.

She could have told me.

I guess telling my father would have been a lot more complicated. That's the kind of thing you're supposed to bring up *before* the wedding, not ten years after.

———

"Where did you go?"

"What?"

"When you were—talking to each other. Where were you?"

"Oh. Out, mostly. She'd meet me somewhere. Odd little restaurants or cafés. Places where she could feel pretty sure she wouldn't see anyone she knew."

Oh.

"I did come over once or twice. Toward the end. I really laid on the guilt, and she finally agreed. Just once or twice. Late. Like a lover. When her husband was out of town and you were up in your room and the neighbors were sound asleep. Their windows were dark, at least.

"She thought she had everything under control. She thought she was protecting herself."

———

"She had everything the way she wanted it. Rich handsome husband. Cute respectable legitimate baby girl. Stability. Peace.

"I was a threat to all of that."

———

"I realized she didn't love *me*. She just loved the idea of being my secret mother.

"But she had a real daughter now. She didn't need me in her life. I'd just get in the way.

"Even getting back at her parents wouldn't be worth it now. It was too late for that.

"I'd complicate things unbearably for her, *now*."

———

"People believed in them, even really recently. It's amazing. There was a family in New England in the late nineteenth century—the *late* 1800s, this was—who thought their teenage daughter was coming back from the grave and feeding off her brother. The townspeople dug her body up and burned her heart and liver and fed her brother the ashes. They thought that would cure him."

M looked a little green. "And . . . did it?"

"Oh no. He died a few months later."

She took a deep breath. "Emily, you know I want you to be happy. And I know you want to give the Dickinson research a break for a while, and I think that's fine. Probably a good idea, even. But do you really think this new interest is, well, healthy?"

"I don't see how revenants are any different from those saint stories of yours."

"Give me a minute and I'll write you a list. A *long* list."

———

"She thought we should just do what we'd been doing. Talking, privately. Seeing each other on the sly. You know—when she had nothing better to do and could get away from her *real* family.

"She'd keep giving me money no one would miss, and trinkets no one knew she owned.

"She didn't understand what more I could want from her."

———

All those conversations in the dining room after Stephen James was killed. Listening to my Hawthorne sisters complain about their nice, annoying, blessedly boring parents. Hearing M coolly mock her decidedly *un*boring mother.

Feeling jealous that I'd never be able to do anything as ordinary as find some imperfection in my own.

Did I think about this that night, or is it only striking me now?

Either way, I guess I got what I wished for.

———

"This was never about revenge. Is that really what you think? Don't you understand?"

If I'd been able to breathe, I might have laughed. She sounded so indignant.

So much trouble and blood, and here I was being *stupid*.

"Have you heard a word I've said? I was trying to *protect* you."

———

Memories shift and I have to write this one down. I'm the only one who can.

I can feel things slipping away from me already.

———

"Don't forget you've got me. My memory's pretty good."

I know, and I'm glad she was there because I don't think I could have brought myself to tell her everything.

What if she blamed me? What if she *hated* me?

What if she didn't want to be anywhere near me after that?

She can leave. She can do anything she wants.

Why does she still want me?

———

"I've already told you you're an idiot. I'll tell you again as often as you need me to."

"Thanks."

M kissed me, gently. "Any warmer?"

"A little."

———

"So all of this was just revenge? I stole our mother from you, so you stole her back?"

———

"How is killing everyone I ever loved protecting me?"

———

My hair isn't really long enough to braid—it barely was before I took the scissors to it that night—but M likes to try anyway. I think it's partly because she can't stand not having everything around her be decorative, and partly because it's a way of being close that doesn't make me freeze up or jump a mile. I like how it feels when she touches my hair, even if she pulls it a bit sometimes.

"I know what you mean," she murmured, trying to make a French braid happen.

"But it isn't right. I'd be able to believe that somebody *else* did what she did. I just can't believe my own mother would."

"Of course not. We all want our mothers to be boring. That's certainly *my* mother's only redeeming quality." M gave up her attempts at braiding and pulled out the sharp, tiny pair of scissors she'd already used to even up what was left of my hair. "I wonder how you'd look with bangs," she murmured, pulling and pushing my hair around.

"Why do I keep thinking so much about that part of it?" I asked. "*Her* part? Considering everything else I know now, why do I keep thinking about what my *mother* did?"

"Because she's your mother and you thought you knew her and it turns out you didn't."

"I didn't think I knew her at all. I didn't know anything about her except that she was my mother."

"That's its own kind of knowing."

———

She seemed surprised that I needed so much explained to me.

"I didn't want you to have to go through what I went through."

"Not having our mother? Or my own father? Or *anyone* to call my own? I *did* go through that. I've been completely alone my whole life—more alone than you ever were. All thanks to you."

I could barely see her, but her voice expressed what must have been on her face: total disbelief. "How can you possibly say that?"

I was numb from sitting in the dark cold for so long, listening to this nightmare. I was wrapped in terror.

"You were adopted," I said. "You got to have a family."

"They weren't my family. Not my *real* family."

"What do you mean? Just because they weren't related to you, why shouldn't they count for something? They still wanted you. Were they mean to you? Did they hurt you?" Did they leave corpses around for you to trip over in the dark?

"No, they weren't 'mean.'" Her tone was mocking. "They weren't anything. Not to me."

"But didn't they care about you? Why did they adopt you if—"

"That isn't the point. Stop sounding like a four-year-old."

"What *is* the point?" And look who was talking like a four-year-old first. *You're not my* real *family.*

"I'm trying to give you the whole picture, and you keep fixating on irrelevant details."

"Fine." I shoved my numb hands under my sweater, against my bare skin. The stab of cold nearly made me shriek, but I couldn't feel any improvement in my fingers. I couldn't feel much of anything. "You want me to look at the whole picture? Well, let's see. You got to grow up and make choices. You made horrible ones." I gave a broken kind of laugh. "To put it mildly. You chose to come back and destroy my life before I got the chance to have one. You've been following me around ever since, making sure I'm completely alone in the world. And now you sound like you're waiting for me to thank you."

I expected rage—I almost would have welcomed it at this point—but instead she just shook her head sorrowfully. "Don't you get it, Emily?"

Don't call me that.

"We're *all* alone. *Every* man is an island. The only way out of loneliness is to be able to trust someone, and I wanted you to grow up knowing what I had to learn the hard way: you can't trust anyone."

"You want me to trust *you*."

"Do I?"

"Don't you?" God, there we were being four years old again.

"I want you to know the truth, that's all."

"About you?"

"About *everyone*. Everyone betrays you in the end. Not just now and then, or accidentally, or because you did something to them first. *Always.* Everyone. People will *always* hurt you if you give them even half a chance."

———

I thought this was all I'd ever wished for.

A sister looking out for me. The truth about what happened. Someone I could talk to without having to pretend to be someone I wasn't.

———

I had tried not to think too much as I slipped out of Hawthorne and down that dark road. I was hoping that if I just kept moving, I wouldn't *have* to think. Wouldn't even be able to, if I got cold and out of breath enough.

It didn't work like that. I couldn't stop wondering what lay ahead. How long before I got hungry enough to beg or scavenge. How far I'd be able to walk until I had to sleep. What I would have to do to keep myself safe when I *did* need to sleep.

These considerations were nothing compared to how it felt when, try as I would to hold them back, thoughts I'd left behind forced their way to the front of my mind. I saw M coming to my room in the morning, full of love and mischief and a million new ideas about our future. I knew exactly how her face would look as she read my letter.

I'd already seen it look that way once. That night in the library when I tried to save her.

I thought this was all the misery one night could hold.

And then *she* brought me her truth.

———

"Enough."

M closed her hand gently around mine, managing to stop my pen without messing up my page.

"No arguing. Your eyes are bulging, and your shoulders are hunched all the way up to your ears. They have been for an hour now, at least. That has to hurt."

"I just—"

"Later." She didn't move her hand. "You don't have to write everything in the world this minute."

———

"Tell me one thing, then."

"I'll tell you anything you want. You know that."

She kept saying things like that. Implying a terrible intimacy between us.

———

"You don't believe in loving or trusting anyone. You think everyone hurts everyone."

"Well?"

"So why me?"

"Why you what?"

"Why care if I had to go through the same pain you say you did? According to your philosophy, I'm just one more horrible person, right? So why would my feelings matter any?"

There was a long silence. I had time to wonder, clinically, if I'd angered her.

"I've already told you," she said at last. "You're the only one I ever loved. The only one I let myself love."

———

I'm carrying everything she refused to pick up.

I feel crazy because she was convinced of her own sanity.

She murdered our mother in a leisurely fashion, and mine are the hands that will never wash clean.

She's buried, and I'm the one who can't stop feeling cold.

———

"She never let me see you. She wouldn't even show me pictures. But she told me how old you were, and I couldn't stop thinking about you. So little. So innocent. I loved you right from the start, before I ever saw you.

"I knew I had to save you, the way I wish someone had saved me."

"You can't use that word. Don't you dare use that word."

"You think because of what I've done I don't know what love means?"

Her hand touched mine in the dark.

"Careful," she added as I wrenched my hand away and almost sent myself rolling down the slope. "You don't want to fall."

That sounded better than continuing this conversation.

"You're out of your mind," I said. "You can't even keep your craziness straight."

"Love isn't crazy."

"Remember that fucked-up mission statement you just played for me? You ruled love out! You've been trying to rule it out of *my* life for as long as I can remember!"

"You're talking about two different things. I never said love was crazy. I said it was a bad idea. A dangerous thing. A weapon you hand to someone right before you paint a target on yourself. You *have* to see the truth in that."

I couldn't speak.

"It's too late for me," she continued. "I learned too late. I'm still weak. Not as much as most people, but I have my soft spots in spite of all my best efforts.

"I wanted better for you. That's what I've been trying to tell you.

"I did it all for you, Emily."

I wish I could doubt her sincerity.

This really was her idea of being that older sister I'd always wanted.

———

"*She* wouldn't let me be any other kind of sister to you, Emily."

Her tone was venomous.

"We couldn't be anything like a real family." She gave an astonished-sounding laugh. "She'd made sure of that right from the beginning. Never telling anyone about me—not even the man she was marrying. Naming you Emily. She said it was so she could say my name every day. It just also happened to make it impossibly awkward for her to ever introduce *both* of us to the same person. 'This is my daughter Emily. And *this* is my daughter Emily. Long story. Care for a cup of tea?'

"Think about that, Emily. *That's* who our mother was. That's what she did to us. That's what she did to *me*—and I think she really believed it when she said she loved me."

———

She kept saying none of it had been about revenge. Acting shocked that I would even use that word.

Funny how not-revenge can look an awful lot like the perfect revenge.

I'm going to take your child away from you and make sure she spends the rest of her life alone, unloved and unloving.

But first I'll let her find what's left of you.

———

This night would never end.

We'd go around and around forever. Each of us convinced we knew what love *really* was. Each of us wanting to protect that one special person who'd slipped through our defenses and won our hearts.

We'd still be here arguing when Ms. Lurie went for her walk. When M found my letter. When the sun rose and the world woke.

We'd be here forever.

Or until she lost her patience and—what? Lashed out at me?

If I'd had no one but me to worry about that night, I think I wouldn't have cared what she did next.

If there weren't anyone else to worry about, I wouldn't have been out there in the first place.

———

"Of course you were angry. I mean, of course you *are* angry. But—"

I stumbled then. I hadn't spoken much during this conversation, and now I knew why.

It turns out that it's really hard to manage more than a short sentence or two when you're talking to someone who needs it explained to her that as a matter of fact, hacking up your mother isn't okay no matter how sad she made you.

"Emily." Her voice was frustrated. "This wasn't about being

angry. God, why can't you understand? I was protecting you from someone who had already destroyed *one* innocent child's life."

———

Someone would come looking for me.

Someone would find *her*.

———

I'd been lying by omission all my life. Now I had to commit my first big out-loud one.

"All right," I said. "I understand."

———

Either I was more convincing than I sounded to my own ears, or she was hearing what she wanted to hear.

At any rate, she believed me.

———

I wanted to live.

I was freezing and stiff and I could barely move, barely think. I felt like I'd been thrown into hell. There was no world outside the tiny ring of light she controlled. There was only unending darkness.

But I suddenly felt more convinced than I ever had that there *was* a world of light somewhere, a place full of risks and warmth and joy.

I knew there was such a place. I'd seen it.

And more than anything, I wanted to be in it.

I wanted to live. Finally.

But if I couldn't spend another moment there myself, I could at least protect the one who'd shown it to me.

That would be a life well spent, indeed.

So I did what I had to do.

She trusted me, so I lied to her.

———

"You have to be kidding me."

M tore the page out of my notebook. I sighed and took it out of her hand and began taping it back in.

"Are you honestly telling me you feel guilty for *lying*? To a *murderer*?"

I shook my head, looking down at my work.

"You do."

"Just let me do this, M. Please."

She raised her voice, almost to a shout. "Where the *hell* is that happily ever after I ordered?"

———

"I understand," I said, and she smiled as if she'd been waiting all her life to hear me say that.

For all I know, she had.

"But there's something else I need to know," I went on.

"Anything," she said.

"I'm sorry I'm having such a hard time. I'm making you spell everything out."

She smiled again, practically beaming.

"I'm happy to be able to explain," she said. "I'm so happy that I can finally tell you all this."

———

I made her happy.

I made *her* happy.

———

"There's something I don't get," I began again. "I mean, everything you've said makes sense now."

"But?"

Her voice was warm, a little teasing. She sounded like we were at one of the slumber parties we never got to have together.

I breathed in deeply, as quietly as I could.

"I still don't understand how Stephen James fits into all this."

———

"You're not her. You're not anything like her. You're not connected to her.

"Yes, all right, you can't stop thinking about her right now. That's because you spent your whole life as the target of some record-setting stalking.

"That's *all* it means. Don't let it mean anything else.

"I'm not kidding, Emily. This part's on you. Don't you dare let her keep defining your life now that you're finally free. It's my life, too, you know, and I say she can't come in.

"We're going to make a life of our own. It's going to be *amazing*. You're not going to believe how fantastic it is. No one will. We'll be the platonic ideal of happiness. Total strangers are going to travel thousands of miles to try to catch a glimpse of what the perfect life looks like.

"We won't let them anywhere near us, of course. But every now and then we'll post pictures of our perfection, just to be nice.

"For now, you're going to finish doing what you need to do. Then, when you're ready, you're going to write all kinds of words that have nothing to do with her. Beautiful words. Words everyone will want to read not because of what happened to you, but because you're that good.

"Meanwhile, I'm going to paint you so you can see how gorgeous you are."

———

"It's complicated."

"I'm listening."

"Well," she said, shifting carefully to get a bit more comfortable. "It had been a long time since—well, since you'd heard from me."

I nodded faintly, glad she didn't seem to expect much of a reply to that.

"And it was your last year at Hawthorne."

I *hated* hearing that name in her voice. My home. My one safe place, however temporary.

"This was the year you'd have to make serious plans for your future."

"And you wanted to make sure I made the right kind of plans." I struggled not to sound sarcastic or accusatory.

Apparently I didn't quite succeed. "This is important, Emily," she said. She sounded like a teacher disappointed in her student—so promising at first, and suddenly so slow.

"I know. I'm sorry. I just—"

"*Do* you know? Do you really understand?"

"I—"

"This isn't a game, Emily." She sounded stern now. "This is life. You're just about to begin yours. It's important you start off on the right foot."

My older sister, giving me a pep talk as I prepare to embark on adulthood. If Hawthorne ever starts having graduation ceremonies, maybe she can give the commencement speech.

"I don't get it," I managed. "I'm sorry."

"What is it you don't get?" Her voice was purposely patient, barely under control.

"What does all this have to do with Stephen James?"

And all control was gone.

"My God, Emily!" she exploded. "Why are you so fixated on him? Why do you keep saying his name? He doesn't matter! He could be anybody! He could be nobody! He *is* nobody, so far as I'm concerned!"

She looked at me and made a visible effort to rein in her temper. "Stephen James—" she said, "since you insist on calling him that—is just a symbol. A warning. A reminder."

"A memento mori," I said cautiously.

She sighed. "Not exactly. But"—magnanimously—"sure. If that's easier for you to understand, think about it that way. Not exactly 'remember you must die,' but remember what can happen if you slip. If you trust. If you let the wrong one in. If you let *any*one in."

I nodded again to keep her from screaming again.

"You shouldn't have to make the mistakes I did."

English wasn't English anymore if she could use it like this.

"I don't want to see you get hurt."

———

I'd been driving myself crazy trying to figure it out.

Now here it was, and my mistake had been not going quite crazy enough.

———

She made the rules that governed my life and then she got bored and destroyed them.

———

Were there others? Murders I didn't hear about, or didn't think twice about if I *did* hear about them?

Did she tell herself it was important to keep her hand in, just in case?

I didn't ask.

I could have. I could have taken just the right tone, and she would have explained how it had all been for me, she was just trying to protect me, and how could she do that if she didn't keep her wits and weapons sharp? She never knew when she might have to act on my behalf again, after all. She couldn't afford to get rusty.

Or maybe she would have found that very idea beneath her. Maybe she thought practice murders would profane her noble mission.

I didn't ask.

I didn't want to know.

———

She was telling me the truth. Finally someone was telling me all the truth I'd ever wanted.

If this was what being set free felt like, I wanted to go back to living in my prison of rules.

———

Stephen James had died because I'd never really been able to keep people like him safe in the first place.

Maybe that should have been a relief.

———

"I wish—"

"What?"

"I guess I wish you'd—I don't know. Told me what was going on. Like you are now. Contacted me somehow."

"I just told you, silly. That's exactly what I did."

I hoped that, wherever Stephen James was, he couldn't hear himself being talked about like this.

"Yes, but—"

"I did what I could with what I had. *You* had to be the one to make the next move."

———

I went too far.

She could believe a lot, now that she thought I was the eager younger sister she'd always wanted, but she wasn't going to buy just *any*thing. Not quite yet.

This was too much too soon.

Maybe I could have gotten away with it a little later.

———

"And now?"

"Now?"

"Well. I made that next move. I came out. I found you. I learned the truth."

"Yes." So softly I could barely hear her. Lovingly.

"So, now what?"

"I suppose that's up to you."

"Me?"

"Is there someone else here?"

———

"You dreamed about her again, didn't you."

She didn't even bother with a question mark.

Was I supposed to apologize?

"I just can't believe she's gone."

About anyone else, that would have sounded desperately sad. Here, it was just desperate.

———

"It's up to you," she said. "What do *you* want now?"

———

I wanted M. I wanted life. I wanted anywhere but here.

I wanted to not know any of this. I wanted to go back to not knowing why my life was the way it was. To having rules. I wanted to go back to being an only child whose life was bad enough that total strangers wanted to read and write about it.

"I want to be with you, of course."

Maybe that "of course" pushed it over the top.

More likely she never would have trusted me. Not completely.

She wanted so much to have me be that one exception to Emily Madwoman's Universal Law of Human Depravity. She wanted me to be the perfect child she'd reared up in the cold darkness of truth. She wanted me to not only forgive her for murdering our mother, but thank her for it.

She wanted to believe in me more than anything, and so of course she couldn't.

"I see."

Her tone had become warm, even eager, when she'd started to think I was on her side. Now she was back to sounding the way she had in the beginning: cool, clinical, a little mocking.

"I always made sure you never had the chance to hurt me."

"I—"

"Don't." She held up one hand. "Don't throw me any nonsense about how you'd never do that."

———

"Maybe I thought you could be different from everyone else. With my help."

I laughed, trying to sound natural. "I *am* different," I said. "Haven't you read the books?"

———

She was so much taller than I am.

I hadn't noticed at first. I had other things on my mind.

She stood up now, and she was the size of an avenging angel.

———

"Tell me the truth," she said.

I stared up at her. I wanted to stand up, too, but I barely felt safe sitting. Gravity is always stronger in the dark.

She didn't seem to notice. She was absentmindedly strong and sure. She loomed over me, and she made standing on that slope look easy.

"Don't you dare lie to me. I've been lied to my whole life."

"No, you haven't," I said before I could stop myself.

———

Even when my words infuriated her, she always seemed fascinated by whatever I had to say.

Her eyes certainly widened at that sentence. Her whole body focused on me, like a cat who wants to pounce while she has the chance but can't help watching the bird play first.

There are people whose interest I'd just as soon not catch, but right at the end I really had hers.

———

"Nobody lied to you. People told you truths you didn't want to hear. That isn't the same thing."

———

"*I* was the one who told the truth."

She was snarling at me now.

"Our mother wanted me to stay in the shadows. She snuck around behind her husband's back to see me. She acted like I was a criminal just by existing.

"Fine. That's what she wanted? That's what I gave her.

"*She* chose that truth. Not me.

"She wanted to live a lie. I wouldn't let her."

———

She'd killed my father almost as an afterthought. She never even mentioned her own.

I guess she didn't care enough to look for him, and our mother never said who he was.

———

"I thought you'd be different," she said, almost in a whisper. "I thought you'd understand.

"You of all people I thought would understand."

———

I couldn't stay sitting anymore, never mind how iffy the ground under my feet was.

Not when my sister was standing above me looking stunned and betrayed.

———

"Why?"

I wasn't sure I wanted to know, but I needed to.

"Why did you think that? How could you?"

———

I was struggling to my feet and she was moving toward me. There wasn't much space between us as it was, but she was closing that gap.

———

"I wanted to take you with me."

———

I think she did. I think she had a dream and I was in it.

———

"I wanted you to understand."

I was just beginning to get up. This was the end and I was going to face it on my feet, even if she proceeded to knock me down.

Maybe she would have.

My foot slipped and I fell back, hard; and then I started to slide into darkness.

It's amazing to me that no matter how hideous things get, there's always room for a little more terror.

———

I could see two things in that near-perfect darkness.

The first was my sister's face, wearing an expression I'll never forget and will spend the rest of my life trying to interpret.

She looked deathly pale, and she was reaching toward me.

———

"Torture is illegal, you know."

At least she wasn't trying to break another of my pens.

"It's allowed if you're the one doing it to yourself."

"Please—"

"I'm almost finished. I promise."

———

She couldn't quite reach me, and I'd have died before I took her hand. If that had been the only thing in the world that could save me, I would have accepted death instead.

I didn't want to die, but now I knew there were worse things, and taking her hand would have been one of them.

I know that's true because that's what was going through my mind in so many words as I slipped and she reached toward me and I couldn't tell if she was reaching to pull or to push.

I really couldn't tell.

It was dark and she was crazy.

Sometimes I hate the idea that there's a God because then what does that say about his world? And sometimes I hope more than anything there's a God so I can ask him: What really happened?

That's the only way I'll know for sure.

———

"It has to be okay. You have to be okay with this. This is the happy ending either way. Not just for you, but for her."

"How is plummeting to her death *happy*?"

"If she was trying to help you, she gave her life to save yours. That shove she gave you on her way down—that's why you didn't go tumbling after her. If that's what she was hoping for, she knew it worked. She fell alone. That's her redemption."

"But—"

"She kept saying everything she did was about protecting you. Well, she finally got it right."

"But I wouldn't have *needed* protecting if it hadn't been for her."

"You really think she'd understand that?"

Silence.

"It's as happy as it could *get*, is what I'm saying. For her."

———

She didn't say anything as she fell. She didn't even cry out.

We were both moving in a confusion of darkness and unforgiving slopes and surfaces, and then I was still and she was falling and she didn't make a sound.

I heard her fall for what seemed like forever, but she'd spoken her last words without getting the chance to plan them.

———

I sat absolutely still.

I was curled so tight I might as well have been just another rock on that slope.

I listened until there was nothing more to hear, and then I sat in that particular silence.

———

"What if she *wasn't* trying to save me?"

"Then she fell because she was being evil. Karma is its own kind of happy ending."

"Not for *her*."

"If she was trying to kill you, she didn't deserve to be happy."

"You said it was a happy ending for her no matter what she was thinking."

"I lied."

———

I haven't told anyone this part.

Alone in that darkness, I wanted to let go and follow her.

I'd lost that brief, glowing sense of life as something beautiful and precious.

I didn't want to live with knowing what she'd told me. I didn't see the point.

I didn't want to live with the memory of her falling.

I didn't see how the world could ever be light or warm, ever again.

I sat in the darkness.

I wouldn't even have to move, really. No need for a big dramatic leap. I could just relax.

The end would be as easy as letting go.

———

That's when I saw something. Just above, where she and I had met and she'd told me her name and I'd thought she was calling mine.

There was a flicker of movement and a flash of light. Blinding whiteness.

"Emily?"

———

"I couldn't have gone after her. I couldn't help her. I would have died, too, if I'd tried."

"That's true. Even if you'd had the equipment and the expertise, there was absolutely nothing you could have done under the circumstances. By the time you'd started, it would already have been too late for her. You'd have been risking your life for nothing."

"I know."

Ms. Lurie looked at me shrewdly. "And do you believe that?"

"No."

———

I don't know if I would have hidden from her voice if I could have gotten away with it.

It was a moot point anyway. M knew I was there.

She'd left Hawthorne not that long after I did. I hadn't been as quiet as I thought when I'd slipped out, and, anyway, she'd half expected me to attempt some kind of escape.

She'd caught up, quietly. We'd have seen her if my sister hadn't made us tuck ourselves away on that slope.

She'd been listening and trying, with what was probably her

lifetime's supply of discretion, to figure out what the best thing to do was. Would speaking up help me, or put us both at risk? But what if listening in silence wasn't any safer?

She'd just about made up her mind to speak up—though she still wasn't sure what on earth she'd have said—when everything happened very quickly and there was no one left to talk to but me.

———

"Emily? Oh, God—are you all right? Do you need help?"

That's what got me moving. That's the only reason I started moving, carefully, and calling out a caution when all I wanted to do forever was stay in the darkness where I belonged.

If I hadn't made that short, weary, stiff-limbed climb and told her that's what I was doing and made her stay right there where she was, she would have tried to help me. With the absolute, blind, impractical determination that had sent her looking for me in the same frivolous nightgown she'd been wearing the night we met, she'd have tried to climb down and save me.

And she damned well would have gotten us both killed.

So I felt my way by inches and made my way up.

———

I had to tell her to stop shining her light right in my damned face for hell's sake.

"Oh, Emily!"

"Just stay there. Shine that just in front of me, so I've got a path."

I was going by feel, but I figured it would calm her down to have something definite to do.

———

Her arms around me almost knocked me over. "Emily. God. Oh, God. You're safe."

I couldn't move.

———

"You heard? You heard her?"

She nodded.

"You know what happened? Everything?" Who I was? Who *she* was?

"Yes."

Her arms were still around me, and that was a shock even on that night.

"Let's go home. Let's get you warm. My God, you're freezing."

"But—"

"We'll figure it all out there. First things first."

———

Ms. Lurie was awake when we got there. That helped.

She didn't scold, and she didn't ask to hear the whole story. She didn't ask *anything* right then, except, "Are you all right? Are you hurt?" That helped a lot.

She brought me into her own room and ran me a bath in her own deep, claw-footed tub, with lots of bubbles for privacy.

That should have been wonderful. At the time, I could barely feel it. I just kept thinking about what I had to do.

———

"Ms. Lurie . . ."

"Take this." A steaming hot mug of tea.

"I have to tell you something."

"I know, dear. But it can wait."

"It's waited too long."

"Is someone in trouble? Is there something I need to do right away?"

I thought about that loud, voiceless fall.

"I don't know."

———

She told the police that a couple of her students had been foolish enough to be out very late and had seen a woman on the side of the road, walking and then falling.

M was able to give her a good idea of where and when.

They looked, and eventually they found.

———

The news didn't scream as loudly as I would have expected. People do fall down these mountains from time to time. She didn't have any ID on her and so there was some puzzling over who she might be, but if they've figured it out nobody's told me.

———

She never told me her last name.

For all I know she had it changed to our mother's birth name, or maybe even her married name. Just to make a point.

Maybe she came up with something completely new, like I did.

At any rate, *my* last name's staying where it is. I'm not going back.

The little girl whose loved ones kept getting murdered until she figured out how not to have any is going to have to stay an unsolved mystery, at least until after I die and these pages can be published safely. Just like I planned, but with a much more complete ending than I ever thought I'd be able to supply.

It still feels a little bit like lying to leave that little girl in the shadows, but I don't see what else I can do.

Not if I want to live—*really* live. And I do.

———

"It doesn't matter if she gets it after Christmas. Before New Year's is still the holiday season. And she'll be glad to hear from you when-ever she gets it, dear. That's what counts."

I didn't know what to say, but the card already had a message printed in it so I just scribbled *Dear Grandma Jean Louise* above that and *Emily* below.

I wanted to say "Love From," but it seemed a little sudden.

I can always say that when I write her a thank-you letter and tell her what I spent her check on. When I finally cash it. I'm still working up the nerve, but M promised to nag me unbearably if I haven't done it by the end of January.

Maybe if I just act like all those years never happened, she will, too, and we can just be grandmother and granddaughter as if we always had been.

And maybe I can ask her to tell me stories about my father. It would be nice to know more about him than his cause of death.

Not just yet, but soon.

———

"You didn't have to get me anything. We already talked about that, remember? This is your practice Christmas. You're still taking notes on how to be normal."

"Thanks."

"You know what I mean."

"I do."

"And, anyway, I'm enjoying spoiling you rotten."

———

I managed to get Ms. Lurie something, to both our great surprise. The fact that she likes bubble bath—and bath salts and scented soaps and all sorts of other bathy things I never would have thought to associate with strong, practical, no-nonsense Ms. Lurie—was one more weird revelation of that night.

I went online and ordered her some really pricey lavender bath stuff. A big basket full of jars and boxes and bottles of pale purple things. I have no idea what most of it's for, but it was pretty and it smelled good when it arrived and I'm sure she can figure it out.

"Thank you, dear," she said on Christmas morning. She looked a little stunned. Well, it was a pretty big basket. You could have fit a baby in there, with room to crawl around.

"It's just—I used up all your bubble bath. When, you know, I came back."

She laughed. "No, not quite all. But thank you. I won't run out anytime soon now."

———

It's weird how easy it was to find something for someone I don't know all that well. It was only right to give something to Miss Miller after all the baking she's done for me, especially since she was spending Christmas at Hawthorne, too.

I gave it to her early in case she wanted to use it before or even during Christmas. (The woman does love to bake.) "I don't know if this is something you'll use, but it's kind of pretty anyway," I said clumsily as I handed her the heavy package. "And it's really old."

She looked startled, and then she tore off the paper and saw the nineteenth-century cast-iron baking tin I'd found online. I hadn't been sure what kind she might like, so I finally got one that was really pricey—there must be a reason for it to cost so much, right?—and old and rare and shaped like flowers, in case she just wanted to hang it up instead of actually baking with it.

I'd had huge second thoughts about that after it arrived and it was too late to change my mind or get her something else. Maybe it was weird to think she'd want to bake in something that old. Creepy or something. Germy?

Miss Miller didn't think so. While I was trying to explain where I'd found it and what it was and why I'd thought of her, she teared up and gave me my first non-M hug since I was a baby, practically.

And then we had flower-shaped muffins—more like little cakes, really—on Christmas morning.

It was kind of embarrassing when she insisted on giving me partial credit for those, especially when she brought the tin out and Ms. Lurie *ooh*ed over it. Even M looked impressed, which surprised me. Well, she does like beautiful things, and it's a legitimate antique.

Should I have gotten *her* one? But M hates cooking. At least I'm pretty sure she does. She set cornflakes on fire once.

That might have just been for fun, though. She was playing around with one of those little kitchen blowtorches. At the breakfast table.

How on earth do I shop for someone when *that's* her idea of a good time?

"Anyway, I didn't exactly *get* you this."

I spent hours and hours online shopping. Or browsing, at least.

I couldn't get her art supplies. I don't know anything about them. And there's a *lot* out there. How do I know what she'd really use? Anyway, she has plenty of money to buy that kind of thing for herself.

If I were any good at buying pretty clothes, I wouldn't be the person who dresses, as M so tactfully puts it, like a stray rain cloud at midnight.

Jewelry? She'd think I was proposing.

Everything I could think of was too big or too small or just plain inadequate. What do you buy for the girl who is everything?

I know her as well as she knows me—okay, other than the whole reading-true-crime-books-about-my-life-before-we-even-met aspect of our relationship—and still I couldn't think of a thing to get her; and she came up with about a million presents for me, and hinted that she'd restrained herself.

It was all really good, too. She made it look easy.

———

"I'm sorry my handwriting isn't as good as yours."

"Don't be stupid. Nobody's handwriting is as good as mine."

She opened that envelope pretty eagerly for someone who kept insisting she didn't want anything.

———

I'd been thinking of ordering some nice thick parchmenty paper and copying out some of my favorite Dickinson poems and letters—original punctuation and capitalization, of course. I'd have used different colored inks to show different moods, and maybe annotated them a little. Not the usual kind of annotation, where the editor talks about what she thinks Dickinson was talking about. Just about why I chose the particular poem or letter, and why it feels as if Dickinson were talking to or about me. Or M. Or us.

I didn't, in the end. Partly because no matter how neat I try to be, my writing just isn't that pretty. It's legible, but no one could call it decorative. And a gift should be pretty.

I can work on that. I could write really slowly and throw in some curlicues. I'd fooled around with a bit of that on normal paper, and it had actually come out looking okay.

But I was so obsessed with Dickinson for so long. She was kind of my job. There's nothing wrong with that, but I'm really tired just now. I want to come back to her when I feel like it, *because* I feel like it.

She'll never stop being the writer I love most, and I hate to betray someone who was there for me when pretty much no one else was—but that's just it. I want to have some time to build up good associations with her. I think that'll be easier when I'm more firmly established in a life where I'm allowed to have good associations with anyone.

It would be a little painful just now to go back through the poems that meant so much to me and have to think about why they meant so much.

She *did* write an awful lot about death.

Anyway, if I'd done a project like this because I had to, all in a rush—because I had to figure out *some*thing to give M for Christmas—my favorite writer would have felt like a chore. And I don't want that.

Maybe I can do this project for M's birthday. That gives me some time. And I have the feeling it's going to take me a while to relax into shopping for her. It'll be good to have a backup plan in place.

———

"Are these the kind of coupons where you promise to wash my car any time I want?"

"You don't *have* a car."

"It's the thought that counts."

"They're not that kind of coupon. They're—truths. You can read them whenever you want and know they're true even when I'm having a hard time talking."

"Oh."

"Don't make fun of my handwriting," I warned again as she opened the stapled-together booklet to the first page.

"Please shut up. I'm trying to have a special moment here."

She paused, and then read aloud. "'You're beautiful.'" And then she actually blushed. A lot. I made M blush. "Oh."

"Keep reading." I'd been kind of dreading this, but now it was turning out to be fun.

She turned to the next one. "'I'm glad you were pushy.' I was *never* pushy."

"You were *only* pushy."

"Well, somebody had to be."

"I said that. In writing. Come on, read some more."

"'I wanted to keep that first rose you gave me, but I was afraid

336

to.' 'I kept the second one even though I was afraid to.' 'Flowers you draw are the only flowers I want.'"

Her voice was a little rough now.

"'Having the chance to be with you is more happiness than I ever dreamed would be possible. It's more happiness than normal people ever get a chance at.'"

That was the last one she read out loud. She finished the rest in silence, and I didn't keep copies so I don't remember what the rest of them said.

Doesn't matter if I don't know, as long as she does.

———

"Thanks a lot," she said in a thick voice. "Brat. I spent a fortune on you, and now I feel like a complete loser."

"You're not. I love everything you got me. Don't you dare take any of it back." I clutched the life-sized stuffed panther so I could feel it purr again. "I just didn't know how to do that for you yet. I told you I'd be bad at this at first."

She said nothing. "I promise I'll buy you normal stuff from now on," I added. "I'll have time to figure that out by the time the next big holiday comes around."

"Yes. You will. And I'll be happy to give you lessons. And plenty of subtle hints."

"Not too subtle."

"No worries."

———

Ms. Lurie made a fire—a big real one with big real logs—in the fireplace in the lounge. She kept it going all day and into the night. Even though the weather wasn't *that* cold, it was nice to wrap up in blankets on the couch and stare at the fire and pretend it was real winter. Cozy.

Ms. Lurie was in her office with a pot of tea, talking Christmas on the phone with her various daughters. None of them were able to make the trip this year and she hadn't wanted to leave Hawthorne. I feel guilty about that, but she insists that's what she would have done anyway. She doesn't like to play favorites, and she can't be four different places at once.

Miss Miller was playing around in the kitchen, so that left just M and me bundled up in front of the fire.

"I don't remember believing in him," I said. "I guess I probably did when I was little. That seems like the kind of thing that—I think my mother would have told me the usual story."

"Mine, too. I was furious when she finally told me the truth."

"Emily Dickinson believed in him. Even when she was our age, she wrote letters to her friends about what Santa had put in her stocking. She was always kind of a kid, even when she grew up."

"I like that."

"Me, too." I paused. "Aunt Paulette couldn't be bothered with fairy tales. Anyway, if she was the one paying for Christmas, she was going to make sure she got full credit for it."

"She sounds like such a lovely woman. Remind me to write a will when I turn eighteen so I can leave her out of it."

"She wasn't *all* awful. Okay, I guess she mostly was. But I mean, she did get a tree and presents and stuff when I lived with her. No stockings—I don't know why. Too personal, I guess. But presents. And lots of candy." I smiled. "And then she'd yell at me for eating too much of it."

"Charming."

"She actually managed to give me some pretty good presents. By accident. She knew I loved reading, so she'd go to the bookstore and tell them how old I was and that I was a girl and then buy whatever they told her to. Same thing at the toy store."

"*My* mother is actually a superb shopper. She doesn't have to know someone at *all*—God knows she doesn't know me—but she can always find a terrifyingly perfect gift for any occasion. She's got a real knack. I've told her she should go into business for herself. There are people who'll pay plenty to have someone else do their shopping for them. But she just thinks I'm making fun of her."

"Can't imagine where she'd get an idea like that."

"No clue."

We were quiet for a minute. Fires are good things to have around to fill in pauses. They give you something to look at and listen to, but they don't interrupt when you want to start talking again.

"After I started going to boarding school," I said finally, slowly, "Aunt Paulette made excuses about why I couldn't come back on holiday breaks. Why I had to stay at school all the time. She never used to travel, but she suddenly started taking all these long trips during the summer, and over winter breaks."

M didn't say anything. She pushed a little closer, very gently, and snuggled her head against my shoulder.

"At first she sent me little presents. For my birthday and for Christmas. I'd always try to send her some kind of thank-you letter, but I could never figure out what to write. So then she just started sending cards, and eventually even that kind of fizzled out. We haven't spoken in years now."

"Doesn't she ever even call you? She *is* your guardian. And your aunt. She could at least pretend that means something."

"She isn't my guardian anymore. No one is. And—I don't think either of us would know what to say. She never liked me, even before she might have figured out she should be afraid to get close to me. I don't blame her for pulling away."

"*I* do."

I thought about it, and then smiled a little. "I guess I do, too."

M shivered and pulled another blanket over us. "There's a long tradition of telling creepy stories at Christmastime," she said. "That's why Dickens wrote about all those ghosts. But the stories weren't supposed to be *this* scary."

———

After M dozed off on my shoulder, I took a look at a book she'd given me. "I scoped out your shelves," she'd said. "If you already have this and you've got it hidden away somewhere, I'll have to throttle you."

I didn't. I'd never even heard of it. "'Revelations of Divine Love,'" I'd read slowly. "Um."

"I know it sounds preachy, but I swear it's not," M said. "I'm not trying to convert you or anything. Especially when I'm still figuring out what *I* think is true."

"Good," I said cautiously.

"She's not a saint exactly," M went on. "The woman who wrote this. But she's *like* a saint. She has a feast day and everything. Maybe she's halfway to being a saint. I'm a little fuzzy on the details."

"You're really selling her, though."

She took the book out of my hand and thwacked me on the upper arm with it. "The point is, she went through some really awful stuff," she said. "She was terribly sick for three days—so sick everyone thought she was going to die. But she lived. And she had all these amazing visions. So she wrote them down. She thought what she'd seen might help other people, too." She handed the book back to me. "The visions were all about how to be happy even when horrible things happen. Or especially when, I guess."

"Not that you're trying to make a point or anything."

"Point?"

I began flipping through the book. "Don't just look at random bits in the middle," M said impatiently. "Start with the *first* page."

I turned to the first page of the first chapter. "The *very* first page," M said. "Oh, give me that."

She grabbed the book out of my hand again and opened it to the apparently really important page. "*Here*."

She'd handwritten something beautifully—calligraphed it, so it looked appropriately old for a book written hundreds of years ago. "Read it to me," she demanded.

I was tempted to start reciting from the text of the book itself, but then she would have killed me and that wouldn't be a merry Christmas for anybody. So I dutifully read her own gorgeous writing aloud. "'All shall be well, and all manner of thing shall be well.'" I smiled. "That's pretty."

"She says it a lot. In the book. It's kind of famous."

"It's beautiful. Thank you."

"So now *this* makes sense." M took a small velvet box out of her skirt pocket and held it out.

"Oh, breathe," she added impatiently. "It's not a *ring*, idiot. I'm not even sure I want to go steady with you."

"It must be bad luck to lie on Christmas."

"I'll take my chances. Okay, look." She snapped the box open. "See? Just a necklace. Nothing scary. I hope you'll like it even if you stop liking me."

A necklace didn't sound so bad. It would take a little getting used to, though. I've never worn jewelry before. My ears aren't even pierced.

"It says—"

"I can *read*, M."

I took the box. The pendant inside was looped oddly—not a ring exactly, but a Möbius strip. I've always liked those.

All shall be well, it read continuously. *All shall be well.*

"So, no symbolism or anything."

"Not a bit."

———

I didn't know M had woken up. Her head was just as heavy on my shoulder, her breathing just as even.

And then she said, "Are you asleep?"

I smiled. "Yes."

"Good. That makes two of us."

"It does." I paused a moment, then added, "I've been thinking about that, actually."

"Sleeping?"

"The two of us."

"I should hope so."

"I mean—who we are." I was quiet for another second. This was harder to say than I'd expected. "I was thinking about changing my name. My first one, this time."

M sat up a little straighter, considering. "Maybe we both should," she said. "There are an awful lot of Emilys littering the landscape."

I wasn't sure if she meant just the two of us, or if she was including my sister in that calculation. Or Dickinson. Or all the Emilys our age whose mothers had somehow separately decided to name their daughters a sweet old-fashioned name that they just happened to like and that then just happened to become the most popular name on those lists M checked that made her sick of being just another Emily.

As if she ever could be.

"You're right," I said.

"I'm always right." She sat up all the way now, stretching. "Should we tell Ms. Lurie about our nefarious plans?"

"Not just yet," I said. "I don't want to move right now."

"Okay."

"Anyway," I added as she rearranged the blanket around us, "I have the feeling that as long as we're at Hawthorne, we'll always be Emily."

AUTHOR'S NOTE

Emily Dickinson's role in this book was an afterthought.

I had my premise. I knew my main character was a damaged, angry, terribly lonely young woman. I had a picture of the impish, insightful woman who would lead her to love and redemption. And, rare for me, I even had the setting. Hawthorne Academy would be a sort of "unschool" hiding in the hills of Topanga and named after my favorite writer's favorite writer (Shirley Jackson and Nathaniel Hawthorne, respectively).

I outlined the plot from beginning to end. I pitched the premise to my agent and received an enthusiastic response. I was ready to begin what felt like a promising project.

The only thing I didn't have was a working title.

I knew that a lot of titles are modified or changed completely by editors. That was fine. I'd just be sure not to get too attached to whatever handful of words I chose.

But I did have to choose *some*thing. And I was drawing a blank.

Our tiny apartment has a *lot* of books. At the time, most of them were not by or about Emily Dickinson. So it was just luck that a volume of her poems happened to be near at hand.

I started thumbing through it in search of a disposable title. Eventually, I decided that "The Letting Go" was good enough to begin with.

And since I was naming my novel after a line from Dickinson, I thought my narrator should be interested in the poet. I added "Don't forget to make main character obsessed with Dickinson" to my notes.

I spent the next few weeks wrestling with important plot issues such as where to leave the body of Stephen James, who should find it, and exactly how many brutal murders had to occur in my narrator's past (too few and she wouldn't be able to figure out "the rules"; too many and I would spend all of what should have been my writing time cheering myself up with chocolate).

Then I hit a point in my writing where I realized that I should, as I put it to myself, do a little research on Dickinson. As luck would have it, I already owned a biography.

Perfect. A biography and one collection of the poems. I was all set.

It sounded like Dickinson's ingredient list for a prairie: you just need "a clover and one bee."

Dickinson was joking. And it turned out I was kidding myself.

The absolutely certain facts we have about Dickinson's life are few, simple, and (mostly) rather dull. The letters and poems she left behind are numerous, enigmatic, and fascinating. The gap between those two statements has been filled with more books than any reasonable person would ever try to read, write, or own.

I am not a reasonable person, a hypothesis I confirmed in the course of writing *The Letting Go.*

As someone whose modest ambition was to learn everything possible about the life and times of the greatest American poet, my timing was excellent. Informative, engaging works addressing All Things Dickinson were coming out on a regular basis. And thanks to e-technology, old works were now accessible even to amateur scholars who had no access to university stacks. Noting the significant disagreements possible when it came to spelling, punctuation, capitalization, word choice, and line breaks, I realized that a driven reader/writer/researcher such as Emily Stone would most certainly base her quotations on the poet's original manuscripts. Which I therefore did myself, with great pleasure and the occasional eye-strain-induced headache.

For anyone who has fallen as far in love with Dickinson as Emily Stone did (and I devoutly hope you have happier reasons for doing so), here is a list of some of the books I found helpful and enjoyable:

Emily Dickinson by Cynthia Griffin Wolff
Emily Dickinson and the Labor of Clothing by Daneen Wardrop
Emily Dickinson Face to Face by Martha Dickinson Bianchi
Emily Dickinson, Friend and Neighbor by MacGregor Jenkins
The Gardens of Emily Dickinson by Judith Farr with Louise Carter
The Gorgeous Nothings by Emily Dickinson, edited by Marta Werner and Jen Bervin
Inscriptions on the Grave Stones in the Grave Yards of Northampton,

and of other towns in the valley of the Connecticut, as Springfield, Amherst, Hadley, Hatfield, Deerfield, &c. by Thomas Bridgman

Kavanagh by Henry Wadsworth Longfellow

Letters of Emily Dickinson by Emily Dickinson, edited by Mabel Loomis Todd

The Life and Letters of Emily Dickinson by Martha Dickinson Bianchi

Lives Like Loaded Guns: Emily Dickinson and her Family's Feuds by Lyndall Gordon

Maid as Muse: How Servants Changed Emily Dickinson's Life and Language by Aífe Murray

The Manuscript Books of Emily Dickinson by Emily Dickinson, edited by R. W. Franklin

The Mother at Home by John Stevens Cabot Abbott

My Wars Are Laid Away In Books: The Life of Emily Dickinson by Alred Habegger

The New England Primer by Benjamin Harris

Poems by Emily Dickinson, Three Series, Complete by Emily Dickinson, edited by Mabel Loomis Todd and T. W. Higginson

The Recognition of Emily Dickinson: Selected Criticism Since 1890 edited by Caesar R. Blane and Carlton F. Wells

The Single Hound by Emily Dickinson, edited by Martha Dickinson Bianchi

The World of Emily Dickinson by Polly Longsworth

ACKNOWLEDGMENTS

"When we were happy she added her crumb, when we were ill all she had was ours; were we grieved, her indignation was hot against whoever or whatever had wounded us." Martha Dickinson Bianchi described her beloved Aunt Emily thus, and I hope my dearest gift of a mother-in-law, Ginnie Bottorff, will allow me to apply the same praise to her. Though she is farther away geographically than either of us would wish, her love and generosity find their way to my home every day.

Her husband, Ron Bottorff, makes talking about politics fun and always has a ray of hope to offer on dark days. Her daughter, my sister Mary Cancilla, is a rock star of an aunt, mother, wife, friend, and honorary dragon (though sorely lacking in the beard department).

My husband Dominick Cancilla and son Markus Cancilla did an amazing job of seeming genuinely interested in every bit of research and every step of progress I made in the course of writing this book. Markus was a patient sounding board on numerous early-morning walks; Dominick was always ready to bail me out if I hit a plot snag, or reassure me that I was indeed on the right track. Without them, I might very well have taken the easy way out and let this project go.

Many thanks to all my long-distance writing friends, with a special shout-out to Kriston Sites Eller, Toni Popoki Reed, Sabrina Alexander, Michelle Sullivan Clay, Natalie West, Lauren Ocean, Shannon Taylor Hodnett, Alessandra Giampaolo (please thank Nic for me!), and of course my loving friend and guardian angel Linda Nielsen. (That cookie-klatsch is going to happen if I have to walk all the way to Idaho to make it so.)

If Kat Alexander, Siobhan Wilder, and Siri Wilder think I'm not going to acknowledge their awesomeness in print now that I finally have the chance, they are entirely mistaken (for what is probably the only time in their gorgeous lives).

Lindsey Strand-Polyak is a brilliant, beautiful, sophisticated, educated world traveler. So, yeah, we have literally nothing in common except a love of baroque violin music. I hope to be her student again and am honored to be her friend.

Emily Denver is queen of the known universe. There. Now everyone can stop wondering.

Colleen Otcasek and her daughter Olivia refuse to divulge how they manage to combine so much stunning elegance with an endless capacity for goofy fun. I'll stop trying to figure it out and just be grateful to have them as friends.

Dear April Walker, Karen Cooper, Efrain Sevilla, Amy Vinroot Wilson, Robin Gonzalez, Adesa Hafford, Jeannine Smith, Barbara Mcminn, and Jeanie Lawrence: "Had we less to say to those we love, perhaps we should say it oftener." (That's Dickinson for "You're totally rad and I appreciate you more than my own words can possibly make clear.")

Many thanks to Kathleen McKernan Whitfield for always having faith in me, even when I'm running perilously low on it myself.

True fact: Leighann Garber is the only human being more huggable than a hedgehog.

Diana Birchall, did you think I'd forget all that tea and sympathy? Okay—coffee and camaraderie? Thank you for being my friend, neighbor, and fellow Janeite.

Finally: heartfelt thanks to special agent Michelle Johnson of Inklings Literary Agency and Rachel Stark of Sky Pony Press.